THE BILLION DOLLAR BOY

THE
BILLION
DOLLAR
BOY

A JUPITER™ NOVEL

CHARLES SHEFFIELD

TOR®

A TOM DOHERTY ASSOCIATES BOOK · NEW YORK

THE BILLION DOLLAR BOY

Copyright © 1997 by Charles Sheffield

A Tor Book
Published by Tom Doherty Associates, Inc.
175 Fifth Avenue
New York, NY 10010

Tor Books on the World Wide Web:
http://www.tor.com

Tor® is a registered trademark of Tom Doherty
Associates, Inc.

Library of Congress Cataloging-in-Publication Data

Sheffield, Charles.
    The billion dollar boy / Charles Sheffield.
        p.   cm/
        ISBN 0-312-86204-0
        I.   Title.
PS3569.H39253B55   1997
813'.54—dc20   96-30716
                                                    CIP

First Edition: April 1997

Printed in the United States of America

0 9 8 7 6 5 4 3 2 1

To Bill and Linda, nontrivial friends.

THE BILLION DOLLAR BOY

CHAPTER ONE

BY NINE-thirty, fifty full breakfasts had been cooked and served. The pans and dishes were cleaned and back in their racks, and the staff of the house were more than ready to relax and enjoy their own meal.

They were sitting at a long wooden table on the basement level. The words that came wafting down to them through the house's internal communications system produced a communal shudder.

"Say, didn't you hear what I told you yesterday?" It was a young male voice, high-pitched and whining. "I like my omelette just a little bit undercooked and runny. What you sent me was firm all the way through. I'll take another one—and you better get it right this time."

The kitchen staff stared at each other, until at last one of them stood up.

"All right, I'll do it." He was a heavily built man in his late fifties with a worn, weather-beaten face. He turned to one of the women at the table. "I thought what I cooked was just the way he liked it. Didn't he eat it?"

"Are you kidding? Young Porky?" She made a grunting noise like a pig. "He ate every scrap. It looked like he licked the plate. You don't get that fat without working at it."

"I thought so." The man stared down at his own untouched food. "Keep this hot for me, would you, Mitzi? I made the first one, so I guess it's my job to give him another. But I won't tell you what I'd *like* to give him."

"And what I'd like to give him, too," said a thin young woman at the end of the table. "Yesterday afternoon, I was all finished cleaning upstairs. Then just when I was set to leave, *he* came in. You know how it had rained. He didn't bother to wipe his boots. He trampled mud all over the rugs and up the stairs, and I had to start over. He knew it, too. He stood there and smirked at me and the mess. I felt like giving him a good one with the vacuum cleaner."

There was a murmur of agreement from around the table. "Pity somebody didn't do that long ago," said another of the maids.

The others chimed in. "A smack on that fat backside would work wonders." "If only his mother had some *control*." "Or his father was around more." "I'm not one for violence, but a whack or two would do him a power of good."

"Don't even think of it." The heavily built man spoke with authority as the senior member of the household staff.

He was over at the long metal-topped range pouring oil into a skillet. "His mother has no control of him, so she won't let anybody else have any, either. If you was so much as to touch His Lordship, you'd be out of this house and off the estate by midday."

"Sometimes I feel like it would be worth it, Branton," said the thin young maid. "There's a limit, you know. A person can only put up with so much."

"You talk like that, Edna, because you've never worked any place but here." Three eggs had been broken into a bowl and were now being beaten vigorously, as though the older man was taking his feelings out on them. "If you'd been in the Pool for years, like me, wondering if you'd ever get a job again, you'd feel different. Cleaning up mud's a whole lot better than lying down and sleeping in it. You'd put up with plenty from God's gift to Earth before you'd be willing to go back to the Pool. If I was—"

"Hey down there." The intercom came to life again. "I said I wanted another omelette. Is anybody listening, or are you guys all asleep?"

Branton sighed and raised his eyes to heaven—or to the upper floors of the house. He went across and flipped the intercom to transmit. "It will be there in just a minute, Mr. Shelby. The eggs are right now going into the pan."

"So get a move on. What's keeping you?"

"I'm sorry, Mr. Shelby. It will be in your room very soon." Branton turned off the intercom and went back to the range. He poured the beaten eggs into the pan and glared down at the sizzling omelette. "You see how it's done," he said. He sounded as though he were talking about the cooking until he went on, as much to himself as to the others, "You put up with any amount of crap. And you tell yourself that, much as you hate the idea, you owe your job to young *Mis-*

ter Shelby and all the others who have more money than you'll ever have. And you console yourself with the thought that one day, maybe it'll be tomorrow, you'll put poison into the little bugger's food. And that will be *that.*"

Mister Shelby—Shelby Crawford Jerome Prescott Cheever, the only child of Constance and J. P. Cheever, head of Cheever Consolidated Enterprises—had finished his second omelette and followed it with half a dozen cupcakes. It was now ten-fifteen on a fine May morning, with blue skies and light breezes. The whole day lay ahead, free to fill with anything that he chose to do.

And Shelby Cheever, fifteen-year-old heir to one of Earth's largest fortunes, was bored. Horribly bored, incredibly bored, terminally bored. The grounds of the walled Virginia compound stretched two miles in each direction, with their sculptured gardens and woods and streams, their stables and game parks and stocked fishponds. There was nothing anywhere in the whole expanse that Shelby had the slightest desire to see or do.

It was more from desperation than the hope of finding anything interesting that he at last went ambling around the inside of the house, starting with the third-floor library and portrait galleries and winding his way down toward the lower levels. The house, as usual, seemed packed with his mother's women friends. He knew better than to look to them for entertainment. He would rather go outside and talk to the horses. At least they wouldn't talk back, or pretend interest they didn't have.

The basement level where the household support staff lived was off-limits to guests, but it never occurred to Shelby that the restriction might apply to him. He wandered down to the kitchen, with its arrays of broilers, spits, blenders, churns, kettles, and ovens. The place was deserted and he passed on through it. A long corridor led to the staff living quarters. He could hear the sound of laughter from that direction.

He came to the recreation room and paused, disappointed, at the threshold. The sound he had heard along the corridor came not from live people, but from a video unit. Two people were sitting in front of it, watching a show and drinking beer straight from the bottles.

"What are you looking at?"

It seemed to Shelby that he had asked a simple enough question. The response was surprising. The woman choked on her beer, while the man jerked upright and glanced rapidly from Shelby to the screen and back.

"It's—it's just a show," he said. "We weren't really watching it."

"I can see it's a show, Branton. I'm not blind, you know." Shelby squeezed uninvited into a chair between the other two. "I meant, *which* show."

"Oh. Well, it's just a comedy. Nothing to be taken seriously." Branton made a move as though to turn it off, but Shelby put a hand on his arm.

"Not yet. What are those people *doing*? Everybody's all ways up." He studied the slapstick action and spinning bodies for a moment. "Hey, I get it! They're supposed to be out in *space*—in free-fall. Isn't that right?"

"It is." Branton made another move as though to change channels, then decided it was too late. "It's just a comedy," he repeated. "Nothing to take seriously."

"Right." Shelby was watching closely, absorbed in the efforts of one of the characters to catch a big round globule of liquid in her mouth while she herself turned end over end.

He laughed. "You know, this is pretty good. Do you think space would really be like that?"

Branton and Mitzi exchanged relieved glances. Apparently it didn't occur to Shelby that this show really had been made in space, and that the free-fall was real rather than simulated. More important from their point of view, Shelby didn't know what made the show so appealing to them: the abundance of machines and labor-saving gadgets on the set that were all designed to replace the work of humans.

Branton nodded at Mitzi, reading her longing look. *If only we were allowed to bring some of* those *down here to Earth. Think how easy they would make our jobs.*

"You know, if real space is anything like this it must be fun." Shelby was hardly aware of the other two. He was grinning so widely that his brown eyes were narrowed to slits in his pasty face. "Oh, look at that! She's going to—"

The woman on the show was approaching another globule of liquid; but this one was so gigantic that instead of her swallowing it, it would engulf her. Unable to stop herself, arms and legs flailing, she plunged into the fluid sphere. It splashed in all directions. Everyone around her was instantly soaked.

Shelby roared with laughter. "That's so great! I never realized that space could be so much fun. You know what? I think I ought to go and take a trip there myself. A little vacation. What do you think?"

Branton had worked for the Cheever household for six years—long enough to know how quickly Shelby's enthusiasms faded. But there was one way to make them last.

"I think you might enjoy the trip a great deal, Mr. Shelby. But I feel sure that your mother, Miss Constance, would never permit you to go to space. Not even for a brief vacation."

The smile was replaced instantly by a scowl. "You think

so? Well, let me tell you something. Any time I ever want to do anything, I can get Mom to go along with the idea. It wouldn't be any different with this. So that shows how much *you* know." Shelby stood up. "Want to bet, Branton?"

"I don't bet, Mr. Shelby."

"Very wise—because you'd lose. Just wait and see. I'm going to talk to Mom this minute about a trip to space."

He hurried out. Branton turned off the video and leaned back in his chair.

"Think he'll be able to do it?" Mitzi asked.

"Without his father here in the house? I'm sure of it. If J.P. were around the Old Man would put his foot down and that would be that. Shelby knows it, too. He's a spoiled brat, but he's not a fool. He'll talk his mother into it."

"He'll probably *hate* space—and he'll blame you for his going."

"I don't think so." Branton picked up another bottle of beer, opened it, and took a long and satisfied swig. "You don't know our Shelby as well as I do. He may have a terrible time—I hope he does—but when he comes back he'll boast to us about how terrific it was. Otherwise, he'd be forced to admit that he was wrong in telling us he wanted to go in the first place."

"What's it *really* like in space?" Mitzi gestured at the blank video screen. "I mean, it can't be like that."

"I'm sure it's not, any more than our comedy shows are like real life. I have no idea what it's like up there."

"With luck it will be hell."

"We can always hope. But you know what?" Branton closed his eyes and smiled in anticipation. "I don't really care. Think of it this way: For a week or a month, or however long His Lordship talks Miss Constance into letting him go, we won't have to deal with Shelby."

Mitzi returned the smile. "You're right. And he thinks that *he'll* be the one getting a vacation."

It took more effort than usual. Constance Cheever didn't know much about space, except that people of her station went there seldom or never. The general NOCD rule—"Not our class, dear"—applied even more strongly to the space-dwelling lower orders than to their teeming brethren on Earth.

"But *why?*" Constance not only had never *been* away from Earth, she knew no one who had. "Everything that you can possibly find there, you can get better here. I'm told that the level of personal service is dreadful. It's often provided by *machines*, rather than real servants. And you couldn't take Branton or our other staff with you."

She was digging in her heels. Next thing you knew she would be talking of calling J. P. Cheever to discuss it. His father would surely kill the whole idea.

Shelby played his trump card. "I thought the trip might do me good. I've not been feeling too well recently."

His mother regarded him anxiously. Shelby's delicate health was her constant and principal concern. Others might look at him and see a strong and hulking youth, fifty pounds overweight and half a head taller than Constance. They might agree on his unhealthy complexion, the result of overindulgence in everything except sleep and exercise. But they would be hard pressed to discover the signs of fatal disease that Constance saw all the time in Shelby's disgruntled countenance.

She moved to place the palm of her hand on his forehead. "Maybe Dr. Linfoot should take another look at you."

"He'll only say the same thing as he did last time. That a change of environment would do me good."

Like Branton, Dr. Linfoot knew how much Shelby's absence could improve the quality of life in the Cheever compound.

"But Shelby, dear, where would you *go?*"

Shelby saw signs of weakening. "I looked it up. There are cruises that leave Earth orbit next Monday and take you on tours of the worked-out mines in the Asteroid Belt. That's where the closest node is, too. That node connects to another one in the Kuiper Belt—a lot farther out, beyond Pluto. One of the cruises, the Aurora line, has an option to take you there. Those mines are still in use. And if you want to, you can use the same nodes to make the transfer to some place *real* far away—"

"Next Monday." Constance Cheever had apparently stopped listening to Shelby after his first sentence. She pulled a little notebook from her purse. "That's six days from now. And let's see, the Symington big reception is in just twenty-three days. Everyone who's anyone will be there. I just have to attend. We would have to be back in time for that."

"We? Mother, you don't have to go with me."

"My dear." Constance patted Shelby's pudgy hand. "Surely you don't think I would let you go so far *without* me? Why, if you went on that cruise and I wasn't there to look after you, and something happened to you, I would just never be able to forgive myself."

He took a deep breath, ready to argue the point, until his mother added, "And as to what your father would say if he knew you had gone without me—well, I daren't even think."

Shelby let out his breath again. The last thing he wanted was to bring his father into this. J. P. Cheever passed through the Cheever compound no more than once a month, and his overnight visits were usually brief; but Shelby admitted, if only to himself, that his father was the one person in the world who made him feel small and scared.

It was time to settle for what he had; and if he couldn't find a way to cut loose from his mother once they were out in space, then his name wasn't Shelby Crawford Jerome Prescott Cheever.

"Both of us, then," Shelby conceded. "It will be great. You don't need to worry about any of the arrangements. I'll work with the staff to take care of those. And I'll tell Branton we'll need the aircar on Sunday afternoon."

"The aircar? Will that take us to space?"

"No, Mother. An aircar can't go to space."

"Why not?"

"It needs air to fly, to support it. There's no air in space. We'll just use the car to fly us to the New Mexico launch site."

"No air?" Constance Cheever looked puzzled. "Then how will we breathe?"

Shelby groaned to himself. And *she* was going to space to look after *him?*

CHAPTER TWO

THE cruise tickets came with so many disclaimers that Shelby took one look and decided not to show them to his mother.

The Aurora cruise line was not responsible for death or injury in the ascent to or descent from space. It was not responsible for motion sickness caused by low-gee or high-gee environments . . . not responsible for death or injury due to natural radiation hazards in space . . . not responsible for delays in schedule caused by the unpredictable occurrence of solar flares . . . not responsible for luggage lost or damaged in space beanstalk operations . . .

The list went on forever.

Actually, Shelby had found the idea of riding the beanstalk to space rather appealing, until he found out how long it would take to reach the cruise liner. The cable cars traveled at what seemed like a reasonable speed, three hundred kilometers an hour. But they had a long way to go. It was thirty-five thousand kilometers to the cruise liner's take-off point from geosynchronous orbit. You would have to sit in one of the unfurnished cars for nearly five days, whereas a laser-boosted rocket from the New Mexico launch site would have you up there in five hours.

No wonder that the beanstalk cars were used only for cargo and maintenance staff. The Cheever luggage had been shipped as early as possible to the foot of the beanstalk in Macapa, on the equator at the mouth of the Amazon. Shelby had watched in disbelief as twelve large trunks were loaded onto the aircar at the Cheever compound. One-half of one trunk held his stuff—the rest were all Constance Cheever's.

For a ten-day tour? What was his mother planning to *do* up there?

It was three days into the cruise before Shelby realized that his mother, by accident or design, had made her travel arrangements much more wisely than he had.

The Aurora cruise line tickets had offered disclaimers against everything—except *boredom*. And that proved to be the biggest danger of all.

The Cheever party, naturally, had reserved the most luxurious staterooms aboard the biggest of the cruise liners. It sounded good, but in practice it translated to a set of rooms for both Shelby and his mother that was about half the size of his own bedroom back home in the compound. The food on the ship was advertised as "all you can eat." Shelby decided, after the first couple of meals, that wasn't very much.

As for the passengers . . .

He should have known. The cruises were expensive. The average member of Earth's fourteen billion humans could no more afford the cost of a cruise liner ticket than fly up to space unassisted.

So who was Shelby supposed to consort with on their four-day trip to the asteroid mines? The same sort of boring well-off brain-dead old fogies that his mother hung around with back on Earth. Anything less like the fun-in-space comedy show that had first drawn his interest was difficult to imagine.

His mother, on the other hand, seemed quite at home. One day was spent in playing a game of cross-connections with the other passengers—"Rawsley. Hmm. Are you by any chance related to the New Hampshire Rawsleys? Really? My godmother's younger sister, she married the oldest son of Willoughby Rawsley. . . ." And then it was on to card-playing, and afternoon soirees, and little formal dinner parties with conversation so stunningly dull that Shelby couldn't bear to be in the same room with it.

He stayed huddled in his own cabin for two days, going through all the material he could find about the ship and the cruise. The idea of an external jaunt in a spacesuit sounded as if it might be fun, until he went aft and mentioned it to a member of the crew.

"It would be more than fun." The crewman, Garrity, was long-limbed and slow-talking, and he looked on Shelby's plum-colored leisure outfit with a skeptical eye. "I could even find a suit big enough to squeeze you into it. But there's a slight problem."

"What's that?"

"The *Bellatrix* is accelerating at a steady half-gee. That's a nice comfortable value, enough so we don't have any worries about free-fall sickness, and high enough to take us out to the Belt, allowing for midpoint turnaround, in four and a half days. But if you were to go outside the ship in a suit you wouldn't have the ship's acceleration anymore. We'd leave you far behind, and you'd go sailing on toward infinity."

Garrity didn't add "you idiot." But Shelby certainly felt the words in his tone of voice.

"Maybe I can do it when the *Bellatrix* gets out to the Belt and the old mines," he mumbled, and retreated to his cabin.

The ship's description of the node network occupied another few hours of his time. It was a pure space development, one which could never be employed with any node that sat in a substantial gravity field. That meant there could not be any nodes on Earth, or closer to the Sun than the Asteroid Belt. The powers-that-be on Earth as a result acted as though the node network did not exist.

But it certainly did, and it offered a near-instantaneous transition between nodes—no matter how far apart they were. A human in a suit or a ship could float into a node chamber in the Asteroid Belt, enter the correct transition sequence into the computer, and pop out in the middle of the Kuiper Belt, far beyond the outermost planet and twenty billion kilometers from the Sun. You could, if the ship's data bank was to be believed, choose a destination much farther away. There were nodes close to—but not too close to—other stars, or even in open space.

Shelby did not understand one word of how the network operated, but the idea of an out-and-back to the Kuiper Belt, while his mother sat playing bridge and drinking tea, had great appeal. A node jump was permitted with his class of ticket. He had checked it soon after they came aboard. Again, though, he could do nothing until they arrived at the Belt— and that was still a full day away.

He went aft to haunt the crew's quarters, just forward of the main engines. After a little pestering, Chief Engineer

Dollfus took him back to show him the Diabelli Omnivores.

"Now, aren't they something?" Dollfus patted one of the six bulbous cylinders with a hairy hand. "Fusion takes place right here, inside this section. We usually burn hydrogen to helium, with an internal temperature as low as ten million degrees. If we need to we can fuse helium to carbon, but that needs at least a hundred million degrees before it's efficient."

Shelby backed away a step. Ten million degrees didn't sound particularly low to him. "What would happen if you were inside that chamber when the fusion started?"

Even before it was out of his mouth he wished he hadn't asked the question. It sounded stupid.

Dollfus regarded dryly Shelby's swelling plum-colored suit.

"Well, let's say that if *you* were in there you'd be nicely rendered down before you came out. But you'd also interfere with the fusion cycle, and the engine would turn off automatically. In practice, you'd never get in. There are a dozen monitoring machines to sound alarms and close off access."

Machines again! Space was *full* of damned machines, more machines than people. There were never enough people to give a customer decent service.

Shelby returned to his cabin in a petulant rage. It was obvious that Dollfus had been deliberately rude to him—to a top-paying passenger! *Rendered down*, indeed.

His first thought was to go right back to the crew's quarters and give Dollfus a tongue-lashing. Then he changed his mind. There were other and more lasting ways of getting your revenge. The Aurora cruise line owners would receive a rocket of their own on the letterhead of Cheever Consolidated Enterprises, just as soon as the sole heir to that organization could find a way to send it. He would teach nonentities like Engineer Dollfus not to mess with the *real* powers in the solar system.

Shelby went across to one of his lockers and pulled out official Cheever stationery. From under a pile of clothes he took a bottle that he had sneaked on board with his hand baggage. He took a swig, gasped as the liquor hit his stomach, and sat down to compose his complaint.

It was just as well that Shelby did not know what went on in the crew's quarters while he sat writing. Four off-duty crew members were sitting around and talking, and Shelby himself was the subject of their conversation.

"Never in his life, if he's to be believed." Krupa was purser of the *Bellatrix*, and her job brought her more than the other crew members into contact with Shelby. "Never made his own bed, never washed his own clothes, never made a meal for himself. Makes you wonder just what he *has* done— other than stuff his face with food while he complains about how it's inedible."

"He's a Cheever," said Garrity. "He's never had to do anything for himself, and he never will. Know what he told me? He gets a hundred million dollars."

"You mean, he'll get it when he's twenty-one?"

"No. He gets a hundred million *a month*—that's what his trust fund produces in interest on investments. Over a billion a year. And when his father dies he'll be a whole lot richer. It's criminal. There's no way he can possibly spend a thousandth of what he makes, while there's ten billion down on Earth going short of a meal every day."

"That's not his fault," Dollfus said. "He didn't *choose* to be born a Cheever. Though I must say, if it was offered to me I wouldn't say no."

"What he needs is *discipline.*" Krupa made a movement with her arm, as though she was slapping somebody with her open palm. "He won't get it from his mother, I can tell you that. He runs her ragged. And it looks like he doesn't see much of his father."

"Too busy making money." Garrity snorted. "Another few tens of billions, while his only child goes downhill. The boy has potential—he's not at all a fool, and he can ask smart questions. But he'll come to nothing without discipline. His father's the one that deserves the smack on the head."

The fourth crew member was a brooding Irishman, Malone, who seldom spoke. Now he roused himself. "I'll agree with ninety percent of what you're saying. But not that about Jerry Cheever."

"Who?"

"The boy's father—Jerome Prescott Cheever. I know him, or at least I used to."

"You never told us that," said Dollfus, in a tone suggesting that he didn't quite believe it.

"There's a lot about me you don't know." Malone sniffed. "I worked for him over twenty-five years ago, when I was still down on Earth and Jerry Cheever hadn't made his first million."

"But that can't be," Krupa protested. "I've stood by in the lounge while Constance Cheever and her friends were playing cards. She talks all the time about 'old money.' "

"No doubt she does. And no doubt she is." Malone shook his dark head. "But not him. Believe it or not, Jerry Cheever started out with no more than me. But he was the smartest man I ever met—and an honest one, too."

"Then he must be double sick," said Dollfus, "to see what a spoiled mass of blubber he's brought into the world. The worst thing is, Shelby Cheever thinks he *deserves* everything he's got. And because he has all that, with people on Earth bowing and scraping and falling over themselves to satisfy his every whim, there's no way he'll ever change."

Garrity reached out a long arm to refill his mug, and regarded Dollfus with a cynical eye. "And would you be any different, Chief, if you had all that?"

"Maybe not. Probably not. Not if I'd been born to it."

Krupa repeated her gesture, swinging her arm in a slapping movement. "That's all the boy needs. Morning and night, and repeat as necessary 'til he acts human."

"Aye. But you can be sure he'll never get it," said Garrity gloomily. "Shel Cheever will always have what he wants, but never what he needs."

For twenty-four hours Shelby had been waiting for the arrival at the Belt mines to break his boredom. It did, but not quite in the way that he had expected.

It had never occurred to him that the comfortable half-gee field inside the *Bellatrix* was entirely the result of the ship's acceleration. On their arrival at the Belt mine, that acceleration had to end. One moment he was standing at a forward port, staring with a high-magnification scope at the disfigured ovoid of an asteroid identified by the ship's computer as CM-67—Company Mine Number 67. The next second his feet were barely touching the deck, and his stomach was floating up into his throat.

It was small consolation to learn over the next few hours that he was one of the lucky ones. He couldn't face the idea of food, but at least he wasn't confined to his cabin like his mother. Constance Cheever was throwing up and wailing to the purser that she was dying, and would Krupa please bring "dear, dear Shelby" to see her so that she could take a last look at him.

Dear, dear Shelby made a token visit to her, but the sights and sounds were disgusting and he left as soon as he could. Since their arrival in free-fall he had been nipping liberally at the bottle in his cabin, hoping to settle his stomach.

It seemed to be working, but the price was a light-headed giddiness that made him long to get outside the confining hull of the *Bellatrix*. When the opportunity came for a space-suited tour of CM-67, he jumped at the chance.

By this time he was not surprised to find that he was the only passenger who was interested in going outside. Anyone who was not throwing up would be playing cards, just as though they had never left Earth. Why did they come? Probably just to talk about it when they got home.

After a training session with Garrity, who showed Shelby how to perform the complete thirty-six-point suit check and then went over everything one more time to make sure it had been done right, the two of them exited through the airlock of the *Bellatrix*. By this time Shelby was feeling not only light-headed but distinctly superior. He alone, of all the passengers, had what it took to handle a space environment. He alone was a natural spacer, coordinated and confident.

He followed Garrity to the looming derelict mine, throwing questions along the way over his suit radio.

"Not for more than a century," Garrity said when Shelby asked if CM-67 was still in use. "The last active mine in this part of the Belt was completely worked out nearly a hundred years ago. It's a matter of economics. There's still ore to be found here, but not as much as in the Kuiper Belt, and not in such high concentrations. You have to go out there to find the action today. There, or with the independents in the Messina Dust Cloud. But for that you'd have to use the node network."

Shelby intended to, but he didn't propose to discuss his plans with Garrity. "What's that?" he asked. He was pointing to a great shining cylinder, a couple of hundred meters long and almost as wide, that floated beside the irregular bulk of CM-67. "Is it a node?"

"Nah." Garrity sounded amused. "We'll be in node territory tomorrow. That's an ore smelter. Works by simultaneous rotation and electric heating of the ore body you put inside it, to separate out metals and slag by a centrifugal field. The technique's less popular than it used to be, because there have been some horrendous accidents. Spin too fast, and the whole smelter can explode."

"Wow. Has that happened near here?"

"Not for a long time. But it's only six years since the Kuiper Belt mines had their worst accident ever with a centrifugal smelter. Two hundred and ninety-seven people died in the Trachten blow-out. And there was just one survivor."

"Boy." Shelby's eyes were wide inside his suit's visor. "It must be great to see something like that—I mean, real close up, when it's actually happening."

"I'm sure." Garrity's tone was carefully neutral. "Unless you're a bit too close. Lucky Jack Linden was the Trachten blow-out survivor. He came through without a scratch, but he never mined again."

"What happened to him?"

"You got me. Before the accident he also had a reputation as the Kuiper Belt's top pilot, but he never flew a ship again. They say that the accident destroyed Lucky Jack's mind. Maybe he got a job back on Earth."

Shelby stared at the crewman. The comment sounded like an insult, but Garrity's face was inscrutable behind his suit visor. Had Shelby imagined the contempt for Earth—and for Shelby himself—in the man's voice?

Suddenly, the whole expedition away from the ship no longer seemed interesting. When Garrity suggested that unless Shelby wanted to take a trip into the mining tunnels that riddled the derelict interior of CM-67 they might as well head back to the *Bellatrix*, Shelby agreed at once.

Worked-out mines were dull. They had been abandoned for decades and nothing was going to happen near them. The real action was farther out, in the Kuiper Belt.

One more day. Shelby couldn't wait for a chance to use the network and take a look.

Thirty hours later he was drinking again in his cabin. He was getting ready to write another letter of complaint to the Aurora cruise line owners.

He had asked politely enough, but Krupa had been totally unreasonable.

"I know *exactly* how your ticket reads," the purser said. She hadn't even given Shelby the courtesy of stopping what she was doing while she talked to him, but had gone on checking the schedule of stewards against cabins. "It does say you can make a trip through the node network to the Kuiper Belt. And you can. But it doesn't say to me, 'Drop everything else the second that a passenger tells you he wants to go.' Of course, if you would be willing to let one of the *machines* take you . . . they're perfectly competent."

"I won't go with a stupid machine. I want a human guide."

"I was afraid you'd say that." Krupa sighed and rubbed her eyes. It was late at night, and she was very tired. "But it gives me a problem, because we're shorthanded at the moment. As soon as Sha-Ming is well enough to come back on duty, he will take you."

"When?"

"Maybe the day after tomorrow."

"That's not good enough." Shelby slammed his fist down on the table. "I paid top dollar. I expect *service.*"

"And you'll get it. Just as soon as I'm able to give it."

Krupa sounded polite, but she wouldn't budge. Shelby had stormed back to his cabin, pulled out the official Cheever stationery with its golden letterhead, and prepared to deliver a blast that would make his first letter sound mild.

"Incompetent staff . . . totally inadequate service . . . disregard of passenger needs . . ."

Those words were all too weak. He needed something that would produce an earthquake when it hit the boardroom of the Aurora line.

He looked for inspiration in the bottle at his side, and was astonished to find only half an inch of liquor left.

Surely he hadn't drunk that much? Someone must have been helping themselves while he was out. A cabin steward, it had to be. He went raging back to the crew quarters, ready to tell Krupa that one of her stewards had to be fired. It was the middle of the sleep period, but he was not going to let that stop him.

She was not there. Only the dark-haired, dark-faced Irish crewman, Malone, and the chief engineer, Dollfus, were sitting across from each other at the long table. They stared up when Shelby burst in.

"And now what?" asked Dollfus.

"There's a thief aboard this ship!"

"Is there now? And what makes you think that?"

"I had a bottle in my cabin. I'm sure that last time I looked it was nearly a quarter full. Now it's just about empty."

"A bottle?" Dollfus caught Malone's eye. "A bottle of what?"

"Kahlúa."

"Ah. You drink, do you?" Dollfus spoke quietly, almost respectfully.

"Sure I do." Shelby stuck out his chest and felt less angry. It was too late to worry about what his mother would say if she found out, and anyway he didn't much care. "I've drunk for years."

"Indeed." Dollfus turned to the other man. "Malone?"

The Irishman shook his head. "If there's a thief aboard the *Bellatrix*, that's something more for Krupa than for me. And I can't offer Kahlúa, for I've nothing like that. But if it's just a drink that you're wanting, as a replacement like, then I can surely oblige. Hold on, now."

He turned and began to rummage in a footlocker at the side of the table. He came up with a bottle filled with a clear brown liquid and set it down on the table.

Shelby stared curiously. The bottle's label was written in a language that he did not recognize. "What is that?"

Malone raised his eyebrows. "Well, that depends who you are. To some people, it's no more than a drink. But to me and my folk, it's *usquebaugh*—which means the water of life. It's no match for your Kahlúa, I'm sure, but maybe it's better than nothing. Chief, will you do the honors?"

Dollfus nodded. He reached behind him to produce three plastic glasses. Malone opened the bottle and poured with a steady hand an exactly equal measure of brown liquid into each. In the low gravity provided by the ship's slow rotation, the fluid moved slowly and sluggishly, seeming far more viscous than it was. Malone handed one glass to Dollfus and one to Shelby.

"To the pride of the Cheevers," he said. He and Dollfus raised their glasses to Shelby and took the liquid down in one gulp.

Shelby tried to copy their actions exactly as he emptied his glass. There was one split second when the drink felt cold in his throat, then it turned to liquid flame. He gasped. He could feel it trickling down into his stomach, starting a fire every inch of the way.

"How is it, then?" Malone asked.

"Just—just fine." Shelby answered through clenched teeth, swallowing saliva between words. "Good strong—flavor."

"I hoped you'd find it acceptable." Malone was pouring again. "One more for us, then the rest of the bottle is yours. Bottoms up, and no heel taps."

This time Shelby closed his eyes. The inner burning wasn't such a shock this time, and it didn't take his breath away.

"You like that, do you?" Malone said. "I hoped you would." He winked at Dollfus.

"It's—it's real great stuff." Shelby took a deep breath and grabbed the bottle as it was thrust at him. "More of a m-man's drink than Kahlúa. But I think I'd better not—I mean, I think I'll have the rest of it—in my cabin."

He turned and hurried out before they could make any other suggestion.

The whole ship was silent and almost dark, and as he passed through the dim-lit interior he began to be filled with the strangest sensation. The warmth that had started in his throat and stomach was spreading steadily through his whole body. And it didn't make him feel bad—quite the opposite. He felt a sense of tremendous well-being and confidence, a knowledge that there was nothing that he could not do. Nothing that he *would* not do. His mind had never been clearer and more forceful.

He came to the middle section of the ship between the passenger and the crew quarters. One of the observation ports was located here, as well as an airlock with an array of suits beside it.

Shelby went to the port and peered out. There it was, so near and yet so far. The node was just kilometers away, the round pearly glow of its entry chamber seemingly close enough to touch. The *Bellatrix* had been carefully parked next to the node, with just enough end-over-end rotation to provide a comfortable pseudo-gravity in the living quarters.

He opened the bottle of *usquebaugh*, lifted it to his lips, and took a tentative sip. It didn't burn at all now on the way down.

Krupa had suggested using a machine to take Shelby through the network, and he had scoffed at the idea. But she didn't have to know. In fact, he wouldn't even *need* a machine. He knew exactly how to put a suit on. His trip with Garrity had proved that there was no big deal to flying in any direction you liked. As for the network entry chamber, from this distance there was no way a person could possibly miss it.

Why not? He had no idea how to get back, but they would take care of that easily enough at the other end. They would *have* to—his ticket clearly called for a two-way trip through the network.

Shelby moved over to the rack of suits and picked out the same one that he had worn on his visit to CM-67. He put it on and puzzled his way through the thirty-six checkpoints, pausing before he closed the helmet for a final mouthful of Malone's whiskey. The suit insisted that two of the seals were wrong. He fiddled with them until the signal came at last that the suit was properly closed.

He was ready to go. Wasn't he?

He stared at his own hand. Whoops! Couldn't take the bottle, it would probably explode when the air was pumped out. He laid Malone's gift, a little reluctantly, on the rack of suits. *Usquebaugh*. The water of life. What a perfect name.

As he entered the airlock, a bizarre machine that looked like a pair of interlocking sets of deer antlers came writhing across to him. Its clucking, clattering, and clicking were nothing more than an annoying buzz in his indifferent ear. He ignored the display unit that it held out insistently toward him.

He'd use a machine when he felt like he *needed* a machine. Right now he certainly didn't. He was able to do anything that a dumb machine could do, and a whole lot better.

Strange. The thought filled his head as the airlock quietly cycled, and hard vacuum replaced the air around him. Strange how *fixated* people in space were with their damned *machines*. He couldn't see any use for them at all. Didn't *need* them at all.

The network node was sitting right in front of him as he drifted out of the lock. It looked as big and chilly as a hunter's moon in his native Virginian sky.

He stared at it until his eyes watered and blurred his vision. Yes, there really was a Virginia, although half the crew of the *Bellatrix* might not realize it. They had not been born on Earth. They probably never went closer to the surface of the planet than low orbit. He knew more about really important things than the lot of them put together.

Where *was* the Earth, anyway?

He peered all around. Several planets over there near the Sun, but which was which? He couldn't tell.

Well, it wouldn't matter in a few minutes. The Kuiper Belt was so far from the sun that only Jupiter, according to the travel brochures, could be seen without a telescope.

Shelby allowed himself to drift slowly toward the node. He was in no hurry. He did not know that an unauthorized exit from the *Bellatrix* had just been recorded. Had he known, it would only have made him move faster. He felt not a trace of guilt about what he was doing. Hadn't the cruise line *promised* a transfer through the node network, for anyone who was interested? It was their fault if he had been forced to take matters into his own hands. Nobody told a Cheever, specially not Shelby Crawford Jerome Prescott Cheever, what he could and couldn't do.

The node was closer now. He guessed that it was at least forty meters across. There would be no problem hitting it dead center—provided that he was *allowed* to. More pesky machines were in his way. They had emerged from within the pearly radiance of the node itself and were right in front of him, trying to block his path. Two of them were holding out funny-looking consoles covered with buttons and little display screens. He waved them out of the way. When they did not move he increased his speed and barged right on through.

They avoided him at the last minute. He could hear excited squeaks on his suit radio. They sounded like pure gibberish. On the other hand, his own head was suddenly spinning and he was not sure he would have understood them regardless of the language.

Come on, machines! He laughed out loud as he soared through the hazy aperture of the node. *Don't give up! Catch me if you can.*

And then suddenly everything was not so fine. As he passed into the node he felt his whole body begin to rotate in one direction while the inside of his head went in another. It made no difference if his eyes were open or closed. The rainbow internal glow of the node was turning a hundred ways at once. He was riding a giant multicolored whirligig that every few seconds chose to vanish and reassemble itself and turn all the different parts of him in multiple different directions.

It was almost a relief when a final spin took him in a direction where there were no directions. He felt himself twisted out of space itself; and in that ultimate nowhere blackness he felt nothing at all.

CHAPTER THREE

SOUND returned before sight. Shelby could squeeze his eyes shut against the bright, bluish light, but there was no way to keep out of his ears the harsh *clunk-clunk-clunk* that came in over his suit radio. It drove hot metallic spikes of pain through his head.

He groaned and muttered, "Stop that. No more." His mouth was dry and clotted, and when he touched his tongue to his front teeth they tasted furred and acid. He knew he had thrown up—how many times?—but his suit could cope with that. It was designed to absorb everything tangible. What it could not do was go inside his head and wipe away the nausea and pain and the taste of vomit.

If only that noise would stop!

He lay until he could stand it no longer, then opened his swollen eyes. At first he saw nothing. He was in some sort of low-acceleration field, and its gentle force was pressing him face-down onto something soft. He lifted his head—there was bag after puffy bag of black plastic beneath him—and peered out through his suit's visor. His first impression was of endless open space. His world had become nothing but a glowing field of swirling blue and indigo. It took a few more seconds to realize that a slender lattice of dark supporting struts imposed a regular pattern upon the chaotic background.

He allowed his head to fall forward onto the padded bags. He must be in a ship, but it was a ship like none he had ever seen or heard of; little more than a framework, a cobweb-thin skeleton of narrow beams that arched up from the floor where he lay to form a curving birdcage above him.

There must be more to it than that. Something below the floor was providing a steady acceleration. And *somebody*, some damnable body, was sending the excruciating thump-thump-thump over his suit's radio that made any form of rest impossible.

Shelby lifted his head again and stared around. He found that the hazy blue background was creeping past the dark lattice of struts. The birdcage he lay in was turning, slowly and steadily. And when he looked more closely he saw that the backdrop was not uniform. Brighter points of light lay scattered within it.

Stars, blazing through a fog of gas and dust? Nothing that he had read about the Kuiper Belt suggested the presence there of a great dust cloud. And no fog or stars could explain the rhythmic clash of sound that still plagued his ears.

Shelby turned his head, wincing at the pain. He lay near the center of a circular floor maybe fifteen meters across. The bags beneath him stretched away on his left to a low circular wall or partition. They were piled up to the top. On his right, though, the floor was still partially clear. As he watched, another bag came sailing over and landed in one of the open spots. Shelby caught a glimpse of the long, spidery arm that had delivered it, but the body of the thrower was hidden on the other side of the wall.

He sighed, lifted himself up, and crawled on hands and knees to his right. When he came to the wall he raised himself farther and peered over the edge.

The arm belonged not to a person but to a machine. It was shaped like an outsized version of Malone's bottle of *usquebaugh*, with a tangled snakes' nest of wires where the cap should have been. Eight skinny arms grew out from the smooth golden sides.

Two of those arms clamped the machine securely to the outside of the wall. Two more were reaching out into space, feeling their way along what seemed like an endless thick black wire. Every forty meters or so, a rough-surfaced sphere about a meter across was hung on the cable like a silver bead on a necklace. The ship was moving along the wire, and as a new bead came within reach an arm of the machine reached out and detached a filled sack from the side of the bead. It hurled it in-board to an unoccupied site on the floor, while another pair of arms neatly attached an empty sack to replace the full one. The rhythmic thump and clatter in Shelby's ears coincided with the detachment of the full bag and its empty replacement.

Shelby stared out along the line of the dark cable. Like a necklace, it was not straight but formed a great arc in space.

The center of the arc seemed to lie in the same direction as the apex of the birdcage arch above him.

He raised his head farther and stared straight up. Sure enough, something was out there. It was partly obscured by the lattice of arching struts, but he saw an ugly, lumpy doughnut shape. The cable seemed to curve all the way from the ship where Shelby lay, to run *behind* the squashed silver ring.

He was feeling more wretched than ever, but his aching brain threw at him an overall image of what he was seeing. The structure that he lay in was traveling steadily along the great circle of the cable. It was moving like this so that the machine clinging to the wall could reach out and take something every few meters from another bead. The silver open disk above his head lay at the center of the cable's arc. The gentle force that held Shelby to the floor was not the acceleration of a drive, as he had at first assumed, but the centrifugal force produced as he and the ship swung around that center like a stone on the end of a string.

It was an explanation that seemed to explain nothing; and although the multi-armed machine might be perfectly comfortable in the near-vacuum of space, there was a limit to how long Shelby could survive inside his suit. His monitor showed that he had only enough air for about one more hour.

Five minutes ago he had felt ready to die; now he was worried that he might. He raised himself higher above the rim of the wall.

"Hey!" His call was feeble and croaking. "Hey! Is anybody there? Can anyone hear this radio?"

No welcome human voice answered, but a screeching noise like high-pitched static added to the regular clanking in his earpiece. The sound was repeated several times, with a twenty-second pause between. The snakes' nest of wires on the machine's head writhed with new energy, but otherwise it seemed to take no notice. It calmly continued its work, lobbing filled sacks past Shelby onto unoccupied areas of the floor. The field of stars and dust cloud continued to turn steadily about them. The disk above neither grew nor shrank in apparent size.

And that was all, for nearly an hour. Shelby was ready to throw himself over the wall into open space—anything was better than sitting helpless until you went into a carbon dioxide coma—when he suddenly found himself in free-fall. The machine stopped throwing bags into the space where he was sitting and swung nimbly in over the wall. Before Shelby had time to worry about floating away into nowhere, a new force pressed him to the floor.

This time, however, it was a true acceleration. Above his head the squashed disk began to grow in size. It was huge, and as they came closer Shelby could see several round openings in the broad outer side of it. The apex of the birdcage was heading straight for one of them.

He expected the ship to fly on through to the interior, and was preparing for that when the struts above him suddenly sprang apart from each other, changing the closed tulip bud of the lattice into the form of a broad open flower. The ship stopped abruptly as the struts met the side of the disk. Shelby, along with the black bags and the bottle-shaped machine and anything else that was not held down, kept going. He flew on helplessly until his forward motion was slowed and halted by a waiting net, springy but strong.

He found himself in pitch darkness. He hung there and groaned aloud in fear and misery.

And a cheerful young voice answered his moan. "See!" it said. "I told you so."

Another voice answered, "You were right, Gracie. And

I thought old Logan was about ready for the scrap heap. Sorry about that, stranger. Welcome aboard!"

Shelby felt a vibration in the net and heard a loud hissing. At the same time a cold blue-white light filled the space around him. He could finally see where he was. He lay in a big, bare-walled chamber, almost buried by filled black plastic bags. There seemed far more of them than he had seen collected by the machine. The aperture through which he had entered was now closed tight, and white jets of fog were emerging from the walls. He hoped that it was air—his supply was down to a few minutes—but his suit's monitor was not yet showing that the atmosphere around him was safe to breathe.

Of the bottle-shaped machine there was no sign. Shelby struggled free of the heaps of soft bags. In what his balance centers told him was down, beneath the net, he saw a pair of suited figures. They stood on a sort of catwalk running across the width of the chamber.

Humans—at last! He had seen enough of machines, here and on the *Bellatrix*, to last him the rest of his life.

Clumsily, he scrambled over to the edge of the net and allowed himself to drop gently down onto the catwalk. One of the figures made a gesture toward his helmet, and they both began to take off their suits.

His suit monitor agreed that there was now breathable air in the chamber. Shelby opened the seals with fingers that felt like somebody else's. It was a huge effort to remove his helmet, but at last he did so.

The other two, astonishingly, were already completely out of their suits. They had managed the whole thing in just a few seconds. Shelby saw a grinning boy of twelve or thirteen, standing next to a girl close to his own age or maybe a bit older.

They came easily across to him while he was still struggling to open the front of his suit.

"Here." The boy reached out. "Let me help with that." And then, when he was close enough to sample the air that was leaking out into the chamber, "Phew! What have you been *doing* in there?"

Shelby saw no need to reply. The smell made it obvious.

"You must be feeling rotten," the girl said seriously. She was neatly and efficiently stripping him out of his suit. "I'm Grace Trask. Welcome aboard the *Harvest Moon*—best ship in the harvester fleet."

"And I'm Doobie Trask," said the boy. "The brains of the family." He took Shelby's suit, placed the helmet inside, and dropped the whole thing casually to the floor. "I guess I owe you an apology. Gracie believed Logan, and I didn't. What can we do for you now?—other than a good long bath."

Shelby was tempted to say *Send me back*. He had a low opinion of the *Bellatrix*, but compared with this place it was a palace. On the other hand, what would Krupa and Malone and Garrity say if they found that he had come all the way out to the Kuiper Belt and then returned without seeing anything more than the inside of his spacesuit? He needed to prove that he had been somewhere and done something.

"Who's Logan?" he asked. "I'd like to meet him, and some more people as well."

"Well, you will," Grace Trask said. "After all, Logan was really the one who saved you. But there's plenty of time for that." She wrinkled her nose. "What else do you need?"

Shelby became aware of his own powerful aroma. The suit had done its best, but that best wasn't nearly good enough. "Well, I guess that a hot shower would feel great."

"A shower, and a meal?" Doobie asked. "We'll be eating soon."

"Maybe." And maybe not. At the mention of food Shelby's mouth, throat, and stomach suddenly resonated with the feel and taste of Malone's fiendish *usquebaugh*. There was one liquid that he would never touch again. "A small meal."

Doobie stared at him curiously. "No offense, but you don't *look* like somebody who eats small meals. But let's get moving and we'll find out. By the way, what's your name?"

"Shelby Cheever. Actually, it's Shelby Crawford *Jerome Prescott Cheever*." Shelby paused expectantly. Anywhere on Earth that name would produce instant attention and respect, and then the question, "Are you related in any way to *the* Jerome Prescott Cheever?"

"Bit of a mouthful," Doobie said casually. "If you don't mind, Gracie and I will just introduce you to people as Shel. All right?"

"Fine." Shelby smiled to himself. Apparently Cheever Consolidated Enterprises was not yet a synonym for wealth and power to teenagers out in the Kuiper Belt. The surprise to Grace and Doobie Trask would be that much greater when they learned the truth.

"A shower, a meal, and meet some people," he went on. "That would be perfect. Let's take maybe four hours. Then I'll have to be heading back."

Grace Trask had been leading the way, moving from the entry chamber along a bare metal-walled corridor that passed from the cargo holds to the living quarters of the *Harvest Moon*. Now she paused. She and Doobie stared at each other, then turned to face Shelby.

"Getting back?" she said.

"To the Asteroid Belt. My ticket promised me a trip through the node network, but I can't stay away too long because Mother will give me hell if I do. She'll say the *Bellatrix* has to finish the cruise and get back to Earth—though I don't know why she'd care. So far she hasn't even looked outside."

"Getting back," Grace said again, as though she hadn't heard one word that Shelby had said. "To the Asteroid Belt and Earth."

"That's right. You got it. We have four hours, maybe five."

"Shel, just where do you think you are?"

"In the Kuiper Belt, in the mining region." Shelby thought suddenly of the swirling cloud of blue and indigo. It was like nothing he had ever heard of—and the sky outside the ship had contained nothing as bright as Sol, even diminished by fifteen billion kilometers of distance.

"Isn't that where I am?" he asked, almost in a whisper; but from their faces he already knew the answer.

"Where you are," said Grace, slowly and carefully, "is not in the Kuiper Belt. It's not anywhere close to the Kuiper Belt. I don't know how you got here or why you came, but you are on board the independent harvester *Harvest Moon*. And we are in the middle of the Messina Dust Cloud. We are twenty-seven light-years from Earth, the Asteroid Belt, the Kuiper Belt, and anything else in the vicinity of Sol."

She moved to stand right in front of him. "I hate to tell you this, Shel. But you're an awful long way from home."

At first Shelby thought that Grace Trask was making a mountain out of nothing.

So he had screwed up using the node network, and accidentally jumped to a node much farther out than his intended goal of the Kuiper Belt. Big deal. That wasn't important. From everything he had heard, physical distance didn't mean much when you used the node network.

You used more energy, of course, and you would receive a bigger bill for the service. But so what? Such things had nothing to do with Shelby. His army of accountants back on Earth were employed to deal with those sorts of matters. As for the cost, he could hop out to the Messina Dust Cloud and back every day for the rest of his life and still not make a dent in his trust funds.

His confidence persisted through a brain-restoring shower followed by a simple meal that he, Grace, and Doobie ate together tucked away in a corner of the *Harvest Moon*'s cramped galley. While Shelby wolfed down food—his appetite had miraculously returned—Doobie prattled nonstop about the superior talents aboard their ship and the marvels of the Messina Cloud.

"Thirty-one independent harvesters at work now," he said, "but not one to match us. Muv knows the Cloud like the back of her hand. She finds the pockets of stable transuranics like she can smell 'em. We're smack in the middle of one now."

Shelby didn't actually know what transuranics were and he was reluctant to ask. "You mean the transuranics come from way out here?" he asked.

"Every last gram of 'em, from the Messina Cloud. Have to." Doobie stared hard at Shelby. "You say you're from Earth. I guess that explains it."

"Explains what?"

"Why you don't seem to know scut about anything. I don't blame you," Doobie went on, with a sweeping generosity that made Shelby fume. "Way I see it, when you're one of fourteen billion trying to figure out where your next meal comes from, you don't have time to worry none about much else."

Shelby decided, in that same instant, that he was somehow going to take Doobie to Earth and show him the Cheever estate; the Cheever model city, too, and the Cheever sea farms, and maybe a few dozen of the Cheever model factories.

"Stable transuranics *only* come from the Messina Cloud," Doobie continued. "In fact, until they put a node here, nobody knew they was even *possible.*"

"But what *are* they?" Shelby didn't mind asking anymore. His time would come to tell Doobie and Grace something of his life on Earth.

"Transuranics?" Doobie stared at Shelby openmouthed. "Whoo! You telling me you don't know even *that?* You do know the table of the elements by heart, don't you?"

"No." Shelby's private tutors had mentioned it, or at least he thought they had. But there seemed no reason why anyone in his right mind would want to commit that sort of thing to memory.

"You will," Doobie said mysteriously. "Anyway, there's ninety-two natural elements. Hydrogen's the lightest, uranium's the heaviest. You can make heavier ones yet, but trouble is, the transuranics aren't stable—they're radioactive, and they decay over time into other things."

"I do know that much." Shelby didn't like Doobie's know-it-all attitude, but what he found harder to take was Grace Trask's sympathetic silence.

"Ah—but sometimes they *don't* decay," said Doobie. "Here, in the Messina Cloud, there are stable transuranic elements."

"But if everywhere else they're not stable—"

"They're not *naturally* stable, even here. Somebody or something *made* them stable, using a technique nobody understands yet. Near as we can figure it"—Doobie spoke with the casual self-confidence of someone who might well have done the research work himself—"something pretty bad happened here maybe two million years ago. That's when the whole dust cloud was created. But we don't really know, because anything around here at that time was *un*created. Who knows? Maybe sometime the same thing will happen again."

"So what are you doing here?" It seemed crazy to Shelby that anyone would discover a danger spot and go there voluntarily.

"I just told you." Doobie spoke as though to a small and backward child. "For the transuranics! People have to make a living, you know. I suppose you don't?"

The temptation was great, but Shelby restrained himself. He would reveal exactly who he was when he had a larger audience. More than two people deserved to watch Doobie Trask's mouth drop open in amazement.

"What I don't see is how you knew the stable transuranics were here," he said mildly. "Twenty-seven light-years is a long way. And finding a network node right where you want it seems too good to be true."

"It would be, if we had." Grace from her close inspection of Shelby seemed to suspect that he was hiding something, but her friendly manner did not change. "Actually, it worked the other way round. Over a century and a half ago the Messina Cloud was noticed as a peculiar little blob in space with strange spectral emission lines. It was only a few light-hours across, and nobody had any idea what might be here. But a photon information packet was sent out at light speed to investigate. When it arrived it discovered the stable transuranics. After that the packet used the cloud's own materials to fabricate the first node. That was just tiny, but with a little one in place materials could be sent through to make it bigger. Everything was bootstrapped like that until there was finally a node big enough for the *Harvest Moon* and the other independent harvesters to come through. And then we were off and running."

Shelby might not know much about transuranics, but his

father's business sense had been delivered with his genes.

"Doesn't figure," he said. "It must have cost a fortune to put that node in place. Who paid for it?"

"We did. And we do." Grace's voice was bitter. "The cost of our node was covered long ago, but every independent harvester who works the Messina Cloud still pays the node tax. That's where most of our profits go—back to some bloodsucking finance shark on Earth. Every gram of transuranics pays its toll, and what do we see in return? Nothing."

Shelby had a vague recollection that Cheever Enterprises held a market corner in bringing superheavy elements down to Earth. It didn't seem the moment to mention that. The arrival of three more people in the galley while Grace was still talking came as a distinct relief.

The newcomers formed a mixed trio. The man leading the way was tall and imposing and overweight. His white hair was receding, but he made up for that with a flourishing set of bushy white side-whiskers that framed a ruddy face. As he walked, he kept turning to the man behind him.

"If I've told you once, I've told you a million times," he grumbled. "The corries are *designed* to dock *themselves*. You don't need to be in there a-doing. You start to dabble and you're *guaranteed* to have trouble."

"Yes, Thurgood. I won't do it again. I promise." The man following was short and of a slight build, and his pale gray eyes and unlined brow gave him a look of guileless innocence.

"You do, do you?" Thurgood's face went redder with frustration. "And haven't you told me that same thing a million times? And still you're at it."

"Maybe. Maybe I have told you that. I'm not sure."

"Well, *I'm* sure." The fat man snorted. "As sure as Doobie there will steal your food from the galley. But every time when we're on final approach, you start in on them controls again and throw me head over teakettle, and I finish smack up in the cargo with even the machines laughing at me. I'm telling you, *Scrimshander Limes*"—the way he spoke the words sounded more like an oath than a name—"I'm telling you that if you do it *one more time*, then as sure as my name's Thurgood Trask I'll—I'll . . ."

It sounded serious, but Shelby saw Grace Trask's delighted grin. Whatever it was between Thurgood Trask and Scrimshander Limes, it had been going on for a long time.

"I won't do it anymore." Scrimshander spoke contritely.

"You better not. Or there'll be consequences." Thurgood Trask turned and caught sight of Doobie, who happened to be winking at Shelby. The big man once more addressed the man walking behind him. "There will be consequences. For instance, you might find, Scrimshander Limes, that instead of being partnered with me, who helps you every way he can, you'll be harvesting the cloud with a young lout who lacks the decency to show respect to his elders and betters even when they happen to be his own flesh and blood and they never ask anything more of him than an uncle should be able to expect from a nephew. You wouldn't want that, would you?"

Scrimshander hesitated. He gave the impression that he had become lost somewhere in the middle of Thurgood Trask's last speech. "No, Thurgood," he said at last. "I wouldn't want that. Would I?"

"You certainly would *not.*"

"Then I wouldn't."

"All right, then. Enough said." Thurgood Trask sniffed and stepped forward to inspect the contents of the galley."

"I cooked that," Doobie said at once. "It's mine."

"Are you going to eat it?"

"I dunno. I might."

"That's quite enough, Doobie." The woman who had entered behind the other two spoke for the first time. "Uncle Thurgood and Scrimshander will eat as much of that food as they like. And you can introduce me to our accidental visitor, and let me welcome him aboard."

She was short and slenderly built, and her voice was low and pleasant. But Shelby had been observing pecking-order ladders since he was an infant. He had no doubt who was in charge.

He stepped toward the woman. "I'm Shelby. Shelby *Cheever*." Again he waited for the name to have its magical effect, and again he was disappointed.

The woman merely held out her hand. "Lana Trask. Captain of the *Harvest Moon;* and mother, for my sins, of these two." She smiled at Grace and Doobie. "I hope they've been looking after you."

"Just fine, thanks." Shelby shook her hand vigorously. "I'm really grateful. And I'll prove it, believe me I will. You may not realize just who your ship has picked up." He stood a little straighter, put one hand in his pocket, and stuck out his belly. He coughed in a self-conscious way. "My full name is Shelby Crawford Jerome Prescott Cheever. When you send me back I'm going to make sure that you get a reward— a big one. Money. And how's a new ship sound to you?" He glanced around the galley with its battered fixtures. "Seems to me the *Harvest Moon*'s a little bit old and dirty and creaky."

Grace Trask's action should have warned him. She turned her head so that Shelby could see her face and Lana Trask could not, and mouthed "No!"

Shelby ignored her. "And jobs back on Earth, too, for all of you that want them. I'm talking good jobs, places within Cheever Enterprises. Maybe on one of the estates, maybe in a factory. I'm sure my old man will swing for that."

Lana Trask's face had tightened when he spoke about

her ship. Now she frowned. "Your old man?"

"My dad. I'm talking about J. P. Cheever. I'm his only son."

"Is that right. And you say you're from Earth?"

"You better believe it."

Lana Trask turned away from Shelby. "Thurgood? You've been there. Does the name Cheever ring a bell with you?"

Thurgood Trask rubbed at his white side-whiskers. "Cheever, Cheever. Let's see. It's been a while—near seven years. Wait a minute, though." He frowned at Shelby. "What kind of business you say your father is in?"

"All kinds. Manufacturing, transportation, health care, agriculture, recreation, computers, minerals, sea farms—"

"Sea farms. Seems to me . . ." Thurgood's brow was furrowed. "Seems to me there *was* a Cheever."

"Rich enough to buy a ship like the *Harvest Moon*?" Lana Trask asked.

"No, no." Thurgood Trask snorted, as though at the very idea. "I remember him now. He ran a fish supply house. Hardly made enough to live on, never mind enough to buy anything. And now I think of it, his name wasn't Cheever at all—it was Seever."

"Did you ever meet *anyone* on Earth rich enough to buy a ship like this one?"

"Never did. Lana, people on Earth aren't like us. They're *poor*. There's fourteen billion of the poor devils, and nine out of ten of 'em go to bed hungry and wake up worse."

"That's what I've heard." Lana Trask turned to Grace and Doobie. "You sure he was all right when you picked him up. No head injuries, no drugs or drink?"

"No injuries." Grace spoke reluctantly. "Drink, though. He stank of it when we opened his suit."

"Drunk, and sick," added Doobie. "But he's all right now. He had a shower and a meal."

"Now just one minute!" Shelby had listened to all the talk about him as though he wasn't there, and he was not going to tolerate any more of it. He stepped closer to Lana Trask. "I'm telling you, my father is J. P. Cheever. He's the head of Cheever Consolidated Enterprises! That makes him one of the richest and most powerful people on Earth. He could buy you and your crew and this crummy old ship a hundred times over, and never even notice. If you know what's good for you, you'd better head back to the node this minute. You'd better send me home, too, just as soon as you can—or you'll regret it. And that's an order."

"Is it now?" Lana Trask said quietly. She was half a head shorter than Shelby, and she had to tilt her face back to stare into his eyes. "An order, you say. Well, you may not know much about life on a harvester ship like this, and you may still be half-drunk. So I'll be easy on you. But here's a free lesson: Only one person on the *Harvest Moon* gives orders; and that person is not an accidental new-aboard, whether he's called Shelby Cheever or anything else."

She took a deep breath and seemed to grow a couple of inches. "And while I'm making a speech, which anyone here will tell you is *not* my natural habit, I'll point out something else to you. Do you have any idea how lucky you are just to be *alive*? From the speed that Logan logged you at when you were first spotted, you must have whistled out of the Messina node a thousand times as fast as it's safe to do it. Who calibrated your source and destination node velocities before you entered back at Sol? Was it you? And were you too reeling drunk to get it right?"

Shelby stared at her.

"I thought so," she went on. "It was sheer dumb luck that

you didn't die right then and there as you came out of the node. And more dumb luck that Logan saw you and was in a position to rescue you. But it wasn't dumb luck for me and for everyone else on the *Harvest Moon*. It was pure dumb *bad* luck, because to save you I had to hold our position fourteen extra hours. That means we've lost our advantage over the other harvesters—all thanks to Shelby Cheever.

"And here's one final piece of learning for you, before you go and sleep it off and wake up rational and reasonable: I can't return you to Earth through the node network at this time, for three good reasons. First, we're heading in exactly the wrong direction. We're on the outward sweep, following the cloud currents with the rest of the harvesters. Our fuel budget doesn't permit the sort of wild maneuver that you're asking. Second, we're carrying a load of pharmaceuticals. I promised to make a drop-off of them when we reach the Confluence, and two ships coming from the more distant reefs will be depending on us. And third, there are mouths to feed on this ship. Who's going to do that if we don't find and take aboard a load of transuranics? Not you, that's for sure. You'll be looked after here, but I didn't ask you to come aboard and I can't risk other people's livelihoods for the sake of an extra unwanted passenger.

"You'll get to Earth right enough—if that's where you really come from. I'll take you back through the node. But I'll do it on *our* schedule, not one made up to suit the whim of the sainted only-son-of-his-father Shelby Cheever."

"When?" Although Lana Trask had never once raised her voice, Shelby felt crushed by the flow of words. "How long before you take me back to the node?"

"That depends on you as well as me. We return to the node as soon as we have a full hold. That's going to be at least a couple more months, probably three, but if you work really hard with us it could be less." Lana Trask nodded to

Grace and Doobie. "Take care of him. Help him to sober up. And we'll talk about the rest of it later."

Maybe it was the aftereffects of the drink, but Shelby felt like crying. He was very on edge, and try as he might he couldn't repress a sniffle.

Oddly enough, Grace and Doobie seemed to find that neither odd nor disgraceful.

"It's Muv," Doobie said. "You know what mothers are like."

Shelby thought of his own mother, vapory and nervous and apparently afraid of everything. He remembered Constance Cheever waking Branton in the middle of the night to come to her suite and remove a small spider, and recalled her screams and wails of terror when Shelby fell off a horse during a riding lesson.

Spiders and falls from horseback might not occur aboard the *Harvest Moon*, but Shelby couldn't see Lana Trask being worried by them if they did. That thought did nothing to make him feel better.

"We don't notice it, of course." Grace was responding to his silence. "Because we've known her all our lives. She's our muv. But others say that the first time you meet her she runs right over you."

"She said I was an idiot," Shelby said sullenly. "And that I was drunk. And she implied I was a *liar*."

There was another long silence, while Grace and Doobie stared at each other.

"Were you?" Grace asked at last.

"No! It's all true, every word of it. I'm sorry I said the *Harvest Moon* is a piece of junk, but my father has enough money to buy a thousand ships like this. Hell, *I* could buy this ship, ten times over."

"But everybody knows that people on Earth are *poor*," said Grace. She looked as though she wanted to believe Shelby but didn't quite see how she could. "Uncle Thurgood was there for a year, and he says there are people starving in the streets. Are you telling us that *he's* lying?"

"No." Shelby had heard the same thing, but he had never seen it. No one that he knew went into the middle cities or anyplace else where the general public had access. The nearest thing to poor people he had ever encountered was in airports, where passengers of the private aircars and the public planes might share a concourse. But anyone who flew was not likely to be going hungry.

"Your uncle isn't lying," he said at last. "There are lots of poor people on Earth. And I guess some of them might be starving. But remember, Earth supports fourteen billion people. Somebody is bound to go short."

"Nobody in space starves or goes short of food," Doobie said flatly.

"They would, if there were enough of you."

"No. We wouldn't let it happen, no matter how many of us there were. *We* look after each other."

"But it's not Shel's fault if it happens on Earth." Grace sensed a rising tension and tried to deflect it. "Is it true, you really are rich enough to buy this ship?"

"I assume that I am. I don't know how much something like this costs."

"Four or five trillion cumes," said Doobie. "That would be buying the ship new, of course."

"I don't know what a cume is."

"A *cume*—you know, C-U-M-E. Cubic meter. Of helium-3, at standard temperature and pressure."

"But I was talking about how much the ship would cost in *money*."

"Cumes *are* money." Doobie stuck his chin out. "The

only sensible standard of money. *Everybody* uses cumes."

"Not on Earth they don't. Sounds dumb to me. What about dollars?"

"What can you do with *dollars*, even if you have 'em? They're just useless mass to lug around with you. Helium-3 is rare enough to be valuable, and everybody uses it for the fusion drives."

"I didn't mean *actual* dollars. I never carry them around, even on Earth. I meant electronic dollars, transferred from one computer to another."

"You can't run a ship's fusion drive on an electronic transfer. You need something *real*—like cumes of helium-3."

"Real physical money is something out of Noah's Ark. Out-of-date for centuries on Earth."

"Yes, and just look at Earth. People starving there. Even you admit it."

"All right." Grace had to step in again. "If you two want to fight, I can't stop you. But you won't do it on *my* time. Look, Shel, it's getting late and you're pretty wasted. You said earlier that you'd like to meet Logan again. Do you want to do that tonight, or would you rather wait until tomorrow morning?"

The word was slipped in so naturally that Shelby almost missed it. "What do you mean, meet Logan *again?* I haven't met Logan at all."

"Of course you have."

"I haven't. I know I haven't."

"You have."

"Now it's you who's at him instead of me," said Doobie. "There's an easy way to settle this. We'll go see Logan and find out who's right."

"I am," said Grace.

"No, I am," said Shelby. He had been sneered at and put down by everybody from the moment that he arrived on the

Harvest Moon, but at last he had something that he was sure about.

But he wasn't sure five minutes later, after Doobie and Grace had led him on a sinuous path from the central habitat of the *Harvest Moon* to one of the outer cargo holds, dim and cavernous.

"Meet Logan—*again*," said Grace.

And Shelby did meet Logan again. For Logan was the multi-armed, wire-headed, bottle-shaped oddity that he had last seen as the birdcage ship docked at the *Harvest Moon*.

CHAPTER FOUR

SHELBY woke up bit by bit, body before brain, memory before mind.

Everything seemed like a bad dream, starting from the moment when he had stepped on board the transfer vessel to take him up to the *Bellatrix*. As soon as he opened his eyes he would surely find himself safe in his own bedroom in the Cheever mansion, with Branton and the other staff waiting downstairs to fill his order for breakfast.

He opened his eyes. He was staring up at a ceiling of grey plastic no more than two feet above him. Sit upright, and he would bang his head. The bunk that he lay in was adequately soft, but it was barely long or wide enough to contain him.

Shelby sighed. For the first time in days he felt concern for his mother. She must know by now that he had vanished into the node network. Since he had not appeared in the Kuiper Belt as planned, she probably assumed that he was dead. And according to Grace and Doobie, until he returned through the node in three months' time there was no way to reassure her.

He sat up carefully and swung his legs over the side of his bed. He had slept in a tiny grey-walled cabin, hardly longer than the bunk and only twice as wide. The entire furnishings were a locker underneath the bunk, a little desk and chair and terminal, and a solid plastic door that could be locked from the inside.

Three months. He was supposed to live like this for three whole months? He would go crazy.

He went outside, unsteady on his feet. The *Harvest Moon* must be under way, because a gentle but steady acceleration provided a sense of up and down and held him to the slightly tilted floor.

Which way to go? He stood in a featureless curving corridor with walls, floor, and ceiling made of the same drab plastic. He could not remember how he had got there the previous night.

With sight and memory of no use, he followed his nose. He could smell food. Sure enough, after following the corridor through a ninety-degree turn and passing four closed doors, he came to a wide opening. It led into the same crowded galley that he had eaten in the previous night. Now that he was less overwhelmed by the strangeness of his surroundings, he could see unfamiliar appliances and gadgets on every wall.

Grace Trask was sitting at the table opposite Thurgood Trask and Scrimshander Limes. They had apparently just finished eating, and Scrimshander was working with a small knife at something in his left hand. He lifted his head as Shelby entered, smiled shyly, and at once hid away what he was holding.

"Good morning, young man," Thurgood Trask said briskly. "Or should I say good *afternoon?* Come on, Scrimshander, come on. Work's a-waiting and time's a-wasting."

He rose from the table and led the other man out, while Grace sat grinning.

"Good morning, *young man,*" she said, as soon as they had gone. "Or should I say good afternoon? How do you feel today, Shel?"

Shelby dropped into the seat opposite her. "What was all that about?"

"Oh, it's just Uncle Thurgood." Grace pushed the dirty plates to the middle of the table. "He overslept, and now he's all bluster. He blames it on me and Scrim for not waking him. If he could he'd blame it on you too."

"But what was Scrimshander doing? He hid something when I came in, as though he didn't want me to see it."

"He didn't. Don't worry. It was nothing bad. He just didn't want you to look at the carving before it was finished."

"That's what he was doing? Carving?"

"How do you think he came to be called Scrimshander? It's not his real name. *Scrimshander* is an old word for the fancy carving that sailors used to do when they were on long voyages on Earth's seas. They used wood and bone and ivory, but you won't find any of those here. Scrim uses plastic. He's very good at it. He does it all the time when he and Uncle Thurgood aren't playing chess together."

"I've never in my whole life seen anyone doing that sort of handcraft work. What was he carving?"

"You'll see it soon enough. Are you hungry?"

"Starving." The change of subject told Shelby that Grace had said as much concerning the carving as she was going to say. He sat waiting, until he realized that she was not about to move.

"What's holding you?" she said at last.

"You asked if I was hungry. I am. I'm waiting for you to give me breakfast."

"Why should I?"

"You fed me last night."

"That was a special case. You seemed sick and lost." Grace put her elbows on the table. "Look, I hope you don't have the crazy idea that I or anyone else here is going to feed you *regularly.*" She waved a hand across to the array of appliances. "Go ahead."

Shelby stared at the strange machines. "I don't know how."

"You don't know how to use a *food synthesizer?* I don't believe it. What do people do when they want breakfast on Earth?"

"In my house, the kitchen staff makes it. I've never cooked a meal for myself in my whole life."

She was staring at him in disbelief. "I see," she said at last. "You know, I daren't tell Muv this, but I think I'm beginning to share your fantasies. The kitchen staff cooks your breakfast. So who cooks *their* breakfast? The kitchen elves? I'd heard about Earth people not using machines much, but I thought it was just spacer talk." She stood up. "Come on. You have to learn sometime. It might as well be now."

She showed Shelby how to program a food synthesizer, first giving him a quick overview and then taking each step in more detail.

"That's just a beginning, of course," she said when she was done. "The food machines are capable of much more than I've shown you. We don't usually cook for ourselves, but we take it in turns. Doobie's the worst cook—or he was, until you came along. Sometimes I think he's bad on purpose, so no one will ask him to do it. When it's my turn I like to produce something really fancy. Of course, I practice the meals on myself first. You'll probably want to do the same."

She returned to the table. Shelby realized that she had meant what she said. He was now supposed to program the synthesizer and eat whatever came out of it. He tentatively made his data entries and at last told the program to execute. The food machine began to gurgle and sizzle.

What emerged didn't look or smell too great. But a person who was really hungry could eat grey bread and purple sausage—especially if he wasn't willing to admit to Grace Trask that he hadn't known much about what he was doing.

She watched him to the last mouthful before she said, "Not bad for a first go, though I don't know if I could have swallowed any of it. Don't worry. You'll improve fast."

"It's called a synthesizer, but it must start from something. What does it start *with*?"

Grace opened her mouth, closed it again, and at last said, "Don't ask. Not yet. Come on. It's time to go to work."

"What do you mean, *work*?"

"While you were snoring your head off Doobie and I did you a big favor. Last night Muv had in mind that you should work and be paid a salary. This morning we persuaded her that wasn't too smart. We said you'd be a lot more motivated and productive if you were on the same basis as everybody else. The crew are all in for a share of the profits that the *Harvest Moon* makes from the voyage—even me and Doobie get some, though Muv just tucks it away for us 'til we're older.

Anyway, she agreed, even if she thinks that until your head clears you'll be crazy as a dust-cloud devil. So you'll be getting a share, too."

"For working? But I've never worked—"

"—in my whole life. Don't you think this is getting a bit monotonous? What *have* you done in your whole life? Anyway, if you can learn to use a food synthesizer, you can learn to work as part of a corry team."

"Quarry team?"

"Not quarry. *Corry.*"

"I've never so much as seen a corry. I don't even know what it is."

"You've not only seen one, you've been in one. It was a corry—a harvester coracle, to be formal—that saved you from dying in space and brought you to the *Harvest Moon.*"

Shelby recalled the birdcage ship. "Oh, *that* thing. That's a corry? You mean that *humans* as well as machines go outside in those?"

"Why not? You were outside in one. I suppose you don't consider yourself human. I can understand that." But the way that Grace was smiling at him took away the sting from her words. It made Shelby wonder why she and Doobie had gone to bat for him with Lana Trask. He couldn't recall any of his friends on Earth going out of their way to do anything for anybody except themselves. On the other hand, Grace Trask, with her casually trimmed hair, easy smile, and slightly grubby hands, was far different from anyone in the socially approved circle of girls of Shelby's age. Definitely NOCD. Constance Cheever would have a fit if she caught Shelby so much as talking to Grace. But the class structure in the Messina Dust Cloud, if one existed at all, must be like nothing on Earth.

He followed Grace as she led the way back along the

winding corridor that he remembered as leading to the outer cargo regions of the *Harvest Moon.*

"Logan again?"

"You've got it." If Grace recalled his first reaction to Logan she showed no sign of it. "We have five corries, but we normally use only three of them. The rest are reserves in case we were ever to lose a couple. Uncle Thurgood and Scrimshander Limes operate one of them. Wait 'til you see them in action! Doobie and Logan and I operate another. It's not fair, but Muv will let Logan operate without us and not us without Logan. Maybe she'll change her mind now that you're here. Jilter Clute—you'll meet him later—runs the other corry. He likes to work alone, except for Ace. Ace is another machine, pretty much like Logan—but you'd better not ever say that to either of them."

"Your mother"—Shelby, even if invited to do so, would never in a million years call Lana Trask *Muv*—"doesn't she work?"

"Not in the corries. Muv's the brains of the *Harvest Moon*, as well as the captain. She sits and sniffs." Grace must have realized that was less than clear, for she went on, "You see, most people think of the Messina Dust Cloud—if they think of it at all—as some sort of great uniform blob of gas and dust sitting in space. It's not like that at all. There's a detailed and complicated structure to it. Also it's in continuous movement, responding to gravitational and electromagnetic forces. Muv says you should think of it as great rolling dust rivers, merging and separating and sometimes overflowing their usual bounds. The dust rivers have never been fully mapped, not even the biggest ones. But that's not the worst part. The materials we're after—the pockets of stable transuranics—wander around in the dust rivers according to their own rules. The geometry is never the same twice. The hardest job for the captain of each harvester is *sniffing*—that's figuring out how the pockets are moving, and where they are likely to show up next. Muv's the fleet's master sniffer, the other harvesters all know it even if they don't admit it. Not even Muv can explain how she does it."

"You mean that you know the other harvesters and their captains, personally?"

"Sure. I mean, we're deadly rivals, but at the same time we have more in common with each other than with anybody else in the universe. We'll all meet in about six more weeks, when we get to the Confluence. That's a place on the other side of the Messina Dust Cloud from the node, where all the major currents meet. You'll see all the ships—the *Southern Cross*, and the *Dancing Lady*, and *Balaclava* and *Hope and Glory* and *Coruscation* and *Sweet Chariot*, and a couple of dozen others. Get to know their crews, too, because there'll be parties." Grace gave Shelby a funny sideways look, almost of embarrassment. "Those parties are important, because they're our main meeting place. Harvester people mostly marry other harvester people, but once they're back through the node in the solar system the ships all go their own separate ways."

They had finally reached the outer cargo holds, and Shelby suspected that if anyone ought to be embarrassed it was his turn. He had excuses—he had been exhausted the previous night, and still partly hungover, and after all it was only a machine. But he didn't feel comfortable. Grace and Doobie had acted as though he had insulted *them*, personally, when he had taken one look at the weird object in front of him and said, *"That's* Logan? You must be kidding. Meeting a stupid machine doesn't count as meeting *someone.*" He had turned and blundered off in a rage, convinced that Grace had deliberately tricked him.

Now he was not so sure. Grace and Doobie spoke of Logan exactly as though the bottle-shaped robot was a real

person, with its own feelings and emotions. Lana Trask had
the same attitude, except maybe more so—*Muv will let Logan
operate without us, and not us without Logan.* That sure sounded
like Lana Trask thought of Logan as a person. And according to Captain Lana it was Logan who had saved his life.

Shelby had met Lana Trask only once, but already he
was deeply impressed. In some inexplicable way she reminded
him of his own father. He resolved to be on his best behav-
ior as he allowed himself to be led forward by Grace to a deep
circular pit. It was partly filled with silvery sand, and squat-
ting motionless in the middle of it like an ancient gilded In-
dian statue was the eight-armed Logan. When Grace called
down, the machine changed at once to a giant spider that
went swarming up the other side of the pit and vanished into
the gloom.

"Oops," said Grace. "Vocal adapter, for a bet. Just a
moment."

Before Shelby had time to ask what she was talking
about, Logan came skittering back and circled the pit to stand
upright in front of them on its bottom two arms.

The wire tendrils writhed. "All right now," said a deep
voice. "I didn't think I would need it this morning."

"You can speak!" exclaimed Shelby. "Why didn't you do
it when I talked to you?"

"You mean, when you first awakened in the corry?"
Logan's speech was articulated with the tiniest pause between words, but it was clear and precise. "For an excellent
reason: I could not. I was on a routine harvest collection and
knew I would be alone in the corry. There seemed not the
remotest possibility that I would have need of a vocal
adapter." Logan raised one arm, to indicate where a small silver box sat below the writhing metallic snakes of its head.
"How was I to know that a human would appear from

nowhere at extreme speed? I was barely able to match velocities and bring you on board the corry. And when you spoke
to me I did my best. I transmitted a signal indicating the fre-
quencies on which I am capable of radio communication.
But you ignored it."

"Not his fault," said Grace. "He was wearing a crummy
Earth-designed suit without any encode/decode feature. He
didn't even know you were sending him a signal. Anyway, you
can talk to each other now. Do you have time to show him
around a bit, Logan? He's going to be working as part of our
corry team, and the refining pit work isn't urgent. I'd do it
myself, but I've got Doobie waiting for me and I'm late already."

"The pleasure will be mine." The wire mop wriggled
and turned in Shelby's direction.

Pleasure? Shelby wondered if the robot was capable of
pleasure—or of sarcasm. If Logan was as smart a machine as
it seemed to be, Shelby's disdain the previous night must have
registered.

He decided to reserve judgment. Grace had left rapidly
without waiting for anyone's reaction, and he and Logan
now stood alone at the edge of the pit.

"I think we ought to begin outside," Logan said, "and
work our way inward. In my experience that is the most effective method with newcomers."

"You've done this sort of thing before?" Shelby allowed
himself to be led away from the pit and up a spiraling stair-
way onto a new level above the cargo holds. He could see an
airlock, and on the wall hung an array of suits.

"Several times. I provided the initial tour to Thurgood
Trask and Scrimshander Limes, when they came here five
years ago."

"You mean they have only been here that long?" It
seemed to Shelby that Uncle Thurgood acted as though he

owned the whole harvester and probably the Messina Cloud as well. "Where were they before that?"

"Mining in the Kuiper Belt. Even if you know nothing of operations here, you will, I suspect, find it easier to adapt than they did. They had much to unlearn. Mining the Belt and harvesting the dust cloud may sound similar in objectives, but they are actually grossly different in procedures. Or so I am told. All my own experience is with the *Harvest Moon.* Although I was fabricated in the solar system, I was not initialized until I arrived here."

The ruby-tipped tendrils that formed Logan's eyes had been watching as Shelby carefully worked his way into and sealed the suit. The design was roughly the same as the one he had arrived in, but there were enough additions and variations to require full concentration. Shelby was relieved and unnaturally pleased when the monitor lights all went out to indicate that the suit was correctly sealed and operating.

Logan approached and placed one spidery arm on the side of the suit helmet. "Channel eight. Although you will not need the circuit until we are outside, I suggest that you change to it now."

Shelby nodded and selected the right channel. Logan's voice, unchanged in either tone or timbre, came over the suit radio: "If you can hear me, then let us proceed through the airlock. Be prepared."

Logan did not say for what. Shelby did not ask, and when the outer door of the airlock opened he did not need to. They were emerging onto the flat outer hull of the *Harvest Moon*'s disk. The Messina Dust Cloud occupied the whole hemisphere above them. Its full glory, which he had been in no state to appreciate when waking in the corry, hit him for the first time like a physical force.

The great blue and purple haze was shot through with streaks and swirls of brighter colors, greens and yellows and glowing crimsons. The rainbow lines and curves defined small currents and whirlpools, which taken together made the outline of a set of broader patterns. These must be the sluggish space rivers that Grace had described, carrying their invisible pockets of valuable transuranics around some unseen center of the Cloud. This was the giant canvas on which Lana Trask practiced her mysterious art.

Shelby could see now that the stars were not *in* the Cloud; they shone through it from much farther away. It was an irresistible urge to turn and scan the sky for one particular object.

"The Sun, and the solar system . . ." He turned to Logan.

"That way." The robot, for whatever reason, had remained silent for a few minutes while Shelby stared spellbound at the heavens. Now it raised one thin arm and pointed. "Invisible, I am afraid, without enhancement to human sight. Even though twenty-seven light-years is no small distance, Sol still appears as a fourth-magnitude star. Normally you would be able to see it, but there is too much scattering and absorption of light by the cloud."

Shelby looked anyway. Over there, unimaginably far away, was the *Bellatrix* and his mother. His father, J. P. Cheever, would be down on Earth, controlling his empires of industry. From this distance both his parents were equally remote.

"You cannot see it, either, but in that direction"—Logan pointed again, through the heart of the Messina Dust Cloud—"lies the Confluence, where all the harvesters will meet in a few weeks' time. The rakehells, too, though Captain Trask prefers that the crew of the *Harvest Moon* should not consort with them."

Confluence, yes. But rakehells? There was an incredible amount to learn, and he was only just beginning. Shelby felt a surge of rebellion—why should he bother to learn any of this stupid stuff? It was useless knowledge that he would never need in his whole life once he returned to Earth. But then Grace's voice, slightly mocking, rose in his mind. *What have you done in your whole life?*

"Rakehells? What are they?"

"Ships and people who like to live dangerously and take big chances. Harvesting is too dull for them. Most of the rakehell crews start out as harvester folk, but once they're on the rakehells they become secretive and paranoid and suspicious of everyone—even of the other rakehells. They are treasure hunters. There are more things to be found in the Messina Cloud than stable transuranics, and more places to go than the great dust rivers. There are regions where Captain Trask will never take the *Harvest Moon*, no matter how the currents are running: dense glowing clots of dust and gas that the rakehells call the hunting grounds. But the harvesters, they call them the reefs."

Logan's mechanical voice was totally without emotion. The nearly superstitious dread that Shelby was feeling had to arise from the bare words and his own imagination.

"What do the rakehells do in the hunting grounds?"

"They seek a rare gemstone with a curious internal structure. It is called a Cauthen starfire, after the woman, Miriam Cauthen, who first found one. Each starfire is as big as a human fist, possesses unworldly clarity and brilliance, and because of its rarity has enormous value throughout the solar system. The rakehells seek the stone constantly. Sometimes they find a starfire, hurry back at once to Sol, and become wealthy. But just as often their ships never return from the reefs. The nearest reef lies in that direction, no more than a day's flight from here."

Logan pointed. Then the robot stood frozen. "One moment, please," it said at last. "I must go to maximum aperture."

As Shelby watched, the tangle of wires on the end of the body widened and stiffened to form a kind of inverted umbrella almost a meter across. The robot stood motionless.

"Ah," Logan said finally. "Not what I suspected, but in some ways even more interesting."

"What?" Shelby had seen nothing.

"I thought at first that I was seeing a rakehell, which could mean that we are nearer to a reef than we suspected. But the object in question is in fact one of the harvesters. Over there."

The robot pointed, and Shelby looked again. "I can't see it."

"That is not surprising. At maximum extension my optical system approaches the performance of a diffraction-limited telescope of one-meter aperture. The other harvester is invisible to you, but believe me, it is there. Come along. We must return inside."

Shelby was all set to refuse—he was finding the experience fascinating, and anyway, since when did humans take orders from machines? Then he had another thought. "Is it dangerous to us?"

"Not at all. But we must inform Captain Trask that we are being observed. Undoubtedly, the other harvester is spying on our movements and hopes to find out where we will go next. Lana Trask finds transuranics when no one else can. I would also like to have access to the *Harvest Moon*'s big telescope. It would be useful to know which harvester that is, and that I cannot determine using my own equipment. Let us proceed inside, if you please."

Shelby followed Logan, but before they could enter the airlock there was another moment of excitement.

"Scrimshander! Scrimshander Limes." Thurgood Trask's voice, loud and exasperated, sounded suddenly over the radio. "Drill and blast it, where are you? I've tried every channel and you're not on any one of them. I need docking help. I hit tar again! I'm blind, and scraping my glove over my visor only makes it worse. Scrimshander!"

There was a crackling sound as Thurgood Trask switched channels.

"There are pockets of hydrocarbon fog within the currents," Logan said quietly. "They are extremely useful, because they provide a source of valuable petrochemicals and they also serve as base materials for the food synthesizers."

Hydrocarbons! There was one of Shelby's earlier questions about food sources answered. He had suspected far worse.

"However," Logan went on, "it is the lighter hydrocarbons that are prized. The heavier ones, thick tars and fuel oils, are a nuisance. They clog faceplates, and coat the outside and inside of the corry, and stick to everything. Regrettably, Thurgood Trask exhibits a positive genius for hitting the densest and most glutinous hydrocarbon fogs. Wait here, if you please, while I determine his receiving channel. I must guide his corry in."

Channel eight fell silent, and Shelby stared around, trying to pick out an approaching corry against the backdrop of glowing colors. He saw it at last, a familiar birdcage shape gradually approaching the side of the *Harvest Moon*. At the same moment his radio crackled again to life.

"Hello?" said a puzzled voice. "Thurgood? I can see you and the corry. But I can't hear you. What channel are you on? Hello? Are you there? Just to be on the safe side, I think I'd better guide you in with an override. And I'll stay right here on this channel."

The corry had been moving slowly and steadily on a direct approach. Now it speeded up and yawed ten degrees. It was still skewed away from the vertical when the open flower of birdcage wires ran into the side of the *Harvest Moon.*

The sound of the collision did not carry through airless space, but Shelby felt the vibration in his boots through the hull of the ship. He also heard the howl of rage over his suit radio.

"Scrimshander!"

"Right here, Thurgood."

"I've told you a million times, when I'm in the blasted corry you're *never* to mess with . . ."

Uncle Thurgood and Scrimshander Limes had finally hit the same channel.

CHAPTER FIVE

IT WAS late at night and Shelby was exhausted. And yet he could not sleep. His brain paraded before him an endless procession of facts and images. He lay on his bunk and his mind reeled.

Perhaps that was the problem. He was tired out, but all day long he had been on the receiving end of the data flow. Whereas he himself had *done* absolutely nothing—unless he counted his botched attempt at cooking breakfast.

Finally he gave up, rose from the bunk, and drifted silently through the interior corridor of the ship. He wanted to get his hands again on the food synthesizer when no one else was around and see if he could make it produce something worth eating. He would need no other authority than his own stomach to tell him if he succeeded.

But even here he was balked. He had felt sure that the galley would be deserted, but Lana Trask was sitting alone at the little table. The captain was in many ways the last person on the *Harvest Moon* that Shelby wanted to see.

He started to retreat, but it was too late. She had spotted him. When she beckoned him in he had no choice but to enter and sit where she indicated.

"How did it go today?" she asked as he dropped into a seat opposite her.

From her manner there was no hint that twenty-four hours earlier she had called him a liar, while at the same time he had tried to order her around in her own ship.

"Lots to learn." Shelby felt obliged to replace that platitude with the truth. "I learned a lot, too. But I also think I annoyed Logan."

Twenty-four hours ago he would have denied that the word "annoyed" could ever apply to the reaction of a machine. Now it was becoming harder and harder to think of Logan as anything but another human, though admittedly an oddly shaped one.

Lana Trask did not seem at all surprised. She merely nodded. "Go on."

"Well, I started to tell Logan about Earth—as an answer to a question. It wasn't my idea. And I said that on Earth I never did see many machines around, but all the ones I knew about were completely primitive compared with Logan. I thought that was a compliment. Only I think somehow I put my foot in it."

"You did. But it was perceptive of you to read the reaction from Logan. I tell Grace and Doobie over and over, listening and reading people is more important than talking. But I don't think it does much good. They blunder on. Anyway, my compliments to you."

Shelby blushed and looked away. A compliment from Lana Trask was the last thing he had expected. "But what did I *do*? What was it I said that irritated Logan?"

"Nothing that you could control. You just reinforced what Logan already knows to be true." Lana Trask rubbed her eyes, and the remote and uninvolved look that Shelby had seen when he entered returned briefly to her face. It occurred to him that it was the middle of the night. What had she been doing, up so late?

"Earth has a dumbing-down policy toward machines," she went on. "The government won't permit a smart one to be made or imported. Naturally, every self-respecting robot away from Earth resents that fact."

"I don't get it. I've seen what Logan can do. Back on Earth, a machine like that could handle the work of a dozen people. Don't we have the technology on Earth to build something like Logan?"

"Without a doubt. The artificial intelligence know-how has been around for over a century, and it's certainly no secret. Earth has as good access to that knowledge as we do. Earth's problem is different—or the government thinks it is. They ask, if there were smart machines to do the work, what would fourteen billion people do?"

"Have an easier life." Shelby knew how easy his own life had been, but he was beginning to realize that he was an exception. He resisted the urge to say more and compare his lot with that of the average Earthling. Grace might be beginning to believe him, but Captain Lana Trask was a different matter.

"An easier life," she said. "Ah, don't we all want that? You might think so. But people have to feel *needed*, too. They want to feel like workers, not just drones. Every time they have a referendum on Earth it always comes out the same: *no smart robots.* You see, it's *people* who have the vote. Machines don't. And if there's ever a test case in court, who do you think wins? People, who have rights, or machines, that don't have rights? Logan knows that even a short trip to Earth would be forbidden."

"Is Logan really as capable as a human?"

"It depends who you talk to. And what you talk about."

"I mean, can Logan do anything that a human can do?" Shelby knew that he was being vague, and added, "I don't mean physical things, like having children. I mean mental powers."

"For anything that calls for pure logic, Logan will run rings round all of us. But Logan finds it hard to understand that humans don't work from logic."

"Some of us do."

"*None* of us do. Sure, we can think logically with our conscious minds. But ninety-five percent of your brain is run by your *unconscious* mind. All our conscious brain does is try to justify, after the fact, whatever half-baked actions we just took. The artificial-intelligence specialists still can't mimic that, because nobody has any idea how it operates. Like what I was doing when you came in. I can't explain it. I just know I can *do* it."

"I wondered if I was interrupting you."

"Not really. I was just about finished. I'd decided earlier that we ought to move the *Harvest Moon.* The information that Logan gave me, that the *Southern Cross* harvester—the one you saw when you were outside—has been hanging around watching us, that was what I needed. When you came in I was working on the final piece."

"But what were you doing?"

"I was deciding where we ought to go. Actually, I was

being a transuranic element." She smiled at the look on Shelby's face. "It may sound crazy, but it's true. I was a molecule of a stable transuranic, asfanium or polkium, drifting through the currents of the Cloud. The basic data are here, in the Cloud survey results." She tapped the sheaf of papers on the table in front of her. "But that's just background. I need more. I sense the cross-tug of different fields, gravity and magnetism and the electric force on my ions. I feel particle impacts, and radiation pressure, and vortex shears from the reefs. I feel the weak bonds that tie atom to atom, and my dipole moment, and my internal quadrupole moment. I respond to all of them. And I move."

"You talk as though the molecules are *conscious*—as though they know what they're doing. But they're not."

"Of course they're not. And I know very well that the molecules are not conscious. They just respond to the total force vector on them. But in terms of what I do, and what the sniffers on the other harvesters do, it makes sense to talk about the way that the molecules might feel. We respond to the *feel* of the situation. I don't know any other way to describe it. My decision is based on my unconscious conclusion as to what the molecules will do. And that's why Logan, or any machine like Logan, can't direct a harvester. Logan is great, and invaluable, but there's a piece missing." She sighed. "Not getting through to you, am I?"

"I guess not. Not really." After struggling to see Logan as human, Shelby was being told to throw out the idea.

"Maybe before you leave you'll take a shot at sniffing for yourself. Then you'll understand how it works. Who knows, maybe you'll be a natural? But for the moment let's try a different approach. Suppose it had been Thurgood and Scrimshander out in the corry who spotted you, rather than Logan. Can you see how it might have been different?"

Shelby hesitated. He certainly could, but he didn't want

to say unkind things about Grace's uncle and his companion. "They might not have saved me," he muttered at last.

Lana grinned at him, as though she knew exactly what he had really been thinking. "I think they would. But that's not the important piece. They would have done the same calculation as Logan did. They would have decided that they could catch you in the corry—barely. They would then have gone after you, just like Logan. But suppose that you had been going too fast to rendezvous with and intercept. What then?"

"I don't know."

"Well, I do. Logan would have checked the calculation and reached the logical conclusion: Don't even try, because the dynamics of the situation say that recovery is impossible. So Logan wouldn't have tried. Thurgood and Scrim would have agreed with the analysis. But they would have gone after you anyway, and probably blown the corry apart trying to reach you. Logan would say, well, that is proof of the inferior reasoning powers of a human. But I would say that is the proof of a human superiority that we don't yet know how to program into a machine. It's the reason why no crew member will ever agree to report to a robot, no matter how smart the machine might be. Can you see that?"

"I think so." Shelby still wasn't sure which he would have preferred: Uncle Thurgood and little Scrimshander, bumbling after him through space. Or Logan, coolly competent, aware to the minute of how much longer Shelby's air supply would last, and calmly continuing to work on the harvester retrieval system to the last quarter-hour.

But Logan hadn't taken into account that Shelby himself was unaware of the machine's state of knowledge. Shelby had been so sure he was going to die that he was ready to throw himself out of the corry when Logan at last headed for the *Harvest Moon*.

Lana Trask was right. Given a choice, Shelby would take Scrimshander and Thurgood's randomness over Logan's logic.

Or rather, Shelby would take whatever Uncle Thurgood decided. Scrim wouldn't have much of a say in things. Thurgood Trask always used an impatient and commanding tone on the other man.

It was a familiar tone. Where had Shelby heard it before?

The answer came to him. That was exactly the way that people at the Cheever mansion—himself included—talked all the time to the support staff.

To escape that unwelcome thought, Shelby blurted out what he was thinking but ought not to have said. "You know, Uncle Thurgood drives Scrimshander pretty hard."

"You think so?" Lana Trask's face changed. She seemed suddenly alert and guarded.

"Yes, I do. I've only been here one day, but I've seen it several times. He really bullies Scrim and orders him around."

"You don't think Scrimshander needs it?"

"Maybe. But he doesn't *deserve* it."

"You'll learn a lot about Thurgood and Scrim," Lana said cryptically. "But not now. Now it's your turn to talk. You know why I was sitting here in the middle of the night. I was planning where to take the *Harvest Moon*. Why did you come here?"

Shelby gestured toward the food synthesizers.

"You mean, you came here for a meal?"

"No. I came here to learn how to use it, when there was no one else around. What I cooked this morning was—not quite right."

"So I heard." Lana Trask stood up. "Are you tired?"

"Yes. But I couldn't sleep."

"I know all about that." She stood staring at him for a

few seconds, her head to one side. "Go ahead. But remember two things. First, any mess you make, you clear up. That's a rule of the galley in any harvester."

Cleaning up anything for himself was an alien thought for Shelby, but he nodded. "I will. What else?"

"A rule of *this* harvester. Anyone can stay up as late as he or she chooses—but duties start at the regular time tomorrow morning. Now, do you still want to work with the synthesizers?"

"Yes."

"Then I'll get out of here. I hate to have people watch over me when I'm working. I doubt if you are any different."

She nodded and left.

At last. Lana Trask probably had no idea how uncomfortable she made him. Shelby turned with relief to the synthesizer and its front display menu—not a menu for food, but the selection key for a voluminous on-line instruction manual.

He began to study it. He was probably going to feel like hell in the morning; but before he left tonight he was determined to produce something that didn't look like it had already been eaten once.

Shelby learned the hard way that Lana Trask meant what she said. He heard a loud sort of whistle through his cabin terminal, but managed to sleep through it. He was still lying in his bunk when Doobie came bustling in and sat down on his feet.

"All right, Lord Shelby. Let's go. I was sent here to get you."

Shelby groaned and pulled the cover over his face. "I knew I ought to have locked my door."

"Wouldn't have made any difference. These cabins are

like sounding boxes—I know. Gracie's got me up often enough. I'd have banged 'til you cried for mercy."

"That's what I'm doing now."

"No chance. Come on, out of there. You want to eat? You have ten minutes."

"How can I get up, when you're sitting on me?" But Shelby pushed back the cover and slowly arose. He had collapsed into his bunk, fully dressed, what seemed like ten minutes ago. The clock told him it was actually three hours. He thought about washing, decided not to bother, and followed Doobie to the galley.

It was deserted. More than that, it—in particular the table—was *empty*. Shelby stared.

"What happened?"

"Happened to what?"

"I made breakfast rolls. Really good ones, ten dozen of them. They were on the table."

"I know. I ate eight or nine myself. You're right, they were great."

"But a *hundred and twenty*."

"Ah. That's Uncle Thurgood. Him and Jilter."

"I thought everybody made their own breakfast."

"That's the theory. But Uncle Thurgood, he has a different theory: What's yours is his, and what's his is his own. You're lucky, though." Doobie went across to an oven, low down, and opened it. "I don't get it with Gracie. I think she must be sweet on you. Anyway, she saved this before Thurgood and Jilter could get near it, and she made me promise not to eat it and not to tell."

It was a sizable enough plate of food, if you ignored the fact that only a miserable two breakfast rolls sat with the rest of the meal. Shelby pondered while he ate. Eight for Doobie, two for him, that left a hundred and ten—and who else was there to eat them?

Grace, Lana, and Thurgood Trask, plus Scrimshander Limes, and the mysterious Jilter Clute. If those five all ate an equal number, which was doubtful, that made twenty-two per person.

"Nah," said Doobie scornfully, when Shelby put the question to him. "I told you, it's Jilter and Uncle Thurgood. You're lucky. If they'd got here first, you'd not have seen a single roll."

Shelby felt like saying he had come close. Instead he asked, "Where's Jilter, and who's Jilter? I think he's the only other person associated with the *Harvest Moon* that I haven't met."

"You'll see him later today. But what you say's not true."

"There are others here?"

"No. But you've never met Dad."

Odd as it seemed, it had never occurred to Shelby that Grace and Doobie must have a male parent. Also, he could not imagine what sort of man might be married to Captain Lana Trask. "You mean your father?"

" 'Course I mean my father. Mungo Trask. Uncle Thurgood's his brother. Who else would I be calling Dad?"

"And he's on board?"

"Never said that. You said *associated* with the *Harvest Moon*. Dad's certainly that. He and Muv bought this ship together, and they share ownership."

"So where is he?"

"Coming to that. Muv's the sniffer. Dad admits he can't compete. But Dad's the expert on markets and prices for what we find. Most trips he stays Sol-side—he's there now—and does his own market analysis. Soon as we get home to the Belt and he sees what we have, he knows exactly the right sort of deal to put together so we can sell at top price." Doobie stared at Shelby with a new curiosity. "Hey, Shel, isn't that what you say your dad does? Makes deals?"

"Kind of." Two days ago Shelby would have raised his nose in the air and pointed out that there was no comparison to be drawn between the massive scale of J. P. Cheever's operations and the piddling little trading of one ship's cargo performed by Mungo Trask. Today he merely said, "Yeah, I guess you could say that. They're pretty much in the same line of work."

"And talking of work." Shelby's plate was empty, and Doobie stood up. "We'd better get to it—soon as we've washed."

"I'm not really dirty."

"Doesn't matter. Ship's rule: wash before duties, even if you're going out solo on a corry. Didn't used to be that way, but two years back Nelly N'Gali shipped out with us." Doobie held his nose. "You've no idea. Three weeks of Dirty Nelly, and Muv made the rule. Nelly's still on one of the harvesters, the *Sweet Chariot*, and from what I hear she's filthy as ever. Maybe you'll meet her at Confluence."

They had reached the bathing area. Shelby's wash was both rapid and superficial. Doobie's was more so. Shelby decided that Nelly N'Gali must have been something special.

Grace was waiting impatiently in the main control room of the *Harvest Moon* when Shel and Doobie got there. Standing next to her was a tall, pale man. His straw-colored hair was cut short and it stood straight up from his scalp like wheat stubble. He nodded at Doobie and stared at Shelby, but he did not speak.

"At last," said Grace. "You certainly took your time."

"Not my fault." Doobie jerked a thumb at his companion. "Him. Harder to get up than I am."

"Tell that to Uncle Thurgood. He's waiting for you on third deck. He's been calling down and shouting at us every two minutes."

"Marvelous. So now he gets to shout at me." Doobie

pulled a face and addressed the straw-haired man. "Jilter, this here is the jetsam, Shelby Cheever. Shel, this is the famous Jilter Clute."

This time the man's nod was at Shelby, but still he did not speak. Instead he turned and led Doobie out of the control room. Finally, at the door, he paused and turned.

"Good rolls," he said, and vanished.

Shelby was left alone with Grace. "What's he mean, *jetsam?*" he asked.

"Doobie's idea of a joke. Jetsam is something you throw overboard from a ship when you're running low on fuel and need to reduce mass. It's a word borrowed from Earth's sailors. They used to throw things overboard when the ship was in danger of sinking. Doobie is suggesting that somebody threw you into the Asteroid Belt node because they wanted to get rid of you." She eyed him curiously. "I assume he's wrong. But some time you'll have to tell me just how you *did* screw up enough to land out here instead of in the Kuiper Belt."

"You already know. I got drunk."

"Too drunk to think? Not very smart."

"So? I suppose you've never done anything that wasn't very smart?"

He was tired and crabby and willing to start an argument. But Grace just looked away and said in a worried voice, "I think I did, two months ago. But I've only just realized it. Hey!" She turned back to Shelby before he could ask her what she meant. There was a fake smile on her face. "Did you put something special into those breakfast rolls?"

A deliberate change of subject. Shelby tucked her comment away for future reference. "A lot of sweat went into those rolls," he said.

That remark sounded disgusting, and too close to his original thoughts about the raw materials of the food synthesizers. "I mean," he explained, "I worked on them for hours and hours, nearly all night. I recycled nine batches before they came out the way I wanted them. Why?"

"Early this morning I arrived in the galley at the same time as Muv. She looked at all the rolls you made, and at the food synthesizer activity log. Then she ate two rolls, very slowly. And then she said something really weird. 'You and Doobie have been pestering me for a year to let you go out on a corry without Logan,' she said. 'I'm going to let you do it, on one condition. If either of you ever goes out without Logan, Shelby Cheever has to be with you.'

"I said, 'But Shel doesn't know the first thing about the Cloud, or how to handle a corry, or transuranics, or anything!' And she said, 'He will. He'll learn. And I'll decide when he's ready. So if you want to go outside, it's in your interests to teach him as fast and as well as possible.' And she took four more rolls and walked out. I think I understand Muv as well as anyone, except for Dad. But this one threw me. Do *you* know what's going on?"

Shelby shook his head. Add one more item to the mystery of Lana Trask. "Your mother's right about one thing. If I'm going to be stuck here for three months I'll go out of my mind unless I have something to do. I'm ready to learn—but I don't know *what* to learn."

"I can help with that. So can Logan and Jilter. One warning: Don't listen to Uncle Thurgood."

"He acts like he knows everything."

"He does know everything—about Kuiper Belt mining. Twenty successful years there, tunneling and blasting and centrifuging for nickel and iron and platinum and iridium. Muv says there's not enough volatiles in the Messina Cloud to wash the ore dust off Uncle Thurgood's mining boots. But transuranics are a different game. Don't go out with Uncle 'less you want to eat tar. Then he's your man."

"But if he was so good at his job in the Kuiper Belt, why did he come out here?"

"He had—reasons." Grace read Shelby's suspicion. "Not what you think. There's no extradition to Sol from the Messina Cloud, and anyway he did nothing criminal."

It occurred to Shelby that Grace could hardly complain if Lana Trask was not always forthcoming with information. Grace was her mother's daughter.

"What about Jilter Clute?" he asked. "Can I rely on him?"

"Like a rock. He's been on the *Harvest Moon* since day one. Jilter doesn't talk much, but he'll answer questions. What he knows, he'll tell you. When he doesn't know something he'll tell you that, and then he'll help you to find out."

"Is he really famous, or was that another of Doobie's stupid jokes?"

"Famous right through the Messina Cloud, harvesters and rakehells alike." Grace looked scrubbed clean and extra neat this morning, and her sudden smile lit up her face. "Just say 'Jilter' to anyone, and they'll grin."

"Who did he jilt?"

"Cynthia Wendover. But that's a long story." Grace glanced at the control room chronometer. "I guess this counts as learning, though I'm not sure it's what Muv had in mind. Tell you what. We'll talk about Jilter, then I'll give you lots of other stuff that you can learn when you're by yourself."

"Thanks," Shelby said dryly. But it was lost on Grace.

"You see," she went on, "Jilter's one hundred percent reliable, but he isn't a man to rush things. About twelve years ago, when he was still known in the Cloud as Rodney Clute, he decided that Cynthia Wendover, of the harvester *Never-Say-Die*, was a very attractive woman. I'm too young to remember it myself, but apparently it took him two years before he got up enough courage to speak to Cynthia. Then they hung around together through the whole of one Confluence, and according to Muv the two of them got along fine. But emotion, which he wasn't used to, just about blew Rodney's mind. For weeks afterward he had no more sense than a ball of steel wool. Muv had to tell him everything six times before it clicked. Cynthia's company had scrambled all his mental circuits—and they hadn't even touched each other.

"After that it was nothing for a whole year, until the next Confluence. Rodney could have gone to see Cynthia when they were back Sol-side, but she was from a very big family and Rodney couldn't stand the thought of all that socializing. It wasn't until they met at the Confluence that he talked to her again. And again they got on very well.

"By the third Confluence, Rodney still hadn't made a real move. Cynthia had been waiting two whole years, wondering where she stood. She had already told her family how much she liked Rodney. She hadn't told them that she'd have jumped right into bed with him if he'd so much as suggested it, because for one thing her family had very old-fashioned views and would have been shocked; for another, Rodney *hadn't* so much as hinted at it.

"So at the Confluence, Cynthia took the lead—this is all from hearsay, you understand, but the whole fleet tells it this same way. It turned out that Rodney had been thinking along the same lines and hadn't dared to mention it. So Cynthia moved them from thought to deed, and again, things went just fine. They must have felt that they needed to make up for lost time, because although they were apparently present for the whole Confluence, no one else so much as saw them.

"By the next Confluence, Cynthia was beginning to get a tiny bit impatient. It was obvious that Rodney was starry-eyed crazy about her, while she knew she didn't want any other man in her life. But he still hadn't said one word about any relationship that went beyond a couple of weeks in bed during Confluence, and letters and calls to each other for the rest of the year.

"Cynthia pinned him down, so to speak, and wormed the truth out of him. He said he couldn't think of anything he'd like more than to be hitched permanently to Cynthia. The thing that he couldn't stand was the idea of a big ceremony, with what seemed to him like an endless army of relatives—I told you she was from a big family—breathing down his neck and watching his every move. He was particularly worried by Wendell Wendover, Cynthia's grandfather and the patriarch of the whole clan. When Rodney was younger old Wendell had pinned him in a corner during Confluence and given him a long lecture about the decadence of youth and the decline in modern morality. Rodney was convinced that Wendell Wendover knew what he and Cynthia had been doing and wouldn't hesitate to condemn Rodney to hellfire if they were both at the ceremony. Wendell was ninety years old but there was plenty of spark left in him.

"By this time Cynthia was getting to understand Rodney pretty well. She knew what he could stand and what was too much for him. She suggested a compromise. They would have a small ceremony, just Cynthia and her parents and her brothers and sisters, plus anyone that Rodney chose to invite. No Wendell Wendover, or anyone else likely to cause trouble. They would record the event, and the rest of her family could watch that.

"Rodney said he didn't want to invite anyone on his side. Cynthia said that was fine, then it would be just her immediate family. Not only that, since Rodney hated the idea of making the arrangements, she would handle them all. He could go off about his usual business, and his only task would be to show up for the ceremony and endure an hour or two with her parents, brothers, and sisters. Then he and Cynthia would go off together for a private celebration and live happily every after.

"Rodney was pretty pleased with the idea. Much less pleased were Cynthia's family. The Confluence isn't the best place to keep a secret. Given the disappearance of Rodney and Cynthia for weeks at a time when the Confluence was taking place, her relatives were convinced that they knew exactly what had been going on. Not only that, word had leaked through to Wendell Wendover. He made his usual speech to the family about the decline in morality and pretty much blamed the whole thing on Rodney, the foul fiend of depravity who had ruined his innocent young granddaughter. Grandpa Wendell had every intention of attending the ceremony and telling Rodney what he thought of him—if the blackguard showed up, which Wendell was ninety-nine percent sure he would not. Men like Rodney used a girl, then abandoned her. Men like that deserved to be horsewhipped, though unfortunately there wasn't a horse or a whip within fifteen billion kilometers.

"Cynthia learned that Grandfather Wendell planned on being there. She decided not to mention it to Rodney. It would only excite him, and he seemed quite agitated enough already. The big danger was that someone else in her family would mention Grandpa's intentions to Rodney, just in passing. The best way to make sure that didn't happen was to insulate Rodney as much as possible from every one of her relatives until the actual day and hour of the event. That ought not to be too difficult, because it fitted in with Rodney's own strong preferences.

"The great day grew nearer. Rodney was in a state of nervous prostration, but Cynthia had expected that so she had everything organized. The ceremony would take place not in a public place, but on one of the Kuiper Belt's smaller planetoids. That was about as private as you could get. She did not propose to tell her family, despite their protests, of the planetoid's ID until the day before the ceremony. They would all travel there in one ship, and Rodney would be waiting. As soon as the ceremony was over, she and he would depart without notice in the ship that he had arrived in. The family could celebrate at the reception without them, and Grandfather Wendell could make as many speeches as he liked.

"Cynthia's family didn't know where Rodney was, but of course she did. He was on one of the Belt's major mining worlds. Two days before the ceremony, she sneaked away from her family and paid Rodney a surprise visit. She had two motives. First, she had to tell Rodney where the ceremony was to take place, and she didn't trust the idea of sending him a message over the standard open channels. Second, Cynthia had been working very hard, and she felt in need of a little rest and recreation. Wendell Wendover's notion of who had led whom astray was about as far wrong as you could get, and Cynthia didn't see why all the R-and-R had to wait until after the ceremony.

"Cynthia found Rodney in terrible shape, a mass of facial tics and bottled-up nervousness. You've seen Rodney. I know it's hard to imagine him like that. But a man whose idea of a crowd is one other person was facing the prospect of a sizable group, every member of which would be concentrating on him.

"Well, she knew a guaranteed way to relax Rodney, one that had always worked in the past. And sure enough, it worked now. It also turned his brains to mush. Cynthia didn't realize how far gone Rodney tended to be after one of their friendly get-togethers, though she knew he got a bit woolly. She told him the ID of the planetoid where the ceremony was to take place, repeated it five or six times, and wrote it down on a piece of paper just to make sure. Then she hurried back to her family. They hadn't noticed her absence, because in spite of her instructions they were making a big thing of it, and when she arrived they were trying on outfits that wouldn't have been out of place at a coronation. There were also six times as many people as she had expected, because her brothers and sisters—did I mention that there were eleven of them?—had assumed that the invitation also applied to their wives, husbands, boyfriends, mistresses, children, and all combinations thereof.

"They somehow squeezed on board the rented cruise ship and headed for Kuiper Belt Planetoid 1181. And there they waited. And waited. Rodney never showed. The male members of the Wendover family swore violent vengeance. Grandfather Wendell made a long speech and had a mild stroke.

"And now you know why everybody calls him Jilter Clute."

Grace paused, after what had seemed to Shelby like one continuous ten-minute sentence.

"But what happened?" he said. "Did he just get too scared, and run for it?"

"Not at all. Rodney had fortified himself with a little drink, summoned up his nerve, and flown off to meet Cynthia and her family. He waited for them for nearly twenty-four hours. The trouble is, he was on Kuiper Belt Planetoid 1811. In his muddled condition he had held Cynthia's note upside-down."

"So they never did have a ceremony."

"Oh, they did. It took a day or two to sort out the confusion, and then they went ahead. The second time was much better. Most of the Wendovers had gone home in disgust, and Grandpa Wendell was too sick to attend. Rodney and Cynthia got together, and they are still together, although she's back Sol-side at the moment having another baby—the

Cloud isn't the best place to have kids. But I don't think any-one in the whole harvester fleet will ever call him Rodney Clute again. For the rest of his life he's *Jilter* Clute."

She glanced at the control room chronometer. "I said it was a long story, but I didn't realize how long. We'd better get to work. For starters, you need to know more about heavy elements. Did you know that three-quarters of the universe is hydrogen, and almost all the rest of it is helium? Anything with atomic weight more than four is rare—and we're after elements with atomic weights above three hundred. Let's go over the list."

That seemed to be the end of the story of Jilter Clute; except that evening, when Shelby was briefly alone with Lana Trask, she said that if Jilter would agree to do a trip out with Shelby it would be educational.

She didn't say "Jilter" the way that Grace and Doobie did. It sounded more like "Dyeelter." After she had said it like that a couple of times, Shelby found the nerve to ask why.

"It's more correct," Lana said. "You'd never know it by looking at him, but Dyeelter's family is from central Asia and they have Turkic names. *Jilter*'s just a lazy way of avoiding that difficult *dyee* sound."

"But the jilting," protested Shelby. And as Lana listened in silence, he repeated as best he could recall it exactly what Grace had told him.

At the end, Lana gazed at him with the wide-spaced eyes that she had passed on to both Grace and Doobie. "Yes, that's another version," she said. "I think I'd better have a word with Grace." And she walked away.

Shelby went raging off to find Grace Trask and murder her, but he didn't manage to track her down before ship op-erations closed for the night. And in the morning, another event made him forget anything as trivial as the origin of a person's name.

CHAPTER SIX

SHELBY'S third day on the *Harvest Moon*, which felt more like his thirty-third, began with the desperate howl of a siren. Convinced that it was a new form of torture from Doobie, he pulled the pillow over his head and tried to ignore the rising and falling wail.

After thirty seconds or so the noise ended. But Shelby's idea seemed to be correct, because very soon there was a hammering on his cabin door and Doobie burst in.

"Shel, get up!"

Shelby hurled his pillow at the tormentor. "Get out of

here! You dummy, I don't have to get up. I'm free today 'til I go outside with Jilter Clute."

"You have it wrong. We've received a Mayday—a distress call. Muv sent me to get you. She thought you might not understand what the siren meant. Come on!"

Shelby tumbled out of bed. He was already—which is to say still—dressed. Pajamas and other sleeping attire were unknown on the *Harvest Moon*. When your clothes were dirty you just dumped them into a laundry machine, and within seconds a new set of the right size rolled out.

"What happened?" he asked, as Doobie led the way at a run toward the main control room.

"Don't know yet. We'll find out."

Already Shelby could tell that something new was happening. He was held to the floor by an increasingly strong force. The *Harvest Moon* was accelerating, harder than he had ever felt it before.

Lana Trask was at the control board and scarcely seemed to register their arrival. But she must have done so, because she said, "Good. Everybody's here. I'll give you an outline, then your assignments. This is going to be touch and go. Thurgood? Fine-tune us, would you?"

Thurgood Trask nodded and took her place without a word at the board. His pudgy fingers ran over the array of switches with surprising speed and delicacy.

"I'll keep it short," said Lana, "then if you need to you can ask questions. Ten minutes ago we had a distress call. It came from Dodman's Reef. One of the rakehells, the *Witch of Agnesi*, is in trouble. They went too near and they think they may have to thread the eye. Only two harvesters are anywhere close to them. Dodman's Reef is three hours away for us and for the *Coruscation*. I expect we will rendezvous there."

"Whoo-whoo! *Coruscation*!" Doobie said, and stared at Grace.

"Not now, Doobie." Lana Trask shook her head reprovingly. "Questions, anybody?"

Shelby had a hundred. Almost every word that the captain had said was pure gibberish. The only thing he was sure of was the blush on Grace Trask's face, and he didn't understand that.

"Assignments?" asked Jilter gruffly—the first uninvited words from him that Shelby had heard. It gave a feel for the seriousness of the situation.

Lana Trask nodded, but she paused with rare uncertainty. "It's not what I'd like," she said at last. "I think we have no choice. Three corries. Thurgood, you'll take one. Jilter, you'll take another—with Shelby. Remember he's a novice. Grace, Doobie, and Logan will handle the third. Scrimshander and I will stay with the *Harvest Moon* and go wherever I think we might be needed."

"Ah—excuse me." Scrimshander Limes raised a hand. His pale grey eyes were apologetic. "I would be more than happy to handle a fourth corry. Or perhaps go with Thurgood?"

Thurgood Trask made a sound between a growl and a snort. Lana waved her brother-in-law to silence. "I know you would, Scrim, and I appreciate your offer. But this ship may be more than I can handle. I would be grateful if you would stay here and assist me."

"Of course." Limes smiled placatingly at Uncle Thurgood, who grunted and subsided. "I will do whatever you think best."

"Then move to stations, everyone." Lana Trask replaced Thurgood at the control board. "Doobie," she said over her shoulder, "you stay with Shelby until the corries go out. Answer his questions."

"How did she know I have questions?" Shelby asked, as he and Doobie left the control room.

"Beats me. Maybe because you've asked ten million already since you arrived here." Doobie was heading toward the cargo holds. "We might as well get into suits and be ready. *Do* you have questions?"

"I guess so. What's your mother mean, *threading the eye?*"

"Just that. You know what a reef is?"

"It's a big, dense blob of gas and dust."

"It is that. But it's more. Do you know why a reef can exist at all?" When Shelby shook his head, Doobie sighed and said, "What do they teach you, back on Earth? Nothing? If you'd been raised here you'd have learned all this when you were two. Not your fault, I suppose."

"Thanks."

"That's all right." Doobie missed the sarcasm in Shelby's voice. "In the middle of every reef—and it's the reason reefs are dangerous—there's a ring vortex. That's like a dense smoke ring of dust and gas, rotating in on itself. Electromagnetic fields hold the ring stable, and usually there's a big cloud of dust around it, so you can't see anything of the vortex ring itself. The eye of the vortex is the hole in the middle of the ring. If you pass through the *exact* center—that's threading the eye—you feel a big change in speed but you don't get hurt. If you go through even slightly off-center, your ship gets torn apart. Only the very best pilots in the whole Cloud dare even consider threading the eye. Muv says she wouldn't try it for a pension, and she's as good as they get. What makes it worse is that near the eye there are strange unpredictable forces that suck you in, and other weird things can happen inside it."

"So why go anywhere near the reefs?"

"For the goodies. You know about Cauthen starfires?"

"Logan told me."

"That's one thing you find around the reefs, and

nowhere else. Then there's big lumps of jet-black stuff that the starfires come embedded in. Shwartzgeld, it's called, and it looks like glittery licorice but it's hard as rock. Even a smallish piece is worth a lot, because people Sol-side keep trying to analyze it and failing. A rakehell who stays clear of reef eyes and has a bit of luck searching will make as much in one season as the *Harvest Moon* makes in ten."

"But why did the *Witch of Agnesi* go so close to the eye, if it's so dangerous?"

"Hey, who knows? Rakehells are rakehells. They're weird."

Doobie seemed to feel that was enough of an explanation. Shelby, struggling with his suit seals and watching with envy as Doobie closed his effortlessly and in seconds, was not so sure. Surely even a rakehell crew must have a sense of self-preservation? More than most people, you would think, if they had to operate in such dangerous places.

"Final approach," said Lana Trask's voice over his suit radio. "Corry stations, please. We have visual and radio contact with the *Coruscation*, and we are patching our general communications systems into each other. Neither one of us is picking up anything from the *Witch of Agnesi.*"

"Which is *bad* news." Doobie headed through the lock for the corry parking level. "If the *Witch* was all right, the crew would still be broadcasting."

The parking level had already been opened to space. The corries were in position. Jilter Clute was waiting. Shelby had more questions, a head full of them, all about Grace and the *Coruscation* and Scrimshander Limes. They would have to wait.

He climbed onto the flat bottom of the corry and lay on his back looking up. He thought again how flimsy the bird-cage struts above him looked, and how unsuitable a corry seemed as a rescue vessel. Then Jilter was at his side and the ship was moving upward, away from the comforting haven of the *Harvest Moon*. Nervous uncertainty took away all Shelby's ability for rational thought.

He had seen them on his first trial run outside with Logan, those tiny swirls of rainbow color which helped the eye to plot out the structure of the Messina Cloud and map the great dust currents within it. The pinwheels had been remote, decorative, and harmless.

Now one of those pretty playthings filled the hemisphere of sky ahead. There was infinite detail to be seen. Within the glowing blue eye of Dodman's Reef, bright bands of green and white and turquoise knotted and braided and shifted as the corry moved closer. Shelby understood now, as words could never define it, the meaning of "threading the eye." At the very center of the bright iris ahead of them sat a black, lifeless pupil. Shelby recalled Logan's words: *There are regions where Captain Trask will never take the* Harvest Moon, *no matter how the currents are running.*

Never, Logan had said. But Logan's faultless logic was wrong. A rescue mission changed the definition of acceptable risk, in a way that a perfectly logical being would never understand. The attempt to save the *Witch of Agnesi* might lead to the destruction of the *Harvest Moon* and the *Coruscation*.

"Got a sighting," said an unfamiliar and laconic voice in Shelby's suit radio. "This is Saul Kramer of the *Coruscation*. Our corry *Mary Mine* has spotted what might be a ship's hull. No signals. We're heading there now. Coordinate and velocity estimates follow. I would appreciate *Harvest Moon* assistance."

"We'll provide it," Lana Trask said quietly. And a few seconds later, "Jilter, you're best situated for direct assistance to the *Mary Mine*. Thurgood and Logan, I'm computing a spread pattern for you. Then we'll divide up the search region among all the corries."

The corry that Shelby was in, to his great discomfort, changed course and headed straight for the staring black pupil. What was Jilter doing? Everyone agreed that the eye of a reef was to be avoided in every way possible.

He must have muttered something, even if no more than a gasp, because Jilter Clute said gruffly, "Private circuit." And, as soon as Shelby had made the switch, "Saul Kramer has his younger brother on that rakehell. I wanted you to know that, so no matter what we find you'll be careful how you speak on open circuit."

"I will." Shelby knew the answer to his next question, but he had to ask it. "Might be a hull, he said—the ship's been destroyed, hasn't it?"

"Afraid so."

"So all the people . . ."

"Maybe, maybe not. They would have been in suits when the *Witch* entered the eye. Tidal forces pull a ship apart, but they're not so deadly on something small. A person in a suit might survive. Thurgood and Logan and the corries from the *Coruscation* will be searching for suits and survivors as soon as Captain Trask gives them the spread pattern. No more, now. We have to get back to open circuit."

For Jilter, it was an astonishingly long speech. Shelby stared ahead of the speeding corry, and his heart sank. He could see it now, outlined against the deadly black eye, a broken thing that had once been a ship. Something had grabbed and crumpled the *Witch of Agnesi* like a paper bag. From the object in front of him Shelby could never have deduced its original appearance. All that was left was a twisted, flattened, and broken hulk.

The *Mary Mine*, a coracle just like those of the *Harvest Moon*, was already hovering beside the wreck of the rakehell. Jilter moored next to them and headed into the debris. Shelby followed, feeling unusually useless.

Two suited figures were already inside, in what had once been the ship's main control room. The chamber had been split all along its length, with the sides of the tear gaping outward through the main hull.

It took Shelby a few seconds to realize that Jilter and the other two were talking to each other. He switched again to the private circuit, and caught the tail-end of an exchange.

"—trapped near the engines when the side imploded," said a woman's voice.

"Ben Kramer?"

One of the suited figures shook her head. "It was Otto Wiessner. Just a kid, first trip out. I know his folks back in the Belt. We'll take his body."

"How about forward?"

"Don't know yet."

"We'll take a look." Jilter grabbed Shelby's arm and helped him to ease through a corridor that had been squeezed in places to less than half a meter wide.

"Crew of four," he said. "One body on board, so there's probably three out—"

"No." Shelby's heart contracted in his chest. He had seen, up near the ceiling, a suited hand. He pointed.

"Stay where you are," Jilter commanded. But Shelby was foolish enough to disobey. He followed close behind and saw what Jilter had already known they would find.

The side passage had been crushed by some terrible force. The man who had been standing inside the passage had been flattened until his suited body was nowhere more than four inches thick. Only his extended left forearm had escaped. Everything else was crushed, and it must have happened instantly because an explosion of blood, freeze-dried and blackened by cold and vacuum, coated all the passage walls.

Shelby swallowed and looked away. Jilter moved closer. The head was quite unrecognizable, but he was trying to see some form of identification on the suit. Finally he shook his head.

"Found another body," he said over his radio. "I'm not sure we can do anything for this one without cutting the whole ship apart. This might have to be a space burial."

"Is it Saul's brother?" asked the woman.

"Can't tell. Too much damage to make an identification. We'd know who it was by elimination if we could find and identify the other two."

"We're monitoring the open circuit and the other corries. They're scanning for suit beacons. Nothing so far. We're going to look again aft."

"We'll try farther forward." Jilter turned to Shelby. "You all right?"

Shelby again swallowed bile and nodded. "I'm fine." It was a big lie, but he forced himself to moved forward along the buckled corridor. He was dreading what other horrors they might find. His relief was indescribable when his radio came to life again.

"Thurgood Trask here, of the *Harvest Moon*." Uncle Thurgood sounded not at all his bluff and blustery self. "I have located two suits, tied together." He cleared his throat. "Both are men. One is dead. But we have one alive. Lost an arm, but the suit sealed at the shoulder. I reckon he'll live."

"Do you have IDs?" Saul Kramer sounded as though he himself had died.

"I'm looking." There was a long, frozen silence, until at last Thurgood spoke again. "I have a definite identification. The survivor is Dieter Landauer. The dead man is Ben Kramer. I'm real sorry, Saul."

"Not your fault, Thurgood. Dieter was a good friend of

Ben's." Kramer's voice cracked on his brother's name. "We'll take Dieter on board here, nurse him 'til we go Sol-side for regeneration of that arm."

"Right." Lana took over. "Thurgood, you head for the *Coruscation*. Saul, if the *Mary Mine* wants to head back, too, we'll handle everything else on what's left of the *Witch*."

"I appreciate that offer, and I accept it." Saul Kramer spoke politely, almost casually, while Shelby marveled. He was used to screaming and wailing whenever he fell down and grazed a knee or cut a finger. How could Saul Kramer accept with such fortitude the death of his own brother? And how— the thought flew in from nowhere—how had Constance Cheever reacted at the news of Shelby's own death? He found it hard to imagine. After just a handful of days, life on Earth in the Cheever compound felt remote and unreal.

"Come on," said Jilter gruffly. "Looks like it's going to be just you and me. Are you up to it?"

"I'll have to be." Shelby was thinking again of Saul Kramer, and he wanted to be as strong. He learned that he was not a few minutes later, when he and Jilter were using an unsealer to separate hull plates and liberate the crushed remains of the dead person. Finally he could see the flattened head. It was not a man at all. The body was that of a woman, young and blond.

The sex of a dead person ought to make no difference, but it did. Shelby found himself crying. A wave of nausea swept over him, and this time he could not hold it back. He began to vomit in his suit, gripped by a dreadful shame and a misery that was worse than the sickness.

"Easy, now." Jilter Clute was standing at his side, his hand sympathetically on Shelby's shoulder. "Your suit will handle whatever you throw at it, so just let it come. I know how you feel. Twenty years ago, when I was still wet behind the ears, I shipped out on the *Bellerophon*. We were the first ship to reach the *Great Northern* after its auxiliary drive exploded. I lost *everything* when we started to go through the wreckage, lunch and breakfast and dinner all the way to three days' back. I know how you feel. Take your time, and let it come."

That was Jilter Clute, who never spoke unless he was spoken to. Shelby, doubled over in misery and anguish, knew what was happening and felt a powerful gratitude. He tried to thank Jilter between spasms, but all that would emerge were dreadful choking noises.

Ten minutes later he felt well enough to continue with the work; but he didn't fully realize how much he owed Jilter until the corry was back at the *Harvest Moon* and the two bodies they had retrieved were stored away for eventual Solside return to the next of kin.

"He did just fine," Jilter told Lana Trask. "No problems at all. I'd be happy to take Shelby out again this minute if you wanted me to."

Lana stared at Shelby's pale and weary face. "Good. Well done, Shel. This wasn't what I expected for your first job outside the ship. But I promise you, everything you do after this is going to seem easy. Go and get some rest. And Jilter, would you take over for a few hours? I want to head over to the *Coruscation* and pay my respects to Saul. He and Ben are Mungo's second cousins. I plan to take Grace with me."

Shelby escaped and went to lie down on his bunk. Within two minutes he was asleep. His head had been filled when he lay down with awful memories of the wreck, but his sleep was easy and dreamless. When he was finally awakened by a rapping on his cabin door, he felt as though the whole terrible episode had itself been a dream.

He went to the door, convinced that it would be Doobie—who else woke him constantly when he was trying to sleep? But he was only half right. Doobie was there, and at his side was the hesitant figure of Scrimshander Limes.

"Told you," Doobie said. "All Shel ever does is snooze. Come on, Shel, you gotta get up. Scrim has something to show you."

"Oh, please, it's nothing." Scrimshander looked pleadingly from Shelby to Doobie and back. "I didn't want to disturb you. I told Doobie I didn't want to disturb you, but he insisted we come."

"You're not disturbing him—now." Doobie jerked his head toward Shelby. "See, he's up and wide awake. Let's go, Shel."

It was almost a pleasure, after what had happened at Dodman's Reef, to find that Doobie at least was his usual self. With Scrimshander trailing along behind they headed for the galley, where Doobie halted.

"All right, Scrim, over to you. It's your show."

"Really, it's nothing." But Scrimshander looked around, as though to make sure that no one else was present, then went across to the locker where the plates were kept. He took something out. "I'd like you to have this, Shelby—if you want it, I mean."

Shelby found himself holding a piece of white plastic about six inches long. He stared down and saw that it was a carving of himself, with every feature accurate from his pointed chin to his rumpled hair. The more he studied it, the more lifelike it seemed.

"This is fantastic," he said—and meant it. "I've never had anything like this before in my whole life."

He realized that his words were true in several different ways. He had been given plenty of things, many of them containing a lot of handwork. But never before had the present been *made* for him by the actual giver.

"It's nothing." Scrimshander blushed and wriggled with

pleasure and embarrassment. "I'm just glad that you like it. But I have to go. Thurgood will be waiting."

He turned and hurried out before anyone could say another word. Shelby stared at Doobie, and then again at the little figurine. "Look at the detail on this! He could make a fortune back on Earth. I wonder why he doesn't go and do it."

"Yeah, well, he has his reasons." Doobie gave a quick sideways glance at the figure. "Scrim might make a fortune—if people on Earth are as rich as you say they are. And provided he did with them like he did with you, and *wasn't* one hundred percent accurate."

"What do you mean?"

"Look at the body. Is that you?"

It was—but only in Shelby's own mental image. The body of the figurine was not overweight. It was lean and strong and muscular.

"You're right. It is a bit thinner than me."

"Yeah? Try about two tons thinner."

"But why did he carve it this way? As flattery?"

"Scrim don't know the meaning of the word. He carves people the way he sees 'em inside his head, not the way they are." Doobie must have somehow known who was coming into the galley, even though he had his back to them, because he deliberately added, "I mean, he don't care nothing about accuracy. Why, Scrim even carved Gracie to look beautiful."

Shelby turned. Grace had entered with her mother. One thing she did not look at the moment was beautiful. There were frown lines in her forehead, and her mouth was compressed and downturned.

"No, Doobie." Lana Trask sounded wearily impatient for the first time since Shelby had known her. "Saul Kramer lost his brother today, and Gunther Thorsten lost his daughter. This is a terrible time for them and for everyone. You'll show a decent sense of respect, or you won't remain on this ship."

"It's all right, Muv." Grace sounded as tired and depressed as she looked. "Doob's upset, I can tell."

"I know he is. But he has to learn to show it in a more suitable way."

"Sorry, Muv," Doobie muttered. "Sorry, Gracie."

Shelby wasn't convinced for a second. Doobie was just a kid. Looking back from the advanced age of almost sixteen, Shelby remembered it well, how little the deaths of people you didn't know meant to you when you were twelve or thirteen. Doobie *knew* what had happened, and he surely wished it hadn't. But he didn't really *care*.

Lana Trask, however, was satisfied—or pretended to be.

"Go on, then," she said. "I don't want to see you until tomorrow morning."

Her order wasn't addressed to Shelby, but he chose to interpret it that way. Although he still needed to have it out with Grace over her lying story about Jilter's name, this wasn't the time for it.

"Guess it must have been pretty bad over there," Doobie muttered when they were out of Lana Trask's hearing. "Usually, when Gracie comes back from visiting the *Coruscation* she has a grin on her face wide enough to fly a corry through. Maybe she didn't see him, or maybe they had a fight. She's been funny the past couple of days."

"Didn't see who?"

"Nicky Rasmussen. That's Saul Kramer's nephew. Gracie's been seeing Nicky the past couple of Confluences. Pretty mushy, if you ask me, but Muv approves. Says it would be a good match between the two harvesters."

"Nicky Rasmussen," Shelby said slowly. "What's he look like?"

"Tall and skinny, with a big nose. First-class freeball player. You'll see him for yourself at Confluence." Doobie, seeking a safe retreat where he could hide away without Lana Trask noticing him, paused. They were approaching a promising alcove furnished with a clutter of assay equipment, but even before they got there it was obvious that it would be no good. Thurgood Trask's voice could be heard, laying down the law.

"Never heard of such a thing in my whole life. Why'd you even think you'd like to be heading outside, in the middle of all today's trouble?"

There was the brisk click of plastic on metal, then Scrimshander's meek voice. "I don't know, Thurgood. I just thought if there was need of an extra pair of hands to do something, or if a person could help to search . . . Check, Thurgood."

"Well, don't you ever start thinking any such thing. Extra pair of hands, indeed! Didn't Lana say as how you'd be more useful here? I bet you weren't even listening to her. Check, you say? Let me see now. Check it is."

There was a long silence, then, "Why, tunnel and blast it, that's not check! It's check*mate*. Scrimshander Limes, you've gone and checkmated me!—when I wasn't looking. If that isn't the most sneaky, du-pli-ci-tous, underhand, unfair, backstabbing—"

"I'm sorry, Thurgood. See, if you hadn't moved the bishop that was protecting your king . . ."

Doobie chuckled and sneaked on past the alcove. "Happens all the time," he whispered to Shelby. "Uncle Thurgood can't stand it. Scrim beats him at chess every time they play. Pretty hard to take, when the way Uncle tells it he knows better than Scrim about everything."

"So why does your uncle play him?"

"Dunno. Maybe Uncle Thurgood thinks that one day

his luck will change. Or maybe he can't believe he loses all the time to somebody who's not firing on all drive units. Either way, any chance they get, the two of them sit down at a board and have at it."

"Your uncle treats Scrim horribly. He bullies him and orders him around all the time. Does Scrim work for him, or owe him something?"

"No." Doobie eyed Shelby thoughtfully. "That the way it is on Earth? Anybody works for somebody else or owes them money, they get bullied and run around all the time?"

"Sometimes." Shelby didn't like the way the talk was going. It was moving too close to home. "I've seen it happen."

"Earth must be a strange place. Try anything like that in the Cloud and you'd get a quick mouthful of knuckles. Here, no one pushes anyone else around. We wouldn't let 'em."

"But no one stops Thurgood, and he does it all the time to Scrimshander."

"Maybe he does. But he has his reasons. Look." Doobie took Shelby's arm as though he was ready to confide something. Then he shook his head and simply repeated, "Uncle Thurgood has his reasons. Good reasons."

Shelby pressed for details, but nothing that he said could persuade Doobie to say more.

Finally Shelby gave up. He decided that when Grace Trask stopped moping over her meeting with Nicky Rasmussen, he would ask her instead.

CHAPTER SEVEN

EARLY one morning, eighteen days after the loss of the *Witch of Agnesi*, Lana Trask was sitting in the *Harvest Moon*'s control room. It was the nerve center of the harvester, linked to every docking facility and every exit point. Lana was staring at one of the displays, where a corry was preparing to leave the ship. Shelby, with Grace Trask's supervision, was in the final stages of departure countdown. He was swarming easily and confidently over the corry's latticework, checking that the top of the corry would fly open automatically upon sensing the presence of the harvester's hull.

"What do you think?" said Lana. She was flanked by Logan and Jilter Clute, and could Shelby have heard her he would have been astonished by the tone of her question. If he had acquired her self-assurance, she had apparently traded it for his uncertainty.

"He has been out in a corry with me five times," said Logan, "not counting the occasion of his original arrival." The robot was not capable of impatience, which was just as well. "As I said a few minutes ago, in all five cases Shelby Cheever performed in excess of expectations."

"Three times with me, every one of them fine." Jilter sniffed. He was quite capable of impatience. "I'd have said something if there was any problem. Let 'em go."

"I suppose you're right." Lana turned to another display, this one showing the input from the harvester's largest scope. "And he seems sane now. He's stopped spouting all that nonsense about his fame and fortune back on Earth. But I'd feel a lot better if *that* wasn't out there."

The display showed, faint and far-off, the tiny image of another harvester.

"Its presence is merely a tribute to your skills at locating transuranics." Logan was also incapable of envy; otherwise, this was the time when it would have been displayed. Lana Trask's inexplicable ability to find stable transuranics was something that even a robot might covet. "If the crew of the *Southern Cross* trail us everywhere, it is only because our leavings are superior to their own findings."

"But is it the only reason?" Lana sat with her finger poised on the transmission circuit to Grace and Shelby's suits. "You believe that you know Pearl Mossman, Logan, but what you see is not the same woman as I see. I've watched her operate for twenty years. She and I came out together on our first trip to the Cloud. She's a very clever woman."

"Obviously, or she would not be the captain of a harvester. But she is not so clever as you, Captain Trask. Otherwise, Pearl Mossman would not pursue our tracks in the hope of filling the cargo holds of the *Southern Cross.*"

"I wasn't using *clever* as a compliment, Logan. Quite the opposite." But Lana at last stabbed down with her finger and said over the open circuit, "Exit permission granted."

"Yes, sir." Grace, knowing that her mother was watching, threw a quick salute. "Exit commencing, Captain."

"And *be careful.*"

"Muv! I'm *always* careful."

"I mean more careful than that."

The corry began its slow ascent, out through the port and away from the body of the harvester. Before it had gone two kilometers, Grace leaned across to Shelby and gestured for him to switch to the suit's personal radio circuit.

"What's wrong?" he said, as he made the change.

"Nothing. But I know Muv. She's back there watching every move we make 'til we get out of range. If she could she'd listen in on every word we say, too. I don't want her to hear us. And this way if she changes her mind, she can order us to come back but we can honestly say we didn't hear her."

Three weeks had been time enough for Shelby to learn a great deal about Grace Trask. On the surface she was cool and rational. Underneath she was wild and impulsive, with a crazy streak that could break out any time and in any direction. He had not yet forgiven her the spontaneous invention of Jilter Clute's colorful past.

"Why should she order us back?" He was not exactly worried, but he suspected that he ought to be. "Where are you planning on taking us?"

"Sightseeing."

As an answer it was designed to be reassuring. Shelby

projected their line of flight, and saw two reefs ahead. The corry's course would take them right between the pair, and already they were close enough to make out the black unwinking eyes.

"The reefs . . ."

Grace nodded. "Lizard Reef, and Portland Reef. Don't worry, we'll stay a long way from both of them. We're quite safe. Look ahead, though, isn't it great?"

It was certainly that. The view forward of the corry was spectacular. Although Lizard Reef and Portland Reef were well separated, there was a constant flow of matter between them, and long iridescent threads of gas twisted their way across the sky ahead, coiled and braided and tangled like golden hair. Dense rings of ionized plasma formed glowing jewels within the strands.

Shelby stared, shivered, and felt an almost superstitious awe. According to Lana Trask, some long-ago race of beings had, by accident or design, *created* the Messina Dust Cloud, space rivers and reefs and Confluence and all. It made everything that humans had ever done, perhaps all that humans would ever do, seem tiny and trivial.

He glanced across to Grace, wanting to share the moment, and found her turning her head from horizon to horizon and even peering behind them over the wall of the open corry, as though seeking the vanished *Harvest Moon.*

Had she seen all this so many times before that she was no longer overwhelmed?

Hard to believe. Shelby felt that he could stare at this space vista forever and never get tired of it. He turned to Grace, and found her gazing fixedly at one point of the sky.

"Grace—"

She waved him to silence. "Don't speak. We're in luck. There's a sounder on the way. Look, and listen."

The tenuous gases of the Messina Cloud seemed to have

thickened around the place that she indicated. There was a curious silvery glitter there, tiny sparkles that dotted the near-vacuum with a billion flecks of light.

Shelby stared, fell silent, and listened. He heard nothing and was all set to complain "Listen to *what*?" when his suit radio, at a sonic frequency so high that it was at the very upper limit of audibility, began to produce a thin bat-chirp. *Shreep-shreep-shreep.*

"Is it a ship?" he whispered.

Grace shook her head without speaking. The sound continued, becoming a little louder. *Shreep-shreep-shreep.* The corry, under Grace's control, made a sudden change of direction and moved at higher acceleration. She raised a gloved arm and pointed to the apex of the birdcage.

Shelby, peering at and beyond the cage of narrow struts, watched the sparks of light at that point dwindle and fade to leave behind emptiness of a curious eye-drawing clarity. Moving in that space was something that he saw in a first moment of panic as a third reef, its black unwinking eye directly ahead of them.

That couldn't be. Reefs were permanent and stable features of the Messina Dust Cloud. There was no way that a new reef could suddenly appear from nowhere. And with that thought Shelby began to see differences.

The object in front of them had the same ring structure as a tiny reef, and at the center sat a similar dark pupil. But this central eye was not round. It had an octagonal shape. Around the perimeter of the ring sat eight ragged blue-white tendrils, pointing outward and thinning gradually to invisibility. Next to the tendrils the pattern of background stars was compressed and distorted, so that the whole object had a rough eightfold symmetry.

And the thing was moving. Not toward the corry, but drifting sideways and slowly turning. As it rotated, Shelby saw that the octagonal ring was merely a part of something bigger, the head on a long, sinuous body. The body itself was black, visible as it occulted the glowing gas clouds behind it. Again, the star patterns nearby were twisted to map out a halo around the dark body.

"Suit radio off," whispered Grace. "All channels."

Shelby followed her instruction. As he did so she moved so that their suit helmets were in direct contact.

"Better to talk like this." Her voice carried faintly from her helmet to his. "I don't want our radio signals to disturb the sounder."

"Disturb it?" Shelby found himself shouting, his voice echoing within the hard helmet. "What do you mean, *disturb* it? It's not alive—is it?"

"Nobody's sure. Some people say that what you are seeing is just a natural phenomenon, no more alive than a reef. I don't believe that. Look at it. Doesn't that sounder seem to *act* alive?"

Shelby stared. It was easy to imagine a living creature, wriggling its way through the gas plumes that stretched between the reefs. Then he reminded himself of where he was. Although there was plenty of gas and dust around them by interstellar standards, this was still close to a perfect vacuum. A human would die in a minute here without a suit. How could anything make a home in the cold of open space?

"The reefs are the absolute best places in the whole Cloud to find sounders," Grace went on in an excited whisper. "They're drawn to the reefs somehow, though no one has any idea how they can appear from nowhere or where they come from. We know that where there happen to be two reefs close together, chances of seeing one are better. That's why I wanted to bring you outside today, before the *Harvest Moon* travels on. It's exactly what I hoped we might find. Isn't it just *great*?"

It was not the word Shelby would have chosen. The corry was still moving closer, and now more details were visible. The slow rotation of the object—creature?—in front of them allowed him to gain an idea of its size. The body trailed out in space, a tapering kilometers-long sack. He could see black lines along its length, and a curious pattern of individual white dots on the side that formed the shape of a running stick-figure man. At the front end the dark eye, which now he saw as an open octagonal maw, was huge. It could easily swallow up not only the corry, but the whole of the *Harvest Moon*.

If the sounder felt inclined to take such an action, there was little that a corry—or a harvester—could do but try to run away. Shelby had learned during his first days on board the *Harvest Moon* that no ship in the Messina Cloud carried any form of weapon.

"Grace, what is it?" he whispered. "And what is it doing?"

"The rakehell crews call them *space sounders*. I thought at first that this one was feeding, because the regions close to the reefs seem to be their feeding grounds—and the mouth is open. Now I'm not so sure."

"Feeding? On what?"

"Gas, dust, whatever it feels like. I don't know."

"Has a space sounder ever eaten a rakehell?"

Grace snorted at him. "Of course not! Why would it eat a ship? Or a corry, either, if that's what you're worried about."

"How do you know? Isn't it true that rakehells are lost all the time?"

"Sure they are—when they go too near a reef and try to thread the eye, like the *Witch of Agnesi* did. I don't know if the sounders realize that our ships exist at all, but if they do they're not unfriendly to them. There have been cases where a sounder flew within a couple of kilometers of a rakehell, took a good look around as though it was sniffing for something it couldn't find, and then just flew away again. Even when the sounders are feeding they don't get upset by the presence of ships. They're completely harmless. Admit it, Shel, you were scared."

"I still am." Shelby was staring at the sounder, which in his view had come uncomfortably close. He could see a fringe of glowing deep red around the gaping maw, and a steady dilation and contraction that gradually increased in amplitude. "How do you *know* it's harmless—harmless all the time?"

"Oh, all right." Grace moved her helmet, turned her radio back on, and gestured to him to do the same. "I'll take us farther away if that will make you feel better. But I wish I knew what this one is doing." Grace pointed to the pulsating maw. "I've never heard a report of a sounder's mouth changing like that. When they feed they usually just get wider and wider."

To Shelby's relief—the gaping mouth was becoming more and more active—the corry began to retreat from the sounder. The movement was imperceptible at first, but gradually he noticed a decrease in apparent size. He was just starting to breathe easy when the acceleration reversed direction.

"Now what are you doing?" Since Grace was holding the controls, he felt quite helpless.

"Look at it, Shel! We can't leave now. The rakehells have never reported anything like this. It's *shrinking* instead of growing."

Shelby looked and realized that she was talking about the sounder's mouth. The great maw was closing in, tightening and puckering down to a small black pinpoint. No longer was it big enough to swallow the corry. As he watched it became smaller yet, shrinking until it was almost invisible.

And the corry was flying in, closer and closer.

"Grace! No nearer."

"Oh, all right. But we really don't have to worry."

As she spoke, he saw another change. "Grace! Back off!"

A swelling was appearing on the sounder's octagonal front end, just as though the tiny mouth was now blowing a shimmering black bubble. As the corry retreated the bubble grew from nothing to become a sphere a couple of meters across. There was a sudden crackle of sound on the suit radio. The bubble separated from the sounder, to hang floating free in space.

And then it was the sounder that had turned and was retreating from the corry. Shelby heard Grace's cry over his suit radio, "It's sounding!"

Space was again thick-flecked with luminous sparks and filled with a diffuse blue fog. The sounder vanished into that glowing mist, while the same *shreep-shreep-shreep* that had announced the sounder's presence came again, fast diminishing in both pitch and volume. Within thirty seconds the sound became inaudible. Space returned to its usual clarity. Shelby stared and stared, but the sounder had vanished.

Beside him, Grace was gasping with excitement. "That's an absolute first. I've heard plenty about sounders feeding, but never of one throwing up."

"How do you know what it was doing?"

"What else could it be? You saw it. Come on, it's safe to take a look now. The sounder's long gone."

The corry crept forward, until the apex was almost in contact with the black sphere. Grace swung easily up the struts, until she was close enough to reach out and touch it.

"Grace! Don't do that. It might be dangerous."

"Phooey. I've never seen anything less dangerous in my whole life. Now, if you'd said *valuable.*"

She had her faceplate almost at the surface of the sphere. As Shelby watched, she reached out and plucked something off it. She held it high in triumph.

"Here's something better than your stupid electronic fund transfers. Here's *real* wealth."

Even in the dim glow of the Messina Dust Cloud, the fist-sized object that she held shimmered and sparkled with its own internal light.

"You wanted to know what a Cauthen starfire looked like?" She thrust it toward him. "Well, now you do. Touch it!"

Shelby reached out gingerly and took the object in his gloved hand. Even in low gravity it had a strange feeling of mass and solidity. He held it close and peered into the smooth surface, seeing hidden fires there.

"It's beautiful!"

"Beautiful? Shel, it's more than that. Ever since cloud exploration began, people have wondered where the Cauthen starfires and the shwartzgeld—the black glitter stuff it was stuck in—originated. Now we know. They're spit out by the sounders. And *only* we know."

Shelby's instincts told him that she was wrong on the last point. Chances were the rakehell crews already knew everything that they had just learned, and a lot more. Anyone with an ounce of commercial sense and a pinch of paranoia would keep such knowledge a close secret.

But there was no stopping Grace. "Shel," she went on. "Don't you see what this means? We're going to be rich!"

In her excitement she put her arms out and hugged him. It was a curiously distant embrace, with two airtight, insulated suits between their bodies, but still Shelby pulled away. In his world, girls did not go around hugging boys.

"I thought everyone on the *Harvest Moon* had a share of everything," he said to hide his embarrassment.

"They do, and they'll do well from this. But it isn't like regular cargo. Cauthen starfires and shwartzgeld are covered by rakehell rules—finders' fifty. That means you and I get fifty percent between us, and everyone shares the other half."

"I didn't do anything to deserve a quarter share. And I'm already rich."

"You still don't get it. I don't mean *pretend* rich, Shel, or little-bit rich. I mean *real* rich, *rich* rich. You and I are going to be rich-rich." She grabbed the starfire out of his hand and clutched it to her chest. "Ooh, it's so gorgeous. I don't mind selling the shwartzgeld, but I wish I could keep this forever."

"Why don't you?"

"How can I? It's worth more than my whole share. We'll have to sell it."

"I'll buy it for you."

"If only you could! Anyway, it's a sweet thought."

She leaned forward and touched her suit visor to his. It seemed like a trivial thing, but it must have had some ritual meaning in the Cloud because he saw her cheeks blush to a fiery pink behind her faceplate. She pulled back and said hurriedly, "We really ought to bring the find on board, and start back. If we don't, Muv will begin to worry and then she'll get mad."

"She'll probably be upset anyway, when she finds out where we went. I mean, when we show up with that"—he gestured to the great lump of shwartzgeld—"won't she know we could only have got it at the reefs?"

"She won't be angry when she sees what we have. Shel, even if we don't collect another gram of transuranics this whole trip, the *Harvest Moon* will make a profit. Muv will be too pleased to worry about anything."

Shelby, helping to maneuver on board the corry the great mass of black glitter, was not so sure. But when they got back to the harvester it seemed at first as though Grace was right. There was half an hour of excitement and rejoicing. Then Lana Trask took Grace off to her own quarters, for a quiet word.

Shelby did not learn, then or ever, what passed between them. But when Grace came back she did not look like the girl who had found gold at the end of the rainbow.

CHAPTER EIGHT

IF GRACE imagined that her newfound wealth would change everything on the *Harvest Moon*, it did not take long to discover that she was wrong. The shwartzgeld was tucked safely away in a cargo hold. Grace was allowed to hold on to the starfire, at least until the harvester returned Sol-side and it was time to sell the cargo and pay everyone's share. She announced that she was going to carry the stone with her everywhere. She dismissed the rumor that starfires carried bad luck with them, unless you immediately took them Sol-side through the node network.

"Stupid rakehell superstition," said Grace to Shelby. She sniffed and held the starfire close, so that she could peer into its changing depths. "What do rakehells know?"

And after a long day in which Doobie and Grace and Shel talked endlessly of reefs and rakehells and sounders and starfires, and Scrimshander Limes looked on wide-eyed, and Uncle Thurgood snorted his disdain and disapproval of anything so far removed from traditional mining, the harvester and its crew went back to the routine but necessary business of tracking down and collecting stable transuranics.

Shelby was at last permitted to make his first solo trip out in a corry. He set a complete circle of cable and collectors around the *Harvest Moon*, waited the necessary twelve hours, and retrieved the plastic bags. He tested one, slowly and carefully.

Lana Trask had done it again. Every sack was filled to bursting with high-grade transuranics.

Shelby cruised back to the harvester after a perfectly routine mission, high on his own success and ready to describe his feat in detail to anybody who would listen.

Finding such a person was not so easy. Jilter Clute was working the cargo hold separators with assistance from Doobie and made it clear with a growled "Get lost" that regardless of teenage preferences there would be no interruptions. Lana Trask was off in isolation, sniffing the Cloud currents and plotting the harvester's final approach route to the Confluence.

Confluence rendezvous was only six days away, and that event seemed to be much on Grace's mind also. Shelby could talk to her, but two or three vague replies were enough to convince him that she was not really listening.

Logan was even worse. He lacked the right circuits and could not even simulate interest or enthusiasm for what Shelby was telling him.

Desperation produces strange solutions. Shelby sought out Uncle Thurgood. He knew that Thurgood was working on his corry, brought into airdock to remove the layer of sticky tar that reflected his latest misadventures in the Messina Cloud. Thurgood was dressed in a dirty boiler suit, and his flushed face seemed redder than ever in its frame of white side-whiskers. Predictably, he was not alone. Shelby could hear the bellow even before he reached the entrance of the dock.

"What are you telling me, that you think I might steal from you?" There was a furious scraping noise, of a strut suffering violence from file and rasper. "That you don't trust me?"

"Never. I would never think any such thing." Scrimshander Limes was pawing ineffectually at the lattice with a blunt scraper.

"Then what's this nonsense about taking your share separate from mine when we get Sol-side?"

"Well." Scrimshander sounded bewildered but persistent. "I know you don't care to visit the Kuiper Belt mines. You have told me so yourself, many times. But I thought I might find them interesting. We will have more money than usual, you say, because of what Grace and Shelby brought back. So rather than trouble you, I thought I would just take some money from my share and use it to go to the Kuiper Belt by myself."

"Never!" Thurgood Trask smashed at the birdcage lattice with his file. The struts twanged like harp strings, and bits of tar sprayed off and stuck to his face and bald head. "Scrimshander Limes, that is the most ridiculous, stupid, wrongheaded, addle-minded, pea-brained notion you've had yet. And you've had some doozies!"

"You mean you would like to go with me?"

"I do *not* mean that I would like to go with you! I mean

I don't want you going off to the Kuiper Belt mines *at all*, alone or with me or with anyone else. I don't want you even *thinking* of going to the Kuiper Belt mines. There's a hundred better places for you and me to visit when we reach Sol-side."

"What do you have in mind?"

"Well, there's—let's see, I guess there's—" Thurgood, gazing wildly about him for inspiration, caught sight of Shelby standing at the entrance. "Now, what the devil are *you* doing here?"

Shelby shook his head. "Nothing." Thurgood Trask in his present mood would be worse than no audience at all.

"Then if you have nothing to do, don't do it here. We happen to have men *working.*" Thurgood, speckled black and filthy from head to foot, scowled horribly. "*And* we are engaged in a private conversation."

"Sorry." Shelby retreated, as Thurgood Trask started in again on his companion.

"Where to go, you ask? I'll tell you where we can go. Where *he* came from—Earth! How about that? If you want to go somewhere different when we're Sol-side, we'll go to Earth."

"I suppose we can do that." Scrimshander sounded more puzzled than ever. "But Thurgood, you've said time and again what a terrible place Earth is."

"When did I ever say any such thing? I never said any such thing!"

But he had. Shelby, hurrying away, recalled Uncle Thurgood's fiery speeches on that very subject. "*Earth?* I'll tell you all about *Earth*!" He would emphasize the accursed word each time he mentioned it with a bang of his big fist on the galley table. "It's the worst planet in the known universe, *Earth* is. The poor devils there are penniless and starving, but they stay there. Why? That's what I'd like to know. Why?"

Then Thurgood would glare around the table as though daring anyone to answer his question. Shelby would remain silent. He was biding his time, and that time would come when the harvester returned Sol-side.

Now, though, Shelby was baffled by what Thurgood was telling Scrimshander. Had he suddenly changed his mind about Earth? Also, Uncle Thurgood had once waxed absolutely lyrical to Grace and Doobie about the wonders and delights of the Kuiper Belt. And what was it that Grace Trask had said? That her uncle had mined for twenty successful years in the Kuiper Belt, and there weren't enough volatiles in the whole Messina Cloud to wash the ore dust off his mining boots.

It was a mystery. But that mystery had to wait until the next day, when Shelby and Grace were hidden away in Doobie's cabin at his invitation. Doobie had taken advantage of a moment of inattention by Thurgood Trask and stolen a dozen pies, piping hot and ready to eat, that Thurgood had just finished baking.

"Payback time," Doobie said as he shared them out. "He'd have done the same thing to us if he'd found ours in the galley."

They were sitting on Doobie's bed, which a combination of disorder and accumulated clutter made the only usable surface in his cabin. Even that was touch and go, because the bed was all hummocks and lumps. The good news was that a few pie crumbs would make little difference to its condition. Shelby, who before reaching the *Harvest Moon* had never in his whole life made a bed, had in his first days aboard been learning the technique from Doobie. He had stopped when Grace found out about that and collapsed into laughter.

She recalled it now, as the pies were gobbled up. "Doobie as bed-making specialist. What would it have been next? Piloting techniques from Scrimshander? Or you might get Uncle Thurgood to give you lessons in calmness and politeness."

"Makes good pies, though," Doobie said with his mouth full. "This is swee-eet. I've waited a long time to get even with him. If you ask me, Uncle Thurgood is worse than ever on this trip."

"I can believe that," said Shelby, "even though I wasn't here before. I saw him yesterday chewing out Scrimshander. He treats him so *rotten*. He bullies him and runs him around, and he never has one good word to say to him no matter how hard Scrim tries. He must know that Scrim's not quite all there. So why is he so cruel?"

He described the meeting from the previous day and concluded, "You'd think that it was some sort of *crime* for Scrim to want to visit the Kuiper Belt. But why shouldn't he, if he wants to and he can afford it? He may not be too bright, but he still has rights."

There was a dead, flat silence. Finally Doobie turned on the bed and stared at Grace. "Your move, Grace."

"I can't. You know I can't."

"You can. You have to. Shel's one of us now, full-fledged harvester crew. You're the one who told *me* that, Gracie. He deserves to know."

"Muv would skin us alive."

"To know *what*?" asked Shelby.

Grace sighed. "All right. But Shel, you have to promise us you'll never tell anybody how you found out."

"I promise."

"All right. You know Scrimshander Limes?"

"Of course I know Scrimshander Limes! What sort of an idiot question is that? I was just talking about him."

"Well, you don't know him. That's the whole point. There is no such person as Scrimshander Limes."

"Then who—"

"Listen closely. This is an awful story, and I don't want to have to tell it more than once. Six years ago, there was a terrible accident back in the Kuiper Belt. A big one. Two hundred and ninety-seven dead."

"I've heard of that! The Trachten blow-out."

That threw Grace, and she paused to stare at Shelby. "Where did you learn that?"

"On the *Bellatrix*, before I came here."

"What else do you know?"

"That only one person survived."

"Correct. There was just one survivor. A man called Jack Linden."

"Lucky Jack Linden."

"That's right. And apparently before the accident he was smart as well as lucky."

"But he never mined again afterward."

"He never did. Because he saw everyone he loved die, right there in front of his eyes, while he looked on; and for all his smartness he couldn't do one thing to help. Lucky Jack, you see, with his luck he'd drawn an assignment outside the mining facility. When the accident happened he was at a safe distance. But his wife and parents and children were blown out into space—still alive, but without suits.

"He could fly over and watch them die, and he did. But he couldn't *help* them. He stood by, useless, and it wiped his mind clean. When he was picked up he didn't remember anything about the accident. Didn't even know who he was. They treated him, but it didn't do any good. Finally they had to release him. It was either that or keep him permanently in a home, and that didn't seem right because everyone was sure he was harmless. He drifted from mine to mine around the Kuiper Belt for close to a year, a kind of human flotsam.

"That's when Uncle Thurgood found him. He told the people who Scrim was living with that he'd find a job for him. Then Uncle gave him a new name and brought him from the Kuiper Belt out to the *Harvest Moon*. They both signed on. Don't ever ask what Uncle told Muv and Dad. They won't say and you'll get into trouble if you so much as mention it.

"Uncle and Scrim have never been back to the Kuiper Belt. Uncle loves the Belt, and everything about it, but he figures that it's the worst possible environment for Scrim, because it might make him remember what happened. He sometimes dreams about it anyway, and that's bad enough. But now you can see why Muv and the others wouldn't let Scrim go anywhere near the wreck of the *Witch of Agnesi*, or any other space accident. And *that's* why Uncle gets so upset when Scrim talks about going for a visit to the Belt."

"He did all that for Scrim?" Shelby asked. And, when Grace and Doobie nodded, "Then why does he treat him so *bad*, like he hates him?"

"He thinks Scrim needs to be chivvied and cared for and pushed along," Grace said, "like a chick and a mother hen. Otherwise Scrim might just sit down and fade away. But don't listen to what Uncle Thurgood *says* to Scrim. Watch his eyes when he talks to him. He guards him night and day, and if anyone ever did or said anything bad to Scrim he would kill them. He loves him better than his own family."

"But *why*?"

"Because he's saving Scrim from something awful, and Uncle knows it even if Scrim doesn't. It's the way of the world. If you were ever to save me, Shel, some way or other, it would make you *responsible* for me. You'd have to look after me forever."

Grace blushed, a fierce inexplicable blush that neither her brother nor Shelby noticed.

"Anyway," she added quickly, "now you know. There's no such person anymore as Lucky Jack Linden. Just Scrimshander Limes."

"Who else knows?"

"Everyone on the *Harvest Moon*, of course. Quite a few people on the other harvesters. We don't tell people, but somehow or other the word gets out."

The little room was silent for a long time. Even Doobie seemed subdued, until at last he stood up. "Come on, Gracie," he said gloomily. "If you want to."

"Come on where?"

"To the galley. I'm going to tell Uncle that we took his pies and that we've eaten the lot. I don't feel right. I can use a Thurgood special steaming."

"Doob, are you crazy?" But Grace followed him out.

So, after a few seconds, did Shelby. No one before had ever laid a finger on him. It seemed a good time to find out what it was like.

CHAPTER NINE

IN THE past two weeks the talk aboard the *Harvest Moon* had been more more about the Confluence, until that word became a muddled mixture in Shelby's mind. What *was* the Confluence?

A location, certainly, a place in space where the multiple great rivers of the Messina Dust Cloud converged and mingled in a way that the crew agreed had to be seen to be believed. It was also a time when all harvesters and many of the rakehells would meet to mark the midpoint of a season. It was an exchange, too, of materials and of news both good and bad. Crews met to commiserate or congratulate or to trade supplies that were running low. And it was also a simple celebration of human beings surviving and thriving so far from Sol.

When a crew member said "Confluence" it could mean any and all of these things. Careful questioning gradually allowed Shelby to sort out which was which.

And then, with Confluence just a day away and everything seemingly well-defined and clear, confusion returned.

Shelby was working with Logan; more accurately, he was watching Logan perform separate activities with each of his eight arms and marveling that the machine could do all that and still talk to him.

"And why should I not?" Logan was braiding eight different types of cable at once, working each one-handed faster than Shelby could have done it with two. As a tutorial it was discouraging, but it was necessary. Lana Trask herself had examined Shelby's cables earlier that day and pronounced them a disgrace.

"You do not find it odd," Logan went on, "that you breathe and perspire and blink and walk and digest and talk and hear and see and feel at the same time. Those are independent activities. If you propose at Confluence to talk only when you sit, to refuse to talk because you are eating, and to dance only when you are silent, then you will surely lack partners and company." Logan handed over a half-braided cable. "Here. You have seen how it is done. Now continue."

Shelby took the braided cable and set to work. "What do you mean when you say *dance*? Does that mean something different in the Cloud?"

"Different from what?"

Logan's logic could be maddening.

"Different from what the word usually means," said

Shelby. "Look, you just mentioned me *dancing* at the Confluence. Define dancing."

"Dancing is a rhythmic movement of humans, usually to music, usually in pairs, but sometimes alone or in larger groups."

"Fine. We agree. But how could that possibly happen at Confluence? The only place on the *Harvest Moon* that's big enough for anyone to dance is the cargo holds, and they're filthy. I can't see much dancing going on there. And I gather that the other harvesters are about the same size."

"That is correct." The wire-mop head nodded, then remained bent over looking down at Shelby's hands. "The Confluence dances will take place in Confluence Center, which as I understand it was designed for just such a purpose. However, since I was not designed with dancing capability I have spent little time in the Center habitat."

"But why do people dance?"

"Do you mean, why do they dance generally or why do they dance specifically at Confluence? Do not bother to reply, since I cannot answer either question. I have pondered it many times, without achieving a resolution." Logan reached out and took the cable from Shelby. "However, I perceive that braiding cable and talking are not two of the things that you are able to perform simultaneously."

Shelby stared at the tangled mess that he had created and that the robot was now holding.

"I must insist," continued Logan, "that all discussion of dancing or other Confluence activities be postponed until after this lesson is completed and Captain Trask has pronounced herself satisfied. Therefore, if you would now be so good as to try again . . ."

Logan offered the cables to Shelby. He glared at them. In less than ten seconds, Logan had completely undone his efforts of the past five minutes. He cursed and started over.

But he couldn't possibly let the matter end there. Even if Logan was no help, somebody must be able to tell him. When Lana Trask appeared to examine his work and pronounce it acceptable—for a first cut—he asked her.

She stared at him. "I thought you knew all about it. Sure, there's a big habitat at the Confluence. The harvester crews built it years ago as a joint effort, and there are dances held in it during every Confluence."

She was using Confluence to mean two different things, a time and a place, but Shelby was getting used to that.

"Why?" he asked. "I mean, why go to all the trouble of building something so far away?"

"Far away from where? We'll be there in another day. Anyway, it was not difficult. There are plenty of raw materials in the Cloud, and machines did all the actual work."

"But why do it at all?"

"We need a place to hold the dance in." Lana saw his frustration. "Shelby, I think I see the piece that's missing for you. Before you understand the habitat and the dance, you need to understand something about Cloud folk. We compete with each other, fiercely, while we're harvesting. But deep down we're a lot alike, with more in common than we have with anyone Sol-side who doesn't know the Cloud. Harvester people who marry each other usually make good matches. The trouble is, there's no natural meeting-place for people like Grace to meet possible partners. Once the harvesters head back through the node, they go their own ways until it's time for the next trip out. And once we're here, the harvesters stay clear of each other because we all follow our own plans for sniffing out the best harvest. The one time and place where everyone meets is at Confluence. For young people, or for unattached older people, the Confluence Center dances are very important. Didn't Grace explain this to you?"

"Not a word."

"Stew that girl. It's time I had a chat with my daughter. Logan, would you go and tell Grace to come here?—right now, and quickly."

"You are a full member of the crew of the *Harvest Moon*, Shelby," she went on as the robot scuttled away on all eight arms. "As someone who is young and unattached, you are expected to attend the Confluence dances. It will be considered very peculiar if you don't. Can you dance?"

"I have danced." Shelby recalled, with no particular pleasure, the formal balls at the Cheever estate. From the age of twelve onward it had been his lot, scrubbed and starched and polished to the point of discomfort, to serve as an escort to some girl with a "right" family background as defined by Constance Cheever. He had felt awkward and ungainly and hated every second.

"I'm not very good at dancing," he added.

"That's all right," said Lana calmly, as Grace entered. She had a nervous look and wouldn't meet Shelby's eye.

"You'll have plenty of company," Lana went on. "The harvesters don't offer much in the way of dance practice. The important thing is to show up and show willing. Now, Shelby, would you please leave us for a few minutes? I need to talk to Grace. Close the door behind you."

Shelby did as he was told. But he hadn't in so many words been told not to listen, and he couldn't resist staying and putting his ear to the crack of the door.

"Why didn't you?" Lana was saying. "You knew I expected you to."

"But Muv, I just couldn't. I mean, we're used to Shel, and we make allowances. But the other ships wouldn't. Stand back and take a look at him, and imagine what they'd say."

"Are you worried on his behalf—or are you worried about what Nicky Rasmussen will think about *you*, if you walk in with Shel?"

"I don't care what Nicky thinks about me. I'm worried what other people will think about Shel. They'll laugh at him. I mean, have you seen his hair? And his clothes! You've seen how baggy they are at the waist. He must have lost seven or eight kilos since he came aboard, but he keeps on with the same old balloon size. He looks like a clown."

"Those are trivial fixes. Fifteen minutes in a cosmetics machine."

"I've tried, Muv. He refuses to go inside one."

"Why?"

"I don't know."

But Shelby did. For six weeks he had been avoiding the cosmetics machines, trimming his own nails and hair and taking clean clothes from the laundry machines, and all the while hoping that no one would notice.

Apparently everyone had. He groaned to himself, as Lana said firmly, "Well, that has to change. For his sake. Let me get him back in here."

Shelby retreated quickly to the other side of the room, and was sitting down as Lana opened the door. She gave him one skeptical glance, then beckoned him inside.

"I understand that you have not been using the cosmetics machines," she said at once, before he could speak. "We can't have that. You must be trim and tidy and well turned out—we all must. We'll be reaching Confluence tomorrow and mingling with people from the other harvesters. The reputation of the *Harvest Moon* as a tightly run professional ship will be at stake." She turned to Grace. "Take Shelby to a cosmetics machine, right now. Show him how to work it. And let me see the result when you are done."

There was no time for argument, and no suggestion that Lana Trask would listen if it were offered. Shelby trailed sheepishly along behind Grace, until she stopped at last before a narrow door.

"This wasn't my idea," she said, "but I'll do the programing for you. Will you be all right inside?"

"I guess so." He didn't want to admit, least of all to Grace, that he had been dreading this moment. Working with a machine like Logan was one thing. You could imagine it was just another person. Getting *inside* a machine, with your whole body, and standing helplessly while it did all manner of intimate things to you, was something else. He felt obliged to add, "I don't have any choice, do I?"

Grace stared at him. "Not unless you're claustrophobic. Are you? I've heard that some Earth people are terrified of being shut up in small spaces. If that's the problem, I could come inside with you."

"It's not that." Shelby finally admitted the truth. "I just don't like the idea of some machine *feeling* me and *measuring* me and *trimming* me."

"Only your hair and nails. But you must have had all this before, back on Earth."

He shook his head. "Never."

"Then how did you . . ."

"People. I had someone to measure me for clothes and make my suits. And someone else did massages, and other people gave me manicures and pedicures and haircuts."

She was staring at him in disbelief. "You won't let a machine near you, but another *person* can cut your toenails? That is *weird*. You couldn't pay me enough to let strangers touch my body or get me to mess around with theirs."

"It's their jobs," Shelby muttered. But Grace's disdain was so obvious that rather than face it any longer he opened the door and stepped through into the cosmetics machine.

He closed his eyes and stood rigid as the door sealed automatically. A hundred unpleasant things were going to be done to him.

The first one was the most disturbing. All his clothes were neatly sliced away and removed from his body. He stood naked and covered with goose bumps, wondering what would have happened if Grace *had* entered the machine with him.

Then scores of delicate fingers were exploring his bare body, feeling his head and fingers and toes, wandering around his arms and legs, measuring his belly and buttocks and chest. He cringed, but he dared not move a millimeter—the touch was far too intimate. Something was snipping at his hair, something was nibbling at fingernails and toenails, and something else was laving and massaging and blow-drying every inch of him with warm air.

It took a few minutes to realize a strange truth: He *liked* the feeling. His personal servants back home had done their best, but they had never operated with such gentle precision; and despite their title, they had never been nearly as personal.

Just as he was beginning to relax, another sequence began. His arms and legs were manipulated into new clothes. Invisible fingers tightened and straightened and made minute adjustments. There was a pause, as though for evaluation. And at last he heard the door behind him slide open.

He turned, stepped out, and saw Grace standing at the door. She had on her face a look of worried anticipation that exactly matched his own feelings.

He stood motionless, waiting, until he saw her smile and heard an explosive "Well! That's more like it."

"Is it all right?"

"All right? It's *great*. You can be a dancing fool all night long in that rig. Come on, Muv has to get an eyeful." She grabbed his hand and towed him away, while he stared down at his new clothes. He was dressed in a uniform of dazzling white, snug across the shoulders and wrinkle-free at the waist. His scuffed and down-at-heel loafers, the same ones he had been wearing inside his suit when he left the *Bellatrix*, had been replaced by uncreased shoes of bright synthetic leather.

Lana Trask was not given to statements of wild enthusiasm. But her cool evaluation, followed by a quiet "Yes, I think so. Now we have a new hand that the *Harvest Moon* can feel proud of," was enough for Shelby. He left the control room as nervous as ever about his ability to dance, but now it might not matter. If nothing more, he could at least stand to one side and hope to be inconspicuous.

"Don't wear them again 'til the dance," were Grace's last words as he left the control room. "I programmed that outfit special, but I designed you casuals as well. Get a set of those out of a laundry machine. Your new size is on file. Take good care of what you're wearing—and whatever you do, don't sleep in 'em!"

Shelby didn't sleep in them. But he did go and find a full-length mirror and spent a few minutes admiring his reflection.

He assured himself, as he prepared for bed and carefully folded his new outfit, that he had no interest in clothes and never would have. But it did seem to him, as an objective and unbiased observer, that he looked pretty damned sharp.

A week or two earlier, Jilter had mentioned to Shelby that on the morning of the arrival at Confluence, it would be "worth getting to an observation port by four in the morning."

Given Jilter's laconic style, that amounted to a major pronouncement. Shelby had made a note of it, and he struggled out of bed bleary-eyed at three-thirty. The corridors of the *Harvest Moon* were silent and deserted as he made his way to the ship's forward observation platform.

He reached it, expecting to be alone so early in the morning. To his surprise, someone was already sitting on the padded bench.

It was Scrimshander Limes. Shelby muttered an awkward "Good morning," then for the next three minutes sat there tongue-tied. Speaking to Scrim used to be no trouble at all. Now he didn't dare to open his mouth.

He was saved by the arrival of Grace Trask. She took in the situation, squeezed onto the bench between him and Scrimshander, and whispered in Shelby's ear a fierce "Act natural, bonehead!" And then in the other direction, "Where's Uncle Thurgood, Scrim?"

"I am not sure. I expected him to be here." Scrimshander frowned. "Oh dear. I wonder if perhaps I was supposed to wake him?"

Grace was right. Scrim was his normal, slightly puzzled self. The problem was with Shelby. He had to learn to behave as though he knew nothing of Scrim's history. With that thought, he was at last able to pay attention to the scene beyond the observation port.

He had been told that the Confluence had to be seen to be believed. It was an understatement. Ahead of them the great space rivers of the Messina Cloud met and merged and swirled about each other, to break the sky into a thousand different shapes. He could see castles and birds and harps and snakes, there a bright-green Christmas ornament, there a pale human face, there a spectral dog chasing after an orange octopus. Friction between gas streams caused ionization and huge potential differences, creating lightning discharges that flickered and danced continuously across the sky. They transformed whatever they touched. A flowering bush was now a dancing bear, now a grinning red demon with horns and forked tail, now a tornado or a crimson flame-wrapped tower.

Shelby sat and marveled. At the same time he puzzled. Surely the sights in front of him were a permanent part of the Confluence, available to be viewed by the harvester crews at any time. Why rise so early in the morning to see them?

As Uncle Thurgood swept in behind the others, puffing and grumbling, Shelby's question was answered. A new pattern, dozens of clusters of white sparks of light, suddenly sprang into existence. They were like new constellations against the dimmer Cloud background.

The other people in the observation room murmured in pleasure. They began to talk all at once.

"There's the *Dancing Lady*," said Grace. "They made it on time, and Doobie loses. I guess that duff drive unit is holding out all right."

"Don't see the *Hope and Glory* anywhere." Uncle Thurgood was scanning the patterns ahead. "Oh, wait a minute, there we are. Now what in Charon's hold are they doing *there*, back of the *Sweet Chariot*? Bad harvest haul, for a bet, and trying to skulk."

"I *think* that must be the *Balaclava*," Scrimshander murmured. "Or is it the *Never-Say-Die*? I am never sure."

"How can you possibly tell who's who?" Shelby asked Grace.

"From the pattern of lights." She pointed. "See. That's *The Pride of Dundee*. No one else has that group of crowns picked out in lights. Every harvester and every rakehell is different. We have our own, too, of course, on the *Harvest Moon*. You'll know all of 'em before Confluence is over. Sometimes it gets tricky, though. Over there is the *Avalon*, but they've lost a few of their lights on the right side and so they look different. Sloppy, to let that go 'til they're right at Confluence. Doob and I will josh them about it at the dance, you wait and see."

She must have been doing a silent count as she spoke, for she frowned and went on, "There's a couple missing—not counting the *Witch of Agnesi*. Wonder if somebody else hit a problem and we never heard about it."

"No problem." That was Jilter, who had quietly entered just after Uncle Thurgood. "It's a full house. The *Coruscation* and the *Southern Cross* arrived late, but they're here and behind us. You can see them from the aft observation port."

He stood in silence, counting and confirming. "Yes," he said at last. "Every one, except the *Witch*. That's good enough for me. I'm for an early breakfast."

He left, soon to be followed by Thurgood Trask and Scrimshander Limes.

"Worth getting up for?" Grace asked Shelby, when just the two of them were left.

"Easily. The thing I don't understand, though, is *why*. I mean, it should be easy to send radio signals to each other, if you want to be sure that every other ship is here."

"Oh, Muv does that. She'd know and tell us as soon as it happened if something disastrous happened to another ship."

"So what's all this business of counting, and identifying the harvesters from their lights, just as though you don't know who's here?"

"It's a *ceremony*, Shel. Don't Earth people understand what a ceremony is? The lighting of the harvester fleet. Always at the same time, and exactly synchronized the way you saw it. It's a sign—a sign that we're here at Confluence, that the season is half over, that we're ready and waiting to meet each other. Everybody on every ship gets up to see the lights go on. I should say, nearly everybody. Doobie will still be snoring his head off."

She stood up from the bench. "That's it for the moment. Next item on the agenda, breakfast. Then we take a good

long break—no duties at all today. Then we get ready. And
then"—she did a tricky little crossover step that Shelby was
sure he could never imitate—"then it's nighttime, and we go
wild at the Confluence Center dance."

CHAPTER TEN

GRACE had described the dance to Shelby in glowing terms. It took him about two minutes from the time they arrived inside the rotating cylinder of the Confluence Center to realize that she had left out a very important fact: He was going to be stared at.

They had flown over, he and Grace and Doobie, in a special little pinnace that he had never seen before on the *Harvest Moon*. Unlike the corries, this ship maintained its own atmosphere. They could put on their dance gear before leaving the harvester, certain that it wouldn't be crumpled and ruined inside a suit. Grace's Cauthen starfire she had left behind, after many agonized attempts to find a place on her where she could fix it without looking ridiculous. A starfire was simply too big for personal adornment. Maybe it could form the jewel centerpiece in a large crown, or, as Shelby suggested, the prize decoration on an elephant's forehead. Grace had frowned and said "Elephant?" as though she suspected a hidden insult.

The habitable cylinder of Confluence Center was huge, about fifty meters long and sixty wide. The pinnace docked inside a big airlock at one end, from which the three passengers could stroll straight out onto the curved inner surface. The effective gravity was a bit low by Shelby's standards, maybe a quarter of a gee. He hoped that might help him to dance better. He had tried a few steps, secretly, on the *Harvest Moon*. Compared with graceful Grace, he felt that he was the lumbering elephant.

They emerged onto Confluence Center's polished floor, which was dotted with small clusters of people from the harvesters and rakehells. Doobie at once headed off toward three other boys of his own age. Shelby stared all around him, fascinated by everything from the glowing light fixtures along the cylinder's central axis to the curved floor that made people halfway around the giant room seem to be standing on their heads. Already self-conscious, he noticed that as soon as anyone looked in his and Grace's direction they would say something to the rest of their group. Then all heads would turn his way. After that there was a louder buzz of conversation that he couldn't make out.

He looked down at his clothing and could see nothing out of the ordinary.

"Grace!" He tried to point out what was happening, without making it too obvious. "Why are they doing that?"

She glanced at a couple of the groups. "It's nothing. Better get used to it, Shel. You're famous."

"Famous? They don't even know me."

"They certainly do. You're famous two ways. First, they know you were picked up in open space, which is unheard-of out here in the Cloud. Second, you're famous because you're rich."

"I thought nobody believed I was rich. I didn't even think that *you* believed me."

"Off and on. But I'm talking real and certified rich. Like you and me. Between us we own half of a Cauthen starfire and a big lump of shwartzgeld, and word on that has spread around the fleet. It's the sort of wealth that people here care about—not the only-son-of-Jerome-Prescott-Cheever sort." She took his arm. "Now, don't get peeved. You know I don't mind one way or the other how rich you are. You're going to meet people, and you have to look pleasant. Can you make idle conversation?"

"Try me." For the first time since arriving at the Messina Cloud, Shelby felt confidence in his abilities. In the social stratum occupied by Constance Cheever, platitude-training preceded potty-training.

Grace did try him. She introduced him randomly to people from the other harvesters. He listened carefully to everyone's name and tried to use it, allowed others to set the direction of the conversation, and restricted his own contribution to occasional harmless comments. After a few minutes with any group he saw the interest in him turning off. He could read their minds as they bade him goodbye: "Just a kid who came here by accident, got lucky, and picked up a starfire."

By the fifth group he had his routine down pat. He hardly needed Grace. So he felt no qualms when she, as another man and woman came strolling toward them across the polished floor, stared off to one side and muttered, "Oh, Lordie. I was afraid of this. Shel, I have to leave you for a while. You're on your own."

As she hurried away he looked after her. He saw her approaching a long-legged male figure whose face was obscured by a large bouquet of blue flowers. That was strange, because Shelby didn't think there were any flowers within light-years. But before he could see what happened next to Grace he had to face the two new arrivals, now standing right in front of him.

"You're Shelby Cheever, aren't you?" the woman said. She was tall and slender and elegantly dressed and about the same age as Lana Trask.

"That's right." He took the hand that she held out toward him.

"I'm Pearl Mossman." She released him and waved to her companion. "And this is Knute Crispin." She added, just as Shelby was convinced that he ought to recognize those names, "We are from the harvester the *Southern Cross.*"

That closed the circuit. "You're the *captain*, aren't you?"

"As a matter of fact, I am. And Knute is my chief assistant." She made a small gesture to Knute Crispin and he nodded at Shelby and left, as Pearl Mossman went on, "But how do you know who I am?"

"Lana Trask has mentioned you a couple of times. She says you are very smart." Shelby was diplomatic enough not to offer the rest of Lana's occasional remarks, that she wished the *Southern Cross* would stop chasing the *Harvest Moon* around the Cloud.

"I can return that compliment, with conviction." Pearl Mossman smiled. "Lana Trask is an exceptional captain and the best sniffer in the Cloud. But I don't want to talk about me and Lana. I want to ask about *you*. Your name, Cheever. Are you by any chance related to J. P. Cheever, of Cheever Consolidated Enterprises?"

"I am." There was a temptation to shout with delight and respond with a great flood of words—someone has heard of me! At last! Hooray! But the experience of the past weeks had made Shelby cautious.

"How do you know about Cheever Industries?" he asked.

"From the time I was on Earth, nine years ago. But tell me, *how* are you related to J. P. Cheever?"

Talking about your family when no one seemed to know or care that they existed was one thing. Answering questions that someone asked you was another.

Shelby began to explain: who he was, where he really lived, how he had come to be in the Messina Dust Cloud. Pearl Mossman made a fine audience, nodding or murmuring sympathetically at all the right moments. Shelby didn't realize how long he had been talking, until he noticed that the dance floor had filled with people and he saw Grace hurrying back toward him. Her eyes were unnaturally bright, and beneath the makeup her face seemed pale.

"It's all right, my dear," Pearl Mossman said as Grace joined them. "I'm not trying to keep him all to myself. Over to you." She turned back to Shelby. "I've really enjoyed talking with you. Maybe we can do it again some time."

Shelby recognized one of his own standard closing lines. He nodded and allowed Grace to lead him away. "What now?" he said. "And what's wrong?"

"Not one single thing is wrong." Grace's hand that held his was trembling. "But I don't want to meet any more people. I want to dance. Come on."

She led him out onto the curved floor, where scores of

other young couples were already moving to the music. Shelby had time for one backward look, to see Pearl Mossman and Knute Crispin standing together and talking, and then all his attention had to be on what he was doing.

Or failing to do. At first he could tell himself that their lack of coordination was at least partly Grace's fault. No matter what she might say, her mind was somewhere else. But gradually she relaxed, and as she began to move less stiffly her attention turned to their awkward progression around the dance floor.

After a few more minutes she shook her head. "You've got it all backward. You're leading with your left leg, and you keep turning widdershins when you should be going clockwise."

Shelby gave her the benefit of the doubt and assumed that her words probably made sense in some language unfamiliar to him.

"Want to tell me what all that means?" he said.

"Never mind." Grace shook her head impatiently. "Forget that we're supposed to be dancing. Just go any way you like, and I'll follow your lead."

Even that was easier said than done. Somehow, no matter how Shelby moved, they came dangerously close to colliding with other couples. The dance floor formed a broad strip that ran most of the way around the curved cylinder, but there never seemed to be enough room. Finally he gave up any attempt at real dancing. He stood, holding Grace close, and made the smallest movements with his feet consistent with not actually standing still. They remained in one spot and they turned, very slowly, but that was all.

"Is this better?" he asked.

"Do you hear me complaining? It's fine." But then Grace added, "I'm sorry. You were quite right. I was upset, but I'm all right now."

"Do you want to tell me what happened?"

"No!" Her tension and stiffness returned. "I definitely do not."

"All right, then." But now Shelby was feeling angry. It hadn't been his idea to come to the stupid Confluence Center party, or to venture out onto the dance floor. He had been forced into it. If Grace was upset, it wasn't his fault. He glared over her shoulder, and noticed someone glaring right back at him.

It was a youth about his own age, but taller and thinner. Definitely not one of the people to whom he had been introduced. So who could it be?

Shelby struggled to make an identification, but then the slow rotation that he and Grace were making on the dance floor carried the youth steadily out of his field of view. He turned his head the other way and saw the stranger's back. He was moving rapidly away. In his place stood Doobie, waving energetically.

Shelby steered Grace carefully in that direction.

"You'll miss the beginning if you don't get a move on," Doobie called when they were still only halfway there. "Swaps start any minute. I wondered where you'd got to."

It was another Confluence ritual, and one that made a lot more sense to Shelby than dancing. Every ship in the Messina Cloud was liable to run short of some supplies, while having an excess of others. Sometimes the problem was known in advance and a deal cut ahead of time. That was the case with the pharmaceuticals that the *Harvest Moon* was carrying. They were already priced and promised to two rakehells, the *Godspell* and the *Once-Over-Lightly*, who had stayed out in the Cloud through the off-season. More often, though, needs became clear at short notice. And then the bargaining began.

"Hurry up, Gracie!" urged Doobie, ready to head for the trading area at the far end of the habitat.

But his sister was holding back. "I don't feel like trading right now. You carry on." She took Shelby's arm and gave him a little push toward Doobie. "Both of you. I'm going to get myself a drink. Maybe I'll join you later."

She didn't wait to see what the others would do but headed off toward the other end of the habitat.

Doobie stared after her, then turned to Shelby. "What have you two been doing? Fighting?"

"No. We've been dancing. At least, I thought we were dancing. I guess I must be pretty bad at it."

"You'd have to be, if you put Gracie off trading. She's the original Trading Queen." Doobie shook his head. "She'd trade her back teeth. I can't believe she's willing to miss the swap sessions. Before we get going, is there anything special you want? The rooms are organized by different departments, and you can start wherever you like."

Was there anything he wanted? It occurred to Shelby that back on Earth he had been given anything he desired, pretty much without limit. And yet within a day or two the coveted object, no matter what it was, had become dull and boring.

"I can't think of anything," he said. "Why don't we just start at the beginning and see what we see?"

"You can do it that way if you want to." Doobie pointed to an archway. "There's the beginning. Me, I want a carved belt. There's a woman on the *Sweet Chariot* who does her own designs, dragons and griffins and unicorns. The cosmetics machines can't touch her for quality. Her work gets snapped up in the first hour. I'll see you later."

Once again, Shelby was left to his own devices. He looked again for Grace, saw no sign of her, and walked forward through the archway. To his astonishment, the first person he saw was Scrimshander Limes. He was sitting behind a table covered with little carvings. At his side was Thurgood Trask.

Thurgood scowled when he saw Shelby. After an initial period of guarded neutrality, he had added Shelby to the list of his natural enemies and tormentors, as much of a menace and food pilferer as Grace and Doobie.

"Well, you can move right along out of here," he said. "Scrim, don't you trade nothing with Shelby Cheever, no matter what he offers. Anything he has he got aboard the *Harvest Moon*—and I'd not like to ask how."

"I'm not trading," said Shelby. "I'm just looking." He bent over to take a closer look at the carvings, astonished again by the detail and accuracy. He saw Doobie to the life, and Jilter, and Lana Trask, along with a carving of himself as he had first appeared on the *Harvest Moon*, hand in pocket and prominent belly stuck out as though he owned the whole harvester. He picked it up, inspected it, and finally laid it down again.

"Scrim, you know I don't look like that any more. You shouldn't be trading it. But you know what's really wrong with this display? You don't have any of Thurgood. Maybe you could do one of him—one where he's making giveaway pies."

He skipped through into the next room before the spluttering Thurgood Trask could rise and seek revenge. Somehow he felt a lot better. There was nothing like an encounter with Thurgood and Scrimshander to make you forget your other worries.

The room that he had entered was long and narrow and at first sight had no people in it. It did, however, have vegetation, tons of it—the first growing things that Shelby had seen since he left Earth. Big-leafed vines snaked and stretched across walls and ceilings. Potted shrubs and tall bamboo-like grasses covered the whole floor. Halfway along he could see a tall bed of familiar deep blue blossoms.

So it had been a bouquet that he had seen, and a real one. He walked over to the flower bed and smelled a powerful and heavy scent. Flowers had never much interested him, but he felt sure that he had seen nothing on the several Cheever estates of quite so deep a blue, or quite so strongly perfumed.

"No charge for sniffing," said a sharp voice. "But if you touch one, it's yours. Want to trade?"

He turned, and saw a brown-faced, gnomelike man, half hidden within a bower of flowering honeysuckle.

"I don't have anything to trade with." Shelby recognized an ironic truth. He might be one of the richest people on Earth, but here in the Messina Cloud he was one of the poorest. He had little but the clothes that he was wearing, and even they were not really his. The only thing he could claim as his own was the little figurine that Scrimshander Limes had given him. He was not about to trade that away for anything.

"You sure? Most people have something." The man emerged from the bower and walked forward to peer up into Shelby's face. "Aren't you the castaway that the *Harvest Moon* picked up six weeks back?"

"That's right."

"The one who found a Cauthen starfire, and a ton of shwarzgeld?"

Shelby nodded, and the man went on, "Well, then, you got more to trade with than anybody. Want some flowers? I grew them myself."

It was a temptation. Shelby could buy a great bunch of the blue flowers and present them to Grace as a surprise. It might bring her out of her bad mood.

A strange caution held him back. Grace had headed off earlier toward a bouquet of blue flowers, and when she came back she was right out of sorts. Maybe the flowers had had something to do with it.

He shook his head. "Not just now. But I might be back."

"Up to you." The gnome retreated into his leafy den. "Your risk. Not my fault if you come again and there's nothing left."

Twenty-seven light-years from Earth, and you meet a man who would be right at home as a gardener on the Cheever Virginia estate. Shelby wandered on to the next connecting room. It was empty, but it had a little side alcove with its own door.

He peered in. Three youths were sitting around a table, heads together. One of them was about Doobie's age, the other two a few years older. They all glanced his way when Shelby appeared, and one of them stood up.

He was at least as tall as Shelby, and he seemed taller because of his thin build and his long, rangy arms and legs. His face had high cheekbones and a long jaw, with dark eyes framed by bushy black eyebrows and a big nose.

It was an arresting face, but Shelby would have recognized it from the eyes alone. They had glared at him from the edge of the dance floor.

"Sorry," he said, and began to back out. "I guess I'm interrupting. I thought this room was part of the trading area."

"See what dropped in on us, Mooks," the thin youth said slowly. "Don't leave us, Shelby Cheever. We'd like to talk to you."

"You know who I am?"

"I used your name, didn't I? Everybody in the harvester fleet knows Shelby Cheever. Snatched up by a corry from open space. Says he's from Earth. Says he's a real big shot there. Says he has enough money to buy a piddling little fleet like ours ten times over. That sound like you?"

Unfortunately, it did. Shelby had said exactly that, six weeks ago. The fact that he wouldn't say it now didn't help—even though every word was perfectly true.

"People exaggerate." Shelby saw that Mooks and the younger boy were moving away from the table, as though they wanted to distance themselves from what was happening. "You know what rumors are like. I am from Earth, though. That part is quite accurate."

It wasn't an apology, but it was a disclaimer and a kind of peace offering. He didn't know these people, and nothing more should be needed.

But the tall boy in front of him was sneering in disbelief. "People exaggerate, do they? I see. Are you telling me that you *didn't* find a Cauthen starfire, along with a great lump of shwartzgeld? That you *don't* own a full quarter share in both of them?"

"Those happen to be true. No credit to me. I was just lucky enough to be there when it happened."

Shelby backed up a step. He wondered what was going on. The dark-haired boy was edging closer, and he seemed to be working himself into a rage for no reason. Was everyone in the harvester fleet so terribly envious of Shelby and Grace's good luck? Apparently they all knew about it. Was *that* why Grace had come back to the dance floor pale and distraught, and why she refused to visit the trading area—because she had suffered an encounter like this one and was afraid of another?

"If you don't mind, I'd like to see what else is being traded." Shelby and the youth were standing face to face, and he backed up another step.

"Oh, but I do mind."

"I'm going." Shelby started to turn.

"Not 'til I say so."

"Nicky!" the younger boy said. Mooks added nervously, "That's enough, Nick."

"You keep out of this." A strong hand seized Shelby's shoulder and held him where he stood.

He turned farther, feeling the fabric of his shirt rip. The other two were running past him toward the door. He tried to take a step that way, but before he could move he was grabbed by the shoulders and twisted violently around. A bony fist hit him under the base of his ribs. It drove all the air out of him. As he doubled over a knee came up to smash into his nose and right eye.

He fell to the floor and lay there, unable to breathe.

"Nick!" said a nervous voice from the doorway.

"He's all right, Mooks." Shelby's attacker stood over him. "He just got what he deserved."

"I'm getting out of here," said the younger boy.

"Me too," added Mooks. "Nick, let's go."

"Yeah. Okay." A foot poked Shelby in the ribs, adding to his multiple discomforts. "Don't worry about him. He's just winded."

Two seconds later the room was empty. Shelby lay on the floor in agony. There was a black curtain in front of his eyes, and his chest felt paralyzed.

As he took a first shuddering breath, blood came trickling down his cheek from his battered nose. He lifted his head and wiped his forearm across his face. The touch of the soft fabric made him wince with pain and brought him fully conscious.

Why? He sat up, slowly and awkwardly. The sleeve of his new shirt, the outfit that Grace had designed with so much pride, was a bloody mess. Why had someone he didn't even know started in on him and beaten him up?

It confirmed what Constance Cheever often said about

people who didn't live on Earth. They were savages, primitive barbarians with no idea of how human beings ought to behave.

He climbed to his feet and leaned on the table until he could breathe easily again. His midriff ached, and his nose was still bleeding. All he wanted to do was get back to his bed aboard the *Harvest Moon*. But how was he going to do that, without everyone seeing him? He didn't want to be a public spectacle.

He dabbed his nose again with infinite delicacy using his sleeve—the shirt was past saving—and walked unsteadily to the door.

The youth called Mooks was hovering just outside it. Shelby eyed him warily.

"It's all right." Mooks came to his side. "I came back to see if you needed help. Can you manage?"

"Why did he do it?"

Mooks shrugged. "You got me. He was all right earlier tonight, but for the past half-hour he's been really weird. I've never seen him do anything like this before." He looked Shelby up and down. "You're a real mess."

"I feel like one." Shelby stared down at his trousers, grimy with dirt from the floor, and at his bloodstained shirt-front. "I want to get back to the *Harvest Moon*. Do you know any way I could make it to the airlock without going across the dance floor?"

"If you don't mind getting dirty." Mooks saw the look on Shelby's face and grinned for the first time. "I guess that's not a problem. I'll show you where to go. It will be good and messy, but you can clean up your clothes when you get there."

He led the way through two more rooms, both deserted, then along a corridor barely narrow enough to walk through. At last he pointed to a descending spiral staircase.

"Service level. Go to the left when you get to the bottom, and follow the line of the cylinder, until in about thirty meters you'll come to another staircase. That will take you up to the area of the big airlock. Watch your head when you go down there. And your balance."

The warning was necessary. The new level was closer to the outside of the rotating cylinder, and as Shelby descended he could feel his weight increasing. The ceiling of the service level was low, and made lower yet in places by the ducting, electrical circuits, and utility service points attached to the ceiling.

It was easy to understand why Mooks had drawn the line at coming along with him. No one but service technicians would come here normally, and apparently the Confluence Center was poorly provided with cleaning machines. Within a few steps Shelby's white suit, already marked at knees and elbows, bore a new layer of filth. He decided that he had nothing to lose. Rather than crouching and bumping his head, he dropped to his knees and scrambled the rest of the way on all fours.

No one was in the airlock when he got there. Although his right eye was swelling shut and he found it harder and harder to see, he refused to seek help. He climbed into the pinnace, flew it slowly and awkwardly to the *Harvest Moon*, and docked it there. Grace and Doobie would have to find another way to get home.

His nose was hurting more and more. He hated the idea of allowing a machine to touch him, but he seemed to have no choice. He headed for the ship's medical center and on the way was lucky—or unlucky—enough to encounter Uncle Thurgood in the crew's recreation and exercise room.

The old miner looked at Shelby and shook his head. "Brawling again! That's all the younger generation wants to do."

"I wasn't brawling. Somebody hit me when I wasn't expecting it."

"And how often have I heard that? Why did he hit you?"

"I don't know. I never met him before."

The bushy white eyebrows went up, but Thurgood Trask said only, "Where were you heading?"

"To the medical center." Shelby indicated his nose, which was throbbing with every heartbeat. "It's getting worse."

"I'm sure it is." Thurgood came close and inspected the damaged organ. "It's broken, you know."

"Can a machine fix it?"

"It could. But I can do a better job. I've done plenty in my time. Aye, and had it done to me a couple of times before I learned that brawling is stupid. Just a second." Before Shelby could reject the idea of anyone touching his nose, Uncle Thurgood threw back his head and bellowed. "Scrimshander! You stay right where you are. I'll be back in a few more minutes."

"No need for him to be involved," he muttered to Shelby, as he took his arm in a powerful grip and led him willy-nilly along the corridor. "This is a one-man job."

Shelby looked at the hand that held his arm. It was meaty and thick-fingered, and no one in his right mind would let it touch a broken nose. He wished that gentle Scrimshander Limes, with his clever and sensitive fingers, were the one holding him.

He realized that he was wrong when Uncle Thurgood sat him down, administered an anesthetic spray, and deftly cleaned and set his nose and packed it with gauze. The whole operation took only a few minutes. It was unpleasant but painless.

"There you go," Uncle Thurgood said cheerfully as he wiped away a smear of blood. "You'll look like a beauty tomorrow—a couple of black eyes guaranteed—and you might get some pain when the spray wears off. I'll give you a pill for it. But your nose will set as good as new. Maybe better. I think a broken nose adds a bit of character to a man's face. Now, are you ready to tell me who did it and why he hit you?"

"I told you before, I don't know."

"Very well. That's up to you. Everything else in working order?"

"Sore middle. But I'll be all right."

"Off you go, then." Thurgood Trask seemed almost ashamed of his gentle handling of Shelby's injury, because he waved his hand and added gruffly, "Get out of here and let me clean up. Don't go back to the Confluence Center, though, if you have a brain in your head—which people your age seldom do. You're in no shape for brawling. No, and not for dancing neither."

"I'm never going to that place again in my life."

"Aye. And haven't I heard that before, too? You'll go straight to bed, if you've any sense. Which I doubt."

In a night that had offered few pleasures, bed sounded to Shelby like the best idea yet. He thanked Thurgood Trask, who seemed more offended than pleased, and limped away to his cabin. Once inside he stripped off his clothing and dropped it in a heap in the corner. He didn't bother to consign it to the laundry machine. If anything could clean and repair that bloodstained, ripped, and crumpled mess, he would be much surprised.

He lay down gratefully on his bunk. There was a faint throbbing behind his eyes, gradually decreasing as Thurgood's pill took effect. His belly was definitely bruised. He was very tired, and it would take more than minor discomfort to keep him awake. As he fell asleep, Thurgood Trask's question came back to perplex him: Who hit you, and why?

Who, he could guess. But why? He didn't know. He did

know that he had never been struck before in anger in his whole life.

He didn't like it at all.

If Shelby had been looking for an excuse not to go to the next Confluence Center meeting, he could hardly have picked a better one. The next morning when he got up he didn't feel too bad but he looked a technicolor mess. His nose was twice the usual size behind its white plaster. Blood had pooled below his swollen eyes, turning the skin to a purplish red. The rest of his face, by contrast, was paler than usual.

The odd thing was that he felt hunger rather than pain. He looked at the clock and saw why. No one had awakened him, although it was now three hours past the ship's regular rising time. He took from a laundry machine the casual suit that Grace had specified and headed for the galley. He didn't want company, at least until he had eaten and made himself a hot drink, so it was good to find the place deserted. He saw evidence that everyone else had already been and gone.

He had almost finished eating when Grace looked in on him. He waved, expecting her to come in and commiserate, or at the very least to ask him what had happened. Instead she stared, her mouth an open O of surprise or horror, and turned to run off along the corridor.

Shelby was left alone again, to think with irritation that he didn't look *that* bad. And even if he did, he deserved sympathy. Was she angry with him because he hadn't returned for her stupid dance? Anyone in her right mind would see that he had had the best reason in the world for vanishing without notice from the Confluence Center.

He moved so that his back was to the doorway and sat there fuming, convinced that for once Constance Cheever had been right. Although you might get occasional kindness here, like that from Thurgood Trask last night, it was an exception. The low-class louts who populated the Kuiper Belt and the Messina Cloud didn't know what real civilization was. He couldn't wait to get back home and tell his mother how much he agreed with her.

A noise from behind made him think that Grace must have reappeared. He turned and found Lana Trask eyeing him calmly.

"It could be worse." She moved to sit across the table from him. "Give it a few days and you'll be right back to normal. Now that you have Grace at your absolute mercy, I want to ask you not to take too much advantage of her."

"She's not at my mercy. She wouldn't even come in and say good morning to me."

"Was she here already?"

"For about a second." Shelby spoke with bitter resentment. "She ran away."

Lana Trask studied him for a few seconds. "I don't think you know what's going on. Do you?"

"I know I did nothing wrong. And some maniac started in on me and hit me for no reason at all, without giving me any chance to defend myself. And I've had no explanations, from Grace or anyone else."

"So I was right. You have no idea what was happening. And of course, Grace didn't want to tell you. I can see that." Lana sighed. "You know, Shel, there are maniacs in the Cloud, as there are anywhere else. I don't deny it. But it wasn't a maniac who hit you. It was Nick Rasmussen."

Shelby had already reached that conclusion for himself. It made everything no less baffling. While he sat and stared, Lana Trask went on, "You never met Nick before, and he never met you. But Grace knows him well. For the past couple of years, at Confluence, Grace and Nick have been regular partners. When Grace and I went over to the *Corusca-*

tion, after the loss of the *Witch of Agnesi*, Grace apparently told Nick that she didn't want to be his partner this year. I wasn't there when she told him, and I only learned of it yesterday. But apparently he took it pretty hard. He didn't accept it. He still thought he could talk her round and they would be partners again this year.

"Until last night—when Grace refused to take the flowers that he had bought for her. Next thing, he saw Grace dancing with you. He knew who you were, because everyone in the fleet does. You can guess what he thought."

"That's crazy. I've never so much as touched Grace."

"I believe you. Or if I'm going to be totally honest, I believe my daughter. She says she likes you, but she insists that nothing has ever happened between you."

"Of course it hasn't. It wasn't even my idea to go to the stupid dance. It was *yours*. You made me do it. And Grace made me dance with her—she told me what a lousy job I did of it, too."

"I know all that. Nick didn't know any of it. But I had no idea what had happened between Grace and Nick. Even Grace didn't realize that he'd lose control the way he did when he saw you together—though maybe she should have shown a bit more imagination and seen that it was possible."

Lana Trask leaned back as though she was finished, but Shelby knew better. He was learning to read her. When she was really done, she left. There was more to come.

"Anyway," she went on. "Now you know. You have every right to be angry, but I hope you won't be too hard on Grace. As for Nick, his father is proposing to send him over to the *Harvest Moon* today and make you a formal apology. I told them I wanted to talk about it with you first. Do you want an apology?"

"I want to smash his face in." Shelby could feel the rage surging inside him.

"I'm sure you do. Very natural. That wasn't my question, though. We're not savages out here in the Cloud, and we don't believe in the eye-for-an-eye-and-a-tooth-for-a-tooth system of justice. But do you want an apology? That much we can do."

Of course he did. He wanted to see Nick Rasmussen grovel and stammer and crawl. Shelby opened his mouth to say yes and found second thoughts creeping in.

He shook his head. "It's pointless. You can make him apologize all you like, but it won't change his mind. He'll hate my guts anyway. He'll think I took something away from him, even though I didn't. Don't you agree?"

"I'm not sure I like to hear my daughter referred to as *something*, as though you two can swap her around any time you choose. But I agree with you. Nick will still hate you. You would have to find another way to sort that one out. On the other hand, I think Nick should apologize."

"I don't need it and I don't want it. What would it do for me?"

"Not a thing. I don't think he ought to apologize for *your* sake—or for Grace's, either. He should apologize for *his* sake. What Uncle Thurgood would refer to as 'the good of his soul.'"

"So why pretend it's *my* decision?"

"Because it is. If you say no, I won't insist."

"He'll think I want him to do it just to humiliate him."

"He may. But you'll know better—won't you?"

Shelby was no longer sure what he knew. He thought, hesitated, and finally shook his head. "I don't want him to come over here and apologize. Even though you think we ought to make him do it, I don't want it."

"All right." This time Lana stood up. "As I said, it was your decision. He won't come. Just one more thing. I'm sure that revenge is on your mind. I want you to know that I won't

stand for it. I don't want you hitting him when he's not expecting it or defending himself—even though that's what he
did to you."

And she was gone. Shelby was left to wonder if he had
done the right thing.

But not for long. Jilter Clute came wandering in. He
nodded to Shelby as though a broken nose was the most natural thing in the world and said, "Lana asked me to drop in
and have a word with you."

"I'm not going to change my mind."

"I don't know what that means, but I feel sure it's not
my department. Lana was wondering if you have had any
training in self-defense. Have you?"

"Where I come from, that sort of thing isn't necessary."

"You're not where you come from. I guess that's a no.
Soon as you feel up to it, I'll teach you a few moves. Shouldn't
take more than a few hours to pick up the rudiments."

"I don't want to learn."

"Suit yourself." Jilter nodded. "Fine by me. But what are
you going to do for the rest of Confluence? Hide away? Or
wonder who'll whack you one next if you go to the Center?
Think about it."

Jilter left the galley. A few minutes later Shelby followed
suit and headed for his cabin. Too many people wanted him
to do what he had no interest in doing. It was the last straw
to open his cabin door and find it occupied.

Grace was lying on her stomach on his bed, a long red
case at her side. She was reading, as though she had been
there for some time.

"What do you want?" His words were cold, although he
felt anything but. She was more to blame for what had happened to him than anyone.

She laid the book on the bed. He noticed that her hands
were trembling.

"I wanted to say that I'm sorry about last night. And I want to ask if you'll come to the Confluence dance with me tonight."

"Looking l-like—like this?" Shelby pointed to his face. He was so angry at the nerve of the girl that he could hardly speak. "You want me to go to the dance again, so everybody can have a good laugh at me? To prove that I'm an idiot twice over?" His anger turned to bitterness. "You say you're sorry. Sure, I'll bet you're sorry. Did your mother order you to come and tell me that?"

"Muv has no idea that I'm here." Grace scrambled off the bed and stood in front of him with her fists clenched. "And no one will think you're an idiot if you go to the dance. They'll think you've got *class*. Mooks and Nick's kid brother Skip saw the whole thing last night, and they've talked. If anyone ought to be scared to go to the dance, it's Nick."

"I'm *not scared*!"

"You could take a swing at him, you know, when he wasn't expecting it."

"Don't kid yourself. Go and talk to your mother if you think I could do that. As for dancing, what do you want me to do? Go to the Confluence Center wearing that?"

He pointed at the heap of bloodied and filthy clothing, still lying in the corner where he had thrown it the previous night.

"No. Go with me—wearing *this*." Grace picked up the red case and opened it. She took out a complete set of clothing, a modified version of what he had worn the previous night. "I got up really early this morning to work on this. You looked good last night, but I thought I could improve it in a couple of places. And I thought black would look better."

"Sure. It wouldn't show the blood so much. Forget it. I came here for a rest. And even if nothing had happened last night, the last thing I want is to go to another stupid dance."

"I guess that's it, then." Grace would not look at him. She picked up her book and hurried out without another word.

She had left behind the black outfit and the red case. Shelby picked it up, sat on his bed, and stared at the clothes for a long time. An amazing amount of work had gone into the new design. It must have taken Grace hours and hours.

He stretched out on his bed and lay there for a long time, until he realized that there was no chance at all that he might fall asleep. At last he rose, left his cabin, and went off to see if Jilter Clute was busy.

CHAPTER ELEVEN

CONFLUENCE was a time for optimism and renewal. It was a guarantee of meeting old friends and a chance to make new ones. Even the crew of a ship that had done poorly on the voyage out could tell themselves, and everyone else, that the second half would be different. The transuranics would never run out, they would be there for the taking forever, and there was always the possibility that lightning would strike in the form of a find of shwartzgeld or starfires. Before they returned Sol-side through the node, they would surely make a fortune.

Confluence was a time for celebration, for courtship, for commitment.

But some commitments are different from others.

Pearl Mossman and Knute Crispin were sitting together at a small table one level higher than the main floor of the Confluence Center. They were watching the young people of the fleet as they formed their tentative pairs. Some of those matches would last only for the length of a single dance; others would endure for a lifetime.

One particular couple, not dancing but standing together at the edge of the dance floor, had Pearl's special attention.

"Trust me," she was saying. "I know it sounds ridiculous, but every word he said was true. I'm sure of it."

"*All* of it?" Knute was a thick-built powerhouse, whose heavy eyebrows and close-set eyes had made a hundred people underestimate him. "What about the underwater sea villas, and the airborne casinos, and the Antarctic resort? Everybody says that Earth is poor."

"Earth has fourteen billion people. Most of them have nothing. A few tens of thousands have a great deal; and a few hundred have so much it's hard to measure it. Jerome Prescott Cheever is in the top ten of the whole planet for individual wealth—maybe he's at the very top. Shelby Cheever"—she gestured to the dance floor below them—"says that he is J. P. Cheever's only child. I believe him. No matter how rich he is today, it's nothing compared with how rich he's going to be. The villas and casinos and resorts are just frosting. The real wealth comes from the industrial power base."

"Then what's he doing out here?" Knute studied the black-clad figure at the edge of the dance floor. "Why didn't he demand to be taken straight home, and say he'd pay for it?"

"He did. Lana Trask is usually a clever woman, but this time she blew it. Nobody on the *Harvest Moon* believed Cheever's story. Nobody in the *fleet* believes it now. You didn't. But even Shelby Cheever misses the real point."

"What's that?"

"How valuable he could be." Pearl drew her chair closer and dropped her voice. "Suppose the *Harvest Moon* takes him back home. J. P. Cheever is grateful, and almost certainly he gives the Trasks a reward. But even if it's a big reward, it's not a real fortune. I can suggest a different scenario. The *Harvest Moon* keeps Cheever here, out in the Cloud. They don't tell J.P. where his only son is, but they take proof back Solside that Shelby is alive. How much do you think J. P. Cheever and Constance Cheever would give to get their kid back in one piece?"

"Ransom?" Knute stared again at Shelby, seeing him in a new light. "Billions. But it won't happen, not 'til hell freezes over. The crew of the *Harvest Moon* wouldn't go along with it. Thurgood Trask would say no, for a start. And he's the most obstinate man in the Cloud."

"Agreed. They would never do such a thing."

"So that's the end of it. The *Harvest Moon* found Shelby. He belongs to them."

"True. As long as the *Harvest Moon* has him, no one else can do a thing. But if Shelby Cheever were to get lost in space again and be picked up by another harvester . . ." Pearl put down her drink and leaned back in her chair. "That would make all the difference, wouldn't it?"

Knute did not answer at once. He had turned away and was watching the dance floor, with its colorful swirling couples. "Agreed," he said at last. "But it would be almost impossible to arrange. Lana Trask is very cautious. You could never do anything to a whole harvester."

"You wouldn't need to. An accident could happen to a

corry. That would be enough, if it had the right person in it."

"Even that would be difficult."

"Did I ever suggest that it would be easy?"

"Difficult, and dangerous."

"Once-in-a-lifetime opportunities tend to be that."

Knute stared again over the crowded dance floor. "It's been a bad season for us," he said at last. "I took a look this morning. Our holds are emptier than you realize."

"I doubt that. I've been careful to hint at the exact opposite around Confluence and suggested that we're having our best-ever season. But I know how little our machines have been coming back with. If we pull this off, though, you and I will never have to worry about transuranics again." She picked up her glass. "Think of it, Knute. A few difficult weeks, at the most. And then you will live just how you like and where you like."

"I am thinking of it. Agreed." Knute lifted his glass and touched it to Pearl's. "To success."

"Very good." Pearl took a thoughtful sip. "And now, as they say, for the details."

Shelby had been convinced before he entered the Confluence Center that every eye would be on him, but as it turned out he was less of a center of attention than on the previous night. *Shelby Cheever again*, the curious glances said. *And he seems to have been foolish enough to break his nose.* Then they turned away to something more interesting.

Grace had her arm tucked through Shelby's. She, even more than he, was on the lookout for one particular person. "Remember what you promised," she said. "If you do meet tonight, whatever happens you won't start a fight."

"I didn't start one last time. He beat me up for nothing."

"It wasn't for nothing. But don't let's get into that again.

I want you and Nick to at least *try* to get on with each other. Why don't you see if you can be friends—for my sake."

"I'll try. But it's not because I'm afraid of him."

"I know. Where is he, though?" She wasn't listening to Shelby anymore, she was scanning the crowd anxiously. "Nick never misses a single night at Confluence. I wonder what's keeping him? Maybe he's been grounded."

"I hope not."

It was a lie. Shelby's feelings were more complex than that. He didn't want to meet Nick Rasmussen, but also he didn't like the idea of postponing what seemed like an inevitable meeting. As Jilter had pointed out, Shelby couldn't hide away right through Confluence.

But what was he supposed to do if Nick picked another fight? Stand and get punched again? He couldn't do that, not even for Grace's sake.

And then he didn't have to worry about theoretical questions anymore, because Nick Rasmussen was there. He was about twenty yards away, standing bolt upright with his arms held by his sides.

Grace had seen him too. "Let's go," she hissed. "If we're going to talk to him, now's the time."

"No." Shelby disengaged his arm from hers. "I'm going to do it. But I want to do it alone."

"Shel!"

"It's all right. I told your mother as well as you, I won't do anything stupid."

"What about Nick? Muv didn't talk to *him*."

"I'll take my chances. Leave us to it." Shelby waited, until after a few moments of hesitation Grace went reluctantly off toward another group of teenagers. Only when she had been absorbed into their midst did Shelby walk across to stand about three feet in front of Nick Rasmussen.

The two stared at each other for a long time without

speaking. At last Nick said, "Look, I didn't want to come here at all tonight."

"So why did you?"

"My old man made me. He's pretty pushy. You know what dads are like."

"Yeah." Shelby could relate to that. He and Nick Rasmussen might have at least on thing in common. If Nick's father was anything like J. P. Cheever, you couldn't argue him down.

Without thinking about it, the two moved gradually away from the dance area to a spot that would later be used for food machines and a buffet service. For the moment it was empty.

"Dad said that he and Captain Trask had agreed," Nick went on. He looked everywhere but at Shelby. "Dad said I was to go over to the *Harvest Moon* yesterday and apologize to you. Then Captain Trask called and said don't bother. What happened?"

"I didn't want you to. It wouldn't have done any good. You'd still think I had something to do with what went on between you and Grace."

"Didn't you?" Nick's gaze met Shelby's. "I thought you did."

"If you know Grace, you know that nobody can make her do anything she doesn't want to do."

"Yeah." Nick nodded ruefully. "I'll buy that. Grace don't budge easy."

"Anyway, I didn't want your stupid apology. What good would an apology do? I wanted to smash your face in, the way you smashed mine. Maybe I ought to do it right now."

Shelby clenched his fists. Whenever he thought about last night he became angry all over again. But instead of getting ready to defend himself, Nick Rasmussen straightened and held his arms rigidly at his sides.

"Well?" Shelby positioned himself in what Jilter had told him was the best position if you had no idea what the other man might do. "Come on. Do we or don't we?"

"I can't." Nick shook his head. "Can't get into a fight, I mean. Look, I'm not scared of you or anything like that. But Dad said if you started something I mustn't fight back. I'm to stand and take it, he said, or he'll kill me. So I guess you've got a free shot, same as I had yesterday." He tightened his mouth, closed his eyes, and winced in anticipation. "Get on with it."

Shelby took a half-step back and raised his fist. With Nick standing in that position he was absolutely defenseless. Shelby could pick his target and hit where and as hard as he liked.

After a few seconds he shook his head and lowered his arm. "You might as well relax. I'm not going to hit you."

Nick opened his eyes to slits and peered warily at Shelby. "Why not?"

"It wouldn't make my nose better any quicker. And I'm from Earth. We're not savages back there. Earth people don't go for that eye-for-an-eye-and-a-tooth-for-a-tooth stuff."

"Nor do we." Nick opened his eyes all the way. "It was my dad's idea, not mine, to let you hit me the way I hit you. I didn't want to be poked."

"Nor did I. But you did it."

"I know. But I was real mad last night about—something. You know what. I'm sorry."

"All right, then." The two stood staring at each other, until Shelby said, "What now?"

In unison they looked over to the dance area. There was no sign of Grace.

"You want to go back there?" Nick asked. "I mean, do you want to go to the dance?"

"Me? No way. I never *did* want to dance. I'm a terrible dancer."

"So why did you do it yesterday? Don't bother to tell me, I can guess. Lots of us on the harvesters don't like to dance."

"So why do *you* do it?"

"As a way to meet girls. Or because the girls want us to. But there's a ton of good things to do at Confluence for people who don't dance."

"Good like what?"

"Good, like treasure hunts, and round-the-fleet races, and human/robot competitions, and team sports. There's swimming, too. The Confluence Center has its own pool. None of the harvesters do, because the water you need for a pool masses too much to have on board a ship. There's even an eating contest. We move that from place to place and keep it pretty quiet, because grown-ups don't like us doing it—the winners always throw up at the end, and most of the losers do, too." Nick paused. "You interested in any of this?"

"I sure am."

"Come on, then." Nick's voice gained enthusiasm. "I'll show you around, introduce you to some of my buddies."

"I already met Mooks and your kid brother."

"I guess you did. Mooks is all right, but Skip is a real pain—he trails around after us and tries to pretend he's as grown-up as we are. He's Doobie's big pal. They both belong in the juvenile moron club. We keep 'em out of our things as much as we can. There's a lot more to do in Confluence Center than you'd ever know if you only talked to little kids like Doobie and Skip—or even if you just talked with Grace."

Shelby allowed Nick to lead him away, heading from the dance floor to an area of the habitat that he had never visited before. Nick's stiffness and formality were vanishing rapidly.

He was talking nonstop about the things to see and places to go in the Confluence Center.

It seemed to Shelby that for a man with a broken heart, Nick was making a pretty speedy recovery.

The dance ended at one in the morning. Other events at Confluence Center went on all night. The *Harvest Moon*, however, had its own rules for anyone under twenty-one. Lana Trask made it clear that, no matter what other harvester teenagers might do, the deadline for Shelby, Grace, and Doobie was to be at the pinnace by two o'clock.

Which Shelby was going to make—just. He came across the curving Confluence Center floor at a dead run. The huge metal cube that he was carrying didn't help his speed, but he would face Lana Trask's anger before he would leave it behind. He had been *given* a thousand things back on Earth, but this was the only thing he had ever *won* in his whole life.

And he had won it fair and square, beating out a scrawny seventeen-year-old on the final spin.

He skidded around the corner that led to the pinnace and ran into Doobie Trask, who was coming just as fast from the other direction.

"What you got?" Doobie was panting hard, but seeing Shelby he relaxed and assumed that they had plenty of time.

"Tell you inside—ten seconds to deadline."

"Yipes!"

They went scrambling into the pinnace, Doobie first, just as the two-o'clock buzzer sounded.

"We're in time," gasped Doobie.

Jilter Clute, standing at the hatch, nodded. "Close enough for me. I'll give you the benefit of the doubt. Stow that, and we're off."

His last words were to Shelby, who put the metal box on the floor and leaned over it to catch his breath.

"What you got?" Doobie asked again.

"Sounder finder. When you're close enough to a reef it's supposed to tell you the distance and direction of the nearest sounder."

"Ah." Doobie pulled a face. "I don't swallow that. It won't work. Will it, Jilter? Can it locate sounders?"

"Nothing has before. But who knows?" Jilter shrugged and started the pinnace drive. "There's a first time for everything."

"I'll believe it when I see it work." Doobie was peering into the open top. "Where'd you get it, Shel?"

"I won it!" Shelby's grin was wide enough to include everyone in the pinnace. Who cared if Doobie was skeptical? "Won it for cross-hurling. I beat Lucas Fosse on the last throw!"

He wasn't going to tell them how lucky he had been. In cross-hurling you threw a spinning hoop at a target away on the other side of Confluence Center. At first the problem seemed straightforward: Things in space move in a straight line. Then you realized that the hoop acted like a gyroscope and stayed flat to maintain a constant direction of rotation. Also, Confluence Center was rotating beneath your feet, which meant that from your point of view the cross-hurl hoop followed a strange curved path. It also seemed as though it turned in midair, an illusion produced by your own motion.

Put all that together with the fact that Shelby had never played before, and there was no way that he could have won.

But he had. His final hoop had soared away to the other side of the big cylinder of Confluence Center and passed around the peg so dead center that the support didn't even wobble. Lucas Fosse's last shot had also tagged the peg, but it was near the hoop edge and you could hear the rattle all the way across at the starting line. Shelby knew that he had won without waiting for the official result.

"Well, I bet this sounder finder won't work." Doobie's head was almost inside the metal cube. "It's dumb. I think you've been gypped. Looks to me like somebody just cobbled this together from bits of old junk."

"You're only jealous." Shelby glanced around for support and noticed Grace for the first time. She was sitting quietly in a corner and had not spoken a word since he and Doobie had arrived.

He went across to her. "Well, I did it."

She glanced up at him coldly. "Did what? I can't read your mind, you know; and I haven't seen you for the past five hours."

"I did what you asked me to do. I met Nick Rasmussen, and I didn't start a fight with him."

"I see."

"In fact, once he took me to the reccy area things went on pretty well between us. He's not a bad guy. We started talking, and when it comes to fathers he and I have a fair bit in common."

"I'm sure you do."

Grace turned pointedly away and faced the wall. She didn't say another word until they reached the *Harvest Moon*, and then it was just a curt "Goodnight."

"What's got into her?" Shelby asked Jilter in bewilderment as she vanished with Doobie close behind her. "I mean, earlier tonight she told me about every two seconds that I was to try to make friends with Nick Rasmussen and I mustn't start a fight. So I do exactly what she says, and now look at her. Do you think she really *wants* the two of us fighting, even though she says she doesn't?"

"Fighting over *her*?" Jilter considered, as the two of

them walked slowly toward their cabins. "I've known stranger things. How many times did you dance with Grace tonight?"

"Dance? Not at all—not with her, not with anybody. I was too busy with other things. Like this." Shelby patted the metal cube that was only just wide enough to pass along the corridor.

"Other things. Any other things involving Grace?"

Shelby shook his head. "I was too busy with Nick and Mooks and their friends. There's nothing wrong with that, is there? I mean, Grace wanted to be at the dance. She told me so. And she insisted that she wanted me to meet Nick."

"I've no doubt she told you exactly that."

"So what's going on?"

"I'm not sure there's a name for it. But it's been around for a long time." Jilter was at the door of his cabin. He nodded to Shelby as he went in. "It's one reason some people—like me, for instance—don't ever get married."

CHAPTER TWELVE

DURING the seven days of Confluence nothing was normal. Regular schedules were ignored in favor of frenzied trading, hard-fought team games, hurried courtships, and continuous carnival.

After all that excitement it was difficult to settle again into steady work. Young members of the harvester crews found it especially hard. In Shelby's case, life on the *Harvest Moon* only returned to reality when, on the third day out from Confluence, Uncle Thurgood and Scrimshander Limes came into the ship's recreation area. They were arguing, in good old pre-Confluence fashion.

"I only wished to point out," Scrimshander was saying, "that the *Southern Cross* is behind us and has been following us for at least two days."

"And what's new about that? Wasn't the *Southern Cross* behind us most of the trip out? And the trip before this one? And before that it was the *Balaclava*. I'll tell you your problem, Scrim*shander* Limes." Thurgood shook a thick finger at his partner. "You're getting above yourself. You think you know everything better than anybody else."

It was a reference to certain events during Confluence. The figurines carved by Scrimshander had become popular with the crews of the other harvesters, and suddenly they were all the rage. Every carving that Scrimshander could produce and put on display—even his old rejects—had been snapped up. To Thurgood's intense disgust and suspicion, Scrimshander became a minor celebrity. Scores of men and women sought him out in his little trading room at the Confluence Center, talking with him about his work, admiring his almost unconscious skill with knife and plastic, and commissioning carvings that did not yet exist.

Thurgood's attempts to shoo people away had been ignored. *He* had been ignored. People didn't want to see Thurgood Trask, and they didn't want to hear Thurgood Trask. They wanted Scrimshander Limes, and they made their views clear.

"What do you suggest?" Thurgood continued. "Do you want to tell everybody that we *own* this part of the Cloud, so the *Southern Cross* and all the other harvesters can't come near it? Is that what you want?"

"Not at all. As I said, I only wished to point out—"

"Well, you *have* pointed out, so that's enough." Uncle

Thurgood noticed that Shelby and Grace were in the recreation room. He scowled at them. "Can't you see that a private conversation is going on here? We don't want you snooping on us and interrupting us. Get the blazes out!"

Grace and Doobie left. As they went through the door Grace snorted, "*Us* interrupting *them*. What's he talking about? We were in there before they were! They were interrupting us."

Shelby decided not to point out the truth: that Scrim and Thurgood had not interrupted anything between him and Grace, because nothing had been happening to interrupt. All through Confluence and for the three days after it, Grace and he had hardly spoken. She had answered questions in a syllable, or not at all. After three or four tries Shelby had given up. For the past half-hour they had ridden side-by-side exercise machines, but never a word or a look had passed between them.

He decided to give it one more try. "According to the charts we're approaching Ushant Reef. I was going to ask your mother if I could take a corry out and do a harvester run for transuranics. Then after that was finished I was thinking of staying out and wandering over closer to the reef."

"Why?"

Another one-syllable reply, but at least this one invited a response.

"I thought I might get lucky again. The last starfire was your discovery, you know, not mine. Even though I got equal benefit I didn't do anything." And, when Grace remained silent, "I don't know if your mother will let me go out alone. I think she'll probably want you to go with me."

"She might."

Two words. Progress. "But even if your mother did say yes to making a harvester run, I'm not sure she'd agree to my going near Ushant Reef. Not even if I promised to stay a safe distance away. What do you think? She's your muv, you know her a lot better than I do."

"I don't know what she'd say." Grace looked at Shelby, and suddenly she smiled. "But there's one easy way to find out. We can go and ask her."

As they headed together toward the control room, Shelby wondered what was going on. A refusal to speak to him for over a week; and then, for no apparent reason, all smiles and everything back to normal. What did it mean? It was what he had hoped for when he mentioned taking a corry outside, so in a way he could claim success. But he didn't know *why.* Here was another question for Jilter.

The visit to Lana Trask, on the other hand, was definitely not a success.

"You can take a corry out for a harvester run," she said. "In fact, if you hadn't come here I'd have been calling both of you. We all have to get to work, there's too much space still in the cargo holds. But you are to stay on the collection circle, and not wander off past it toward Ushant Reef. You hear me?"

"We weren't planning on going close, Muv."

"Your idea of close and mine are not the same. I can forgive Shel, he's a newcomer, but you, Gracie, you ought to know better. Ushant Reef is the least mapped and most dangerous reef in the Cloud. More rakehells have been lost there than anywhere else."

"More Cauthen starfires found there, too."

"That's not the point. You two have got your starfire. Be satisfied with it."

As usual, Grace was wearing the stone in a pouch hung from her belt. She reached inside to take out the fist-sized gem and rub it and press it, something she did at least a hundred times a day. The starfire responded with a brighter display of its ever-changing inner fire. Thurgood Trask had told Grace that what they saw was nothing but a piezoelectric effect, but his words did nothing to explain the stone's beauty. This afternoon it glowed a cold and brilliant blue-green.

"It would be great to find another." Grace stared down into the luminous depths. "No one in the harvester fleet owns a piece of two of them. I'd like to be the first."

"Sure you would. That's called greed, and you ought to be ashamed of yourself." But Lana Trask must have felt something of the same urge herself, because she went on, "I'll tell you what. Two weeks from now we'll be back near the Portland and Lizard reefs, the place where you two made your find. It's a safer area, and I know it better. I just *may* consider allowing the two of you to make an exploration trip when we get there—if you work extra hard all the way until then."

"We will." Grace and Shelby spoke in unison.

"Good. Then get started on today's work—right now. Scat."

"Do you really think she will?" asked Shelby, as they left the control room and headed for the cargo holds.

"Let us explore, you mean?" Grace nodded. "If we work extra hard she will. You have to know Muv. She's too logical to live. Work real hard, and we explore the Portland and Lizard when we get there. Don't work real hard, and we can forget the exploration. So I guess we have to work. Let's get to it."

She sounded resigned. Compared with the excitement of cruising out to a reef, harvesting transuranics was no treat for Grace. For Shelby, on the other hand, all tasks on the harvesters still had the fascination of newness. He wasn't much disappointed by Lana Trask's ruling.

The outer collection cable had been deployed by Logan

late the previous night. Now it was Grace and Shelby's job to follow the line along its multiple-hundred-kilometer length, examining the widely spaced collector spheres and bringing in-board any sack with an acceptable mass of transuranics. The detailed analysis of samples, with their clues as to where the harvester might want to go next, would be done later on board the main ship.

It was hard work physically, with a required rhythm that made it essential for the two of them to work closely together. As they did so they could talk about anything they chose over the suit radios, either on the general channels or on the short-range and scrambled personal channel that guaranteed privacy. Grace, after her ten-day silence, was unusually chatty.

"Muv's not lying, exactly," she said, "but she's stretching the truth. I checked with Uncle Thurgood, and he says we've never done as well before this early in the season. Keep it up, he says, and we'll be full hold and first through the node to Sol-side—again."

"It happened last year?"

"Sure did. Third year running. Muv's the best sniffer in the fleet. And there's your proof of it."

She pointed out past the collection cable. Shelby, to his surprise, saw an unfamiliar corry outlined against the Cloud's blue glow. It was floating no more than a kilometer away.

"That doesn't look like one of ours."

"It isn't. Different design. For a bet it's from the *Southern Cross.* Wonder how long it's been there? Still trailing along behind us, and still trying to figure out how we do it. Uncle Thurgood gets mad 'til he's nearly foaming at the mouth, but Muv says he should relax and accept it as a compliment. We'll know for sure who it is in a few minutes— looks like they're coming this way."

"What do they want?"

"Maybe to compare notes. Maybe just being sociable. I don't think they're in any kind of trouble, because they're acting too casual."

The other corry approached steadily until it was no more than thirty meters away, drifting on the other side of the collection cable. It halted and a suited figure waved an arm from the open floor.

"Go to channel sixty-six, Shel," said Grace. "That's standard corry-to-corry."

"Good afternoon to you," said a familiar and pleasant voice, as Shelby switched channels. "How are the pickings?"

"Hi, Captain Mossman," Grace waved in reply. "We're getting a good haul. Anything we can do for you?"

"No. I'm just out here sightseeing and taking a little constitutional. Really pretty today. Did you notice the pinwheel?"

"Yeah. Very strange. We had a good look, too." The Cloud beyond the *Harvest Moon* contained a strange swirl of hot pink, a striking feature that Grace swore had not been there on the way to Confluence. "Don't mind us if we keep on working."

Their corry was crabbing its way steadily along the collection cable, with Grace and Shelby loading collectors as they went. The corry from the other ship kept pace. Pearl Mossman was watching them closely and edging a little nearer.

"Who's that with you, Grace? I know from the style that it's not Thurgood or Scrimshander."

"Give me a break." Grace laughed. "Do you see me coming out with Uncle Thurgood? Tar doesn't suit my complexion. This is Shel Cheever. He's our newest crew member."

"We already met, back at Confluence." Pearl Mossman waved again, this time just for Shelby. "Hi, Shel. Welcome to corry work, the curse of the Cloud. Are you two regular partners?"

The question sounded as if it were addressed to Shelby, but after the last ten days he wasn't sure of the answer. He turned to Grace. "Are we?"

"I guess so." They looked at each other.

"And hoping to find another starfire, I'll bet," said Pearl. She was now no more than ten meters away and edging nearer, close enough to study the smallest changes in facial expression.

"Could be," Grace admitted, after another glance at Shelby.

"Well, watch your step if you're heading for Ushant Reef."

"We won't be going anywhere near it."

"Me neither." The other corry slowly began to drift away from the collection cable. "I'll probably see you two outside again. Good hunting. Say hello to Jilter and Lana. And remind Scrim that he promised to make me look really beautiful when he carves me."

"We'll tell him." Grace watched the little ship move off into the distance until it was no more than a darker dot against the blue glow. "I think Muv will find that little episode very interesting," she said slowly.

"I thought you were used to the *Southern Cross* following you around."

"Oh, we are. It's not that. It's that Pearl's corry didn't have any sign that it was working. They use machines for almost everything on the *Southern Cross*, but I didn't see a robot anywhere on board the corry. And you saw the bare floor."

"She said she was out sightseeing."

"I know. But harvester people don't *go* sightseeing during the season—not unless they're working at the same time. And she wasn't."

"What do you think it means?"

"Your guess is as good as mine. That's why I want to talk to Muv."

"Right now?" Shelby's arms were aching, and he wouldn't mind at all if Grace said they had to hurry back instantly to the parent ship.

"Sure—go home and get skinned by Muv and Uncle Thurgood for stopping halfway through a collection. We'd be sent right out again. Come on, Shel, back to the grind. A hundred kilometers to go." Grace leaned over the cable, leaving Shelby to try to puzzle out for himself what had just happened. Why would Pearl Mossman bring her corry sauntering around their collection system?

Shelby couldn't think of anything plausible. There was no way that Pearl could hope to steal from their collectors and get away with it.

Lana Trask, when they returned to the *Harvest Moon* with their corry loaded to the limit, at first seemed equally puzzled.

"*Sightseeing?*" She shook her head at Grace. "That's a new one. I've known Pearl for a long time, and she cares even less for sightseeing than I do."

"It's what she said. And she sure wasn't working."

They were eating dinner, and now Lana laid down her knife and stared at the wall. "You know, it could make sense— if something that I heard at Confluence, and didn't believe, turned out to be true."

"Full holds?" Jilter said quietly.

"You heard it too?" Lana turned to Grace and Shelby. "No harvester has ever managed to fill the cargo holds by the time it gets to Confluence. Most don't come close until they're almost all the way back to the node. But it's not impossible. And during Confluence Pearl Mossman was going around and hinting that they were so close to full holds that all they needed was a few more days."

Shelby had no idea what it took to fill a harvester's hold, but his commercial instinct took over with an automatic question. "Wouldn't any ship that filled its holds make straight for the node and head Sol-side with its harvest ahead of the rest? It wouldn't hang around to go looking at Cloud pictures."

Lana stared at him as though she had never quite seen him before. "Good for you, Shel. You're absolutely right. A full harvester would be out of here with its tail on fire—unless it had other reasons to stick around in the Cloud. Thurgood? You spent a lot of time at the Confluence trading sessions. Any other deals going on for Mossman and Crispin that would make them stay Cloud-side when they had full holds?"

"Never heard of a one." Thurgood shook his big balding head. "There were side deals involving *Dancing Lady* and *Hope and Glory*. And let's see now, I heard some rumors about *Sweet Chariot* and *Coruscation* and *Once-Over-Lightly*. The *Southern Cross*, though, not a murmur."

"Which would make sense, if there really *was* some supersecret deal." Lana picked up her knife. "Well, if there is one it's going to remain a secret. We can't let speculation on what they might be doing affect our own plans. One other thing, though. Would you take a look through the scope, Doobie, and see if the *Southern Cross* is still sitting on our coattails?"

Doobie was the fastest eater on the ship and his meal was long gone. He nodded and hustled out.

Three minutes later he was back. The *Southern Cross* was still there, but it was at the limit of the range of their scope and was now little more than a silver dot. Assuming that the other harvester had the same viewing equipment on board as the *Harvest Moon*, the chance of Pearl Mossman gaining useful information about what they were doing was an absolute zero.

"Which is as it should be, and about time." Uncle Thurgood was the only person who seemed really pleased by the news. "Tunnel and blast 'em, they've spied on us too much already."

Everyone nodded. But they were more interested in Lana's next question. "Very true, Thurgood. So they're still trailing us, but they're too far away to learn a thing about our harvest. What are they up to?"

No one could offer an answer.

The two people who could have provided the answer were not about to do so. Pearl Mossman and Knute Crispin, comfortable in the automated interior of the *Southern Cross*, were reviewing the situation.

"Now that I've seen things close up," Pearl said, "I'm even more sure that if it's done at all it has to be with the corry. Unless we're willing to go aboard the *Harvest Moon* and capture the whole place."

"Which you're not."

Pearl shook her head. "I'm not. Too many of them, and only two of us. You couldn't possibly watch all of them while I'm back Sol-side talking to J. P. Cheever. But we may have to take Grace Trask as well as the Cheever kid."

"No problem. I can easy handle the two of 'em. Did you see any good way of making the grab? Preferably something that could be taken for an accident."

"I know how to do it if we're willing to sacrifice a couple of our machines."

"Permanently?"

"I'm afraid so. Don't worry about that, Knute. Once we trade Cheever you'll never need robots again. You'll have human servants anytime you feel like them. But we'd have to leave the machines behind."

"You mean, where the *Harvest Moon* could ask them what happened? That's sounds like a bad idea. The machines would tell 'em how to track us."

"Not necessarily. Can't you fix it so there's a complete memory wipe of each robot five minutes after its part of the operation is finished? That way the Trasks may guess what we did, but they'll never know for sure from our machines."

"A timed memory erasure? I can arrange that, no problem. But what's your scheme? Is there any risk to us, or to the *Southern Cross?*"

"Not a smidgeon. Not if we wait and time it right." Pearl pulled a blank sheet to where Knute could see what she drew. "Here's the *Harvest Moon.*" She made a small dot in the middle of the page. "And this is that ship's collection system, at its maximum extension." She drew a rough circle centered on the harvester, then shaded a long figure-eight loop far off to the right. "And here are the Portland and Lizard Reefs, and their overlap region."

"We're nearly two weeks away from them. There's no guarantee that the *Harvest Moon* will pass that way to reach the node."

"They've been there coming and going on that route for at least the past three seasons. They've done well so far this year, so I don't see why Lana Trask would change a successful plan. But if they do change, then we'll change, too. Let me tell you the rest of it." Pearl marked the point of the *Harvest Moon*'s collection circle closest to the twin reefs of Portland and Lizard and held her pen steady there. "We wait until Cheever and Grace Trask go out for a harvest collection— we know the look of their corry—and we keep waiting until they've been right around the cable and have come to this point. It's a signal dead spot because of interference from the two reefs. No matter what they send from their suit radios, the transmission will arrive garbled at the *Harvest Moon.*"

"Where are we, then?" Knute was peering at the diagram. "If we're not careful we'll be in a dead spot, too."

"We will. I'm counting on it. The Trasks won't know we're anywhere close. But we'll be waiting *here.*" She marked a point even closer to the shaded double loop of the reefs. "Say, a hundred kilometers beyond the collection circle."

"Takes energy to stay there." Knute was looking dubious. "We'll feel a strong pull from both reefs."

"We will—and so will the corry with Cheever in it. The corry won't move toward us or the reefs, of course, because it will be electromagnetically held to a collection cable centered on the *Harvest Moon.* But that's where our machines come in. We send them *here* and *here*"—Pearl marked two other points on the collection circle, one on each side of where Shelby and Grace were assumed to be—"and at the right moment, they sever the cable next to them simultaneously. I don't have to tell you what happens next."

"The crew of the *Harvest Moon* go out of their mind, trying to save the severed collection cable." Knute finally seemed happy. "With the reef fields working on it it's going to tie itself up like a ball of string. And the corry comes slingshot out toward the *Southern Cross.* You said we'd be a hundred kilometers away? It will really be zipping out of there when it gets to us. Think we can catch it?"

"That's your department. You tell me. The hundred kilometers is nominal. If we have to wait closer to the collection cable, that's what we'll do. You make arrangements to catch the corry with Cheever in it. The moment you tell me you have it, I take us out of there."

"But if you head back toward the *Harvest Moon*—"

"I don't. I take us between the reefs." She saw his expression. "*Not* threading the eye of either, because I value my skin more than that. I'll take us along an equipotential between the two reefs, where the disturbing field is a minimum."

Knute looked dubious. "That puts us smack in the middle of a sounder alley."

"It does, but that's all right. We won't be disturbing any sounders we might see and there's no reason for them to take any interest in us. The main point is we'll be in a blackout region for the *Harvest Moon*. So far as they're concerned, their corry and a length of collection cable will simply have vanished. With any luck they'll assume Cheever and Grace Trask went into one or other of the reefs. Not even Lana Trask will follow them there."

"I don't like it, Pearl." Knute Crispin was bending low over the page, his eyebrows in a single black line. "At least two rakehells, the *Galway Galleon* and the *Smiling Buddha*, disappeared in that sounder alley between Portland and Lizard."

"After they spent weeks there, looking for starfires and shwartzgeld. Probably got sucked into a reef eye by going too close. We'll just be passing through, straight in and straight out." Pearl Mossman picked up the piece of paper sitting between them and held it out across the table. "Look, Knute, either we do this at the max or we don't do it at all. When things get hot we won't have time to give each other pep talks. Which are you? In or out?"

"I'm in. You know me." Knute shrugged. He took the paper and smoothed it on the table surface. "I'd rather ride to hell in a dogcart than sit and do nothing. But I like to be sure we're prepared for the downside."

"Prepare all you like." Pearl Mossman stood up. "Take a look at that sheet, too. You'll have plenty of time for it, because I don't propose to bother with any more of this damned harvesting. Shelby Cheever is a bigger fish than twenty holdfuls."

"You bet. Catch him"—Knute made a grabbing movement with both hands—"and we'll be richer than any harvester crew in history."

"Catch him *alive*, Knute." Pearl turned to leave the cabin and added over her shoulder, "Just try to remember that detail when you get your hands on him, and hold down your enthusiasm. Cheever's not good for much when he's alive; but he's of no use at all to us dead."

CHAPTER THIRTEEN

"Dodman's and Plymouth to Portland and Lizard,
Tacking past Beachy from Ushant or Wight . . ."

THE longest corry session was over, and Grace was singing to herself as Doobie and Shel tallied the final few dozen bags. It was already far past the usual working hours, and the boys were drooping with fatigue. Grace sat in her shirtsleeves at the very apex of the corry, looking down on the two youths working below. Her voice was not loud, but it was clear and true and it echoed splendidly off the bare walls.

Doobie squinted up at her in the gloom. "Hoy! You wailing up there. What you think you're doing? When you coming down to do your share?"

"I am doing my share—first-class entertainment for you, free of charge." But Grace climbed gracefully down the struts to deck level. "All right, Doob, I'll take over. It's nearly the last time. One more this year, according to Jilter, and we'll be all done."

"We're that near full holds?" Doobie bowed and stretched at the hips, easing his aching back. "I don't believe it. We weren't that close this time last year."

"Go ask, if you don't believe me." Grace grinned at Shelby as Doobie instantly turned and headed out of the cargo hold. "Now that was a tactical error. Little brother won't be back 'til we're long done tallying and stowing."

"What *were* you doing up at the apex?"

"Now don't *you* start." Grace paused with the automatic tallier in her hand. "I was singing. Are you going to tell me people don't sing where you come from?"

It occurred to Shelby that in his immediate circle they did not—not, at least, from sheer happiness. He had heard more spontaneous singing in two months with the harvester fleet than in all the rest of his life.

"I didn't mean that," he said. "Of course I know you were singing. But that song—with the names of the reefs in it. Did you make it up yourself?"

He went on tallying as he spoke, and without the use of the tallier. It had been a surprise and a peculiar pleasure to learn that he was the only person on board who could maintain a running count in his head and never lose it, while talking about anything else at the same time—even about numbers.

"I didn't make up that song," Grace said. "Wish I had. But it's not about reefs in the Messina Cloud. It's hundreds of years old, and it's about places on Earth."

"But those are real reef names. We passed Ushant Reef a couple of weeks ago, and tomorrow we'll be approaching Portland and Lizard."

"That's just an accident. I guess that when the Cloud was first being explored, people got lazy. They went back and gave names to the reefs out of history books, from the seas and ports and danger points of Earth. And they stole the tunes, too, from old sea chanteys."

"So there's really no such thing as genuine Cloud songs, made for here and sung here?"

"Not yet. Not good ones. One day, though, there will be. There's a Cloud poetry competition every year at Confluence. Of course, *you* were too busy running around with Nicky Rasmussen and his friends to think of going"—a touch of resentment still in her voice—"but anyone can enter. I went to it."

"And you entered?"

"No. I didn't have the nerve."

"So who won?"

"Nobody. There's a standing rule: Unless some poem is judged really, really good, no one will be declared a winner."

"But if everyone is afraid to enter . . ."

"They're not all like me." Grace realized that she had admitted, for the first time to anyone except her mother, that she wrote poetry. "Some people enter, and instead of being really, really good they are really, really awful. I'd be ashamed to stand up there and spout what they wrote, but they don't seem embarrassed at all. They might not seem so bad, except that there's first-rate Cloud verse to compare them with."

She had given up any pretense of tallying. Now she stood perfectly still, closed her eyes, and declaimed: "*It is ours to sweep through the ringing deep where Azrael's outposts are, Or buffet a path through the Pit's red wrath when God goes out to war, Or hang with the reckless Seraphim on the rein of a red-maned star.* Well? What do you think of that?"

"It's gibberish. It doesn't mean anything."

"You want bells on it? It's the *sound* that matters. And it describes *us*. We do sweep through the *ringing deep*. We do go *further than rebel comet dared*—that's from another verse of the same poem—every time we jump through the node network to reach the Cloud."

"Recite some more to me." And when Grace did so, a quite different and sad poem that began, *These were never your true love's eyes, why do you feign that you love them?*, and then still another and very strange one, *When I left Rome for Lalage's sake, by the Legions' Road to Rimini*, he shook his head and said, "You're right. It's the sounds more than the sense. But I thought you said there were no good Cloud poets?"

"That isn't by a Cloud poet. It's an old Earth poet. I know a fair amount of his poetry, but if you really want to hear it you should ask Uncle Thurgood."

"*Thurgood*?" That was the last name Shelby would have guessed for a person interested in poetry. The bluff red face and bushy white side-whiskers seemed the very opposite of the romantic mush that Shelby had learned to think of as "poetic."

"You heard right. Uncle Thurgood knows whole long poems by heart. He'll sit there and recite 'McAndrew's Hymn' or 'The Mary Gloster' for as long as you'll sit and listen. One of the big disappointments of his life was to go to Earth and learn that the work of his favorite poet is banned there."

"I've never heard of any of the poems that you quoted. But *banned*—on Earth?"

"I'm not joking. Muv says it's because the poet told the truth about women, that we defeat men hands down any time it comes to a real crunch. We're more focused and more ruthless. But Uncle Thurgood says no, that's not the reason. It's that the writer liked machines and people who work with machines, he respected what they do, and he wrote poems showing that the lives of engineers and miners and pilots have their own excitement and romance. That's exactly the way people feel in the Kuiper Belt, or out here in the Cloud. But the people who run Earth can't stand that idea, Uncle Thurgood says, because they do everything in their power to *prevent* the use of machines there. It's as though they want everyone to stay poor, when we could all be rich."

The people who run Earth. That sounded suspiciously like J. P. Cheever, of Cheever Consolidated Enterprises. Did anyone on Earth have *more* to do with the running of the planet? For the first time in weeks Shelby thought of Earth and of his own family. It was just as well that no one except Grace believed what he had told them. If they had believed, he might have received not their respect but their contempt.

Grace yawned, a gigantic gape that showed her tongue and her back teeth. She pointed the tallier at a last pile of bags. "Let's compare counts and get this over with. I'd like to hit Muv with a status report before she goes to sleep. We've certainly done our bit. I want to make sure she keeps her side of the bargain."

Shelby found himself yawning in sympathy. He shivered, allowed the yawn to stretch to its luxurious completion, and said, "Two thousand and seventy-nine, according to my tally. Not counting the bag that came up empty because of a collector defect."

"Right on the button." Grace stared at her tallier, and

then at Shelby's empty hands. "With no tallier. You've got to teach me how you do that."

"Sure. As soon as you teach me to sing in tune." Shelby entered the final tally in the wall terminal. "Go see your mother before anyone else does. If we're really so close to full holds, the last collection run is going to be done right by the Portland and Lizard Reefs. We don't want Thurgood or Scrimshander jumping in to take our place." He pointed to the pouch on Grace's belt, where the Cauthen starfire hung in its usual place. "I don't deserve my share of that. But I'd like the chance to earn a piece of one for myself."

Lana Trask had not reneged on her promise. What she had done, facing the enticing prospect of full holds before any other harvester, was add a little insurance policy.

It was Grace who came to Shelby with a scowling face, saying, "We can go out today. But we won't be the only ones. Muv is expecting that what we bring back will give us full holds, but she thinks two other ships, the *Coruscation* and *The Pride of Dundee*, may be close to the same state. She wants to make sure that all cables are reeled and stored by the time we're done, so that the *Harvest Moon* can head for the node the moment the tally is completed. Scrim is going to be out there, too, in his own corry. He'll be reeling in cables."

And it was Shelby who brought Grace back to reality, saying, "Come off it, Grace. You're worried about *Scrim*? Can you imagine him finding a starfire, even if he tripped over one? Think yourself lucky that it's Scrimshander Limes who'll be out there with us, and not somebody like Jilter."

Grace nodded, slowly and reluctantly; but her real reassurance came only when they were outside, swinging in their corry along the dark length of the outer collection cable. Scrimshander was working the inner cable more than thirty kilometers away, closer to the *Harvest Moon*, but even from that distance they could see his corry's wild swings away from its assigned position. Every wrong move was followed at once by a violent overcompensation. The cable he was attached to and trying to reel in jerked and writhed like a live snake.

"Yea!" Grace said. "Yippee! Ride 'em, Scrimmy!" But she spoke over the private channel, so that only Shelby could hear her and be so convulsed with laughter that he could not do his own job properly. It should not much matter. He had checked before they came outside, and the harvester was already so close to full holds that Grace and Shelby could return with half a load and still put the *Harvest Moon* over the top in the amount of stored transuranics. The only thing that could now make a noticeable difference to the commercial success of the voyage would be the finding of another starfire, and in fifteen more minutes they would be free to release the corry from the cable and fly over to test their luck nearer to the Portland and Lizard Reefs. Shelby could hardly wait. Already the field tugging at the corry was more than a standard gravity, and only their coupling with the thick collection cable held them in position.

Shelby gave a short pulse of the corry's drive, just to get a feel for the forces on them. He felt a new sympathy for Scrimshander Limes. The presence of the reefs made the response of the corries quite different from usual. He switched to the general communication channel, intending to compare notes with Scrim, and heard only a blare of random noise.

"Don't waste your time, Shel," Grace said over the private channel. She had guessed what he was doing. "We're in a communications dead spot between the reefs. Signals over any sort of distance are blotted out by static. Just relax and let the cable hold us steady."

She was leaning over the side and inspecting the state of the next collector as she spoke, and her voice rose suddenly in pitch and volume. "Didn't you hear me? I said *steady*!"

There was a good reason for her scream. Shelby had not touched the drive controls, but he felt random acceleration forces as the whole sky began to roll dizzily about him. At first he thought that the corry must have come completely loose. Then he saw the collection cable. They were still attached to it, but the continuous six-hundred-kilometer loop of hawser whose constant curvature permitted the corry a smooth progression along it was gone. In its place was a short section of a few kilometers that writhed and twisted and snapped at both ends like a whip. Collection beads were flung clear and vanished into space. It was simple luck that pinned Shelby and Grace to the corry's floor, rather than casting them free into open space or flinging them against the cable.

"Don't touch the drive!" Grace shouted. She, like Shelby, had realized the problem. The cable had broken, and until the transients of released tension had died down it was not safe to apply any other forces. Clinging to handholds on the flat floor, she came crawling across to the corry's control boss, where Shelby was holding on desperately. Beyond her he could see the changing sky. The corry was hurtling away from the *Harvest Moon*, heading toward the dark vortices of the Lizard and Portland Reefs. It was impossible from his viewing angle to tell if they were going to fly right into one of them.

He looked back the way that they had come. With the outer cable broken—but how could a cable possibly break in two places at once?—the crew of the *Harvest Moon* would have their hands full for quite a while. He and Grace had to find their own way back to the harvester. The return flight would have been trivial in ordinary open space. But here, in the anomalous fields created by the two reefs, he didn't know how difficult it might be.

Grace was finally by his side, clinging as he was to the

central control boss of the corry. She did what Shelby ought to have done at once, hitting the release sequence that separated the corry from the writhing length of broken cable. The irregular movements ended in an instant. They were flying, smoothly but fast, along a line that passed right between the two reefs.

Shelby found that he could breathe again. They had been lucky. It should not be difficult to turn the corry around and head right back the way they had come.

Grace must have been thinking the same thing. She was at the controls, steadying and gently rotating the corry. Shelby, conditioned by two months of life aboard a harvester, automatically checked his own suit monitor and leaned over to see Grace's. They each had enough air for at least twenty-four hours. It should be ample. If they were not back aboard the *Harvest Moon* in that time, they would never get there.

"How far?" he asked Grace, not really expecting an answer. He just wanted to hear her voice. "How far do you think we are from home?"

"I don't know." Like him she peered back the way that they had come, although they both knew that they could not possibly see the *Harvest Moon* at such a distance. "We're still moving really fast. Maybe a couple of thousand kilometers?"

And it was at that precise moment, just as Grace said the word "thousand," that Shelby felt reality slip away completely. Because there, moving across the sky in front of them, he saw a familiar shape. It was the *Harvest Moon*—not two thousand kilometers away, but apparently close enough to touch.

Grace, with her years of experience in the Cloud, saw at once what Shelby could not. To him all harvesters looked the same. She knew them as individuals. They had small structural differences and unique patterns of lights.

"We're in luck, Shel," she cried, while he was still struggling to understand how the *Harvest Moon* could pop up right in front of them. "It's the *Southern Cross*. They've seen us. They'll take us back home."

The other harvester was matching their course and steadily coming nearer. Shelby saw a suited figure in one of the main hatches, waving to them.

"They're telling us to come aboard." Grace was busy again at the corry controls. "Wave back, Shel, and show them that we understand."

If there was a special harvester signal that carried such a message, Shelby didn't know it. He simply waved both arms and kept on waving until the corry slid in through the port and he lost sight of the other figure. As the hatch slid shut behind them he saw the familiar white fog as jets of air entered the cold chamber. He and Grace waited impatiently through the two minutes needed to achieve a breathable atmosphere. They stepped together onto the catwalk.

"Our collection cable broke." Grace started to gabble at top speed even before her helmet was fully open. "Thank heaven you were close by to help us. I was wondering if we would be able to make it back home on our own, because this is closer to a reef than I've ever been in my whole life. I didn't even think we'd be able to send a message back to say what happened to us, because we're in a communications blind spot here."

The man facing them was nodding slowly. Shelby recognized him. It was the thickset individual who had been with Pearl Mossman that first night at Confluence Center. Knute Crispin. He had an oddly wary expression on his face—not at all the satisfaction that a man ought to feel on saving someone from a tricky situation in space.

Grace didn't seem to notice. "I suppose it's just as bad

a blind spot for you," she went on. "So the quicker you can take us home, the better. As soon as they get the broken cable under control Muv will start going out of her mind with worry, wondering what's happened to us, and wondering—"

"Grace," Shelby placed his hand on her arm. He had been watching the other man's eyes. "Wait just a minute."

"Why shouldn't I—"

"Try listening to your boyfriend, Grace." Knute Crispin had come closer, but he remained a good four steps away from them. He studied Shelby's face. "You've got damn good instincts, Cheever, I'll say that. I can see I'm going to have to be careful with you."

Grace glanced quickly from one to the other. "What's going on here? Do you know, Shel?"

"Not really." Shelby did not take his eyes away from Knute. "But ever since the accident happened I've been asking myself how a collection cable could possibly break in two places at once, when it's supposedly made of the toughest material available. I don't think it *could* break like that by accident. But it could be cut—on purpose."

"Now, that's really rather paranoid." Knute Crispin had a little half-smile on his face. "Why would anyone ever think to do such a thing?"

"I don't know." Shelby hesitated. "To slow the *Harvest Moon* down for a day or two, because you are close to full holds and want to be first to go Sol-side? But that doesn't make sense. If you were near full holds you wouldn't wait to pick up our corry."

"Quite right. If we had full holds we'd have been out of here before this." Knute Crispin seemed to be enjoying himself. "Any other suggestions?"

Shelby shook his head.

"Then I guess I'll have to tell you, won't I? Before that,

though, and just so you won't get any ideas . . ." Knute reached out and picked up a long cylindrical pipe that had been hanging on the wall of the hold. "Do you know that this is?"

It was strange to Shelby, but Grace said at once, "It's a patching gun."

"It is indeed. You've probably never seen one used, Cheever, because it's only for emergency fixes. But Grace has. She can tell you what it does. It drives a rivet through a pair of hull plates and holds them together until they can be properly welded or cold-sealed. Isn't that right, Grace?"

Grace nodded slowly.

"Of course," Knute went on, "it doesn't have to be hull plates, or internal ship partitions. It could just as well be a rib cage, or maybe a skull." He raised the pipe. "This is already charged, of course. Twenty rivets. People will tell you there's no weapons in the Cloud, but that's nonsense. Anything can be a weapon, including teeth and fists. And just to be sure there's nothing on you that might serve . . ." He waved the rivet gun at Grace and Shelby. "Take off your suits. Don't worry, it will only be for a minute. I want to be sure there's no surprises inside them."

Shelby stood, stubborn and scowling, until Grace said, "Do it, Shel. He's telling the truth about what a rivet gun can do. It would make a hole right through you." She removed her helmet completely and began to ease her way out of the rest of her suit. Shelby did the same, until he was halted by a barked command from Knute Crispin: "Hold it right there!"

Shelby froze, wondering what he had done now. But the other man's attention was on Grace. Knute walked forward, still covering them with the rivet gun, and gestured toward her midriff. "Is that what I think it might be? I've heard rumors. Whatever's in there, bring it out—slowly."

Reluctantly, Grace put her hand into the pouch that hung from her belt. She withdrew it holding the starfire. Even in the dim light of the hold, the fist-size jewel glowed with its own inner light.

"Very nice indeed. Just toss it this way, and gently." Knute caught the starfire as it came toward him, but the rivet gun's aim did not waver.

"So that's it!" Grace burst out. "You did all this to get your thieving hands on our starfire!"

"Wrong. This is just a nice little bonus." Knute thrust the starfire out of sight into one of his own suit pockets. He studied his captives for another half-minute while they removed the rest of their suits. "All right," he said at last. "You both seem to be clean. You can put your suits back on now. You're going to need them." As they silently sealed the suits, and placed their helmets again in position, he added, "You still don't get it, do you? You still don't know why you're here."

"If it's not to delay the *Harvest Moon*," Shelby said slowly, "and it's not for the starfire, then . . ."

"Then? Keep going."

"Then it's something else that you want. Something that you think is valuable." Shelby looked at Grace and back at Knute. He took a long, deep breath. "You didn't need to take Grace at all, you know. You can let her go."

"No way to get one of you without the other. We thought about that." Knute shrugged. "Anyway, that's an academic point. It's too late now. You're both here."

"Will one of you tell me what the devil you are *talking about*!" Grace had been watching the other two with increasing confusion. "Something else valuable—what?"

"Me," Shel said quietly. "To hold for ransom. They want me so they can demand a ransom from my family. I'm an idiot. I've spent my whole life back on Earth being guarded night and day, so nobody could ever have a chance to kidnap me. Then I come out here and forget every warning that I was ever given. Why was I stupid enough to think things would be different in the Cloud?" He glared at Knute Crispin. "You don't know what trouble you're getting yourselves into. For one thing, you daren't use that rivet gun. I'm no use to you unless I'm alive."

"Quite true, Cheever. We need you alive. But I can still use the gun if I have to." Knute reached out and pressed the pipe to Grace's chest. His finger was tight against the rivet gun's trigger. "If you want to keep Grace alive, too, you'll do exactly as I say. She's expendable, you see. We don't need *her* around to get a big ransom for you."

Grace stood frozen, afraid to breathe. Finally Shelby nodded. "Take it away. Don't touch her. I'll do whatever you tell me to do."

"Now you're being sensible." Knute took a couple of steps backward. "Let me explain what's going to happen next. And let me give you my word: If you do your part right for a few more weeks, you'll both come out of this alive and well and without a mark on you.

"First—and obviously—the *Southern Cross* won't be taking you back to your harvester. We're going the other way, right along the line between the Portland and Lizard Reefs. That keeps us nicely in the communications dead spot so far as the *Harvest Moon* is concerned, so even if you found a way to call for help it wouldn't get through.

"After that it's very simple. While we're still between the reefs the three of us will leave the *Southern Cross*. We'll take this ship's pinnace and head back to the Confluence Center. It will be deserted at this time of the season, so we'll have a nice restful time there—you can think of it as a little vacation, with nothing to do but take it easy and use the recreational facilities. I imagine you'll be able to fill in the rest of the story for yourselves."

"It's pretty obvious," Shelby said bitterly. "We go to the Confluence Center, and nobody except Captain Mossman knows we are there. She takes the *Southern Cross* Sol-side, heads for Earth, and tells my family that if they want to see me alive again they'd better pay whatever she asks."

"And will they pay, do you think?"

"Of course they will." Shelby sighed. "I'm Shel Cheever—Shelby Crawford Jerome Prescott Cheever, the only son of J. P. Cheever, head of Cheever Consolidated Enterprises. Damn it."

"No need to curse your good fortune—and ours. But there you have it. Neat, clean, and foolproof." Knute waved the rivet gun. "So let's get on with it. The pinnace is in the next chamber. Lead the way. And remember, I'll be watching every step that you take."

Shelby went first, thinking furiously and hopelessly. Since they were now going through an airlock, presumably the pinnace was held in a chamber containing a vacuum. It was almost certainly exposed to space. He and Grace were both in their suits. The moment that they emerged from the lock into the other chamber, they could jet away from Knute and head toward the outside.

And then what?

Knute might shoot one or both of them with the rivet gun. Or he might follow them at his leisure in a corry or a pinnace, find them, and capture them again. Or he might not find them at all. In which case they would die floating in open space in their suits, as their air supply ran out.

"It won't work, Shel," Grace said. She had guessed the direction of his thoughts. "None of it will work."

"Quite right," Knute added from behind them. "Listen

to the lady, Cheever. The smart thing to do is exactly what I tell you. As a first move, you will help to free the pinnace from its moorings. Pearl Mossman is waiting for us to give a go-ahead before the *Southern Cross* turns on its drive. I don't have to tell you we'd better be well away before that happens."

Obeying Knute's careful instructions, Shelby and Grace moved together to cancel the electromagnetic moorings that held the pinnace. As the little ship edged toward open space, they followed close behind. Knute did not allow them to get more than a couple of meters apart from each other, and there was never a moment when he did not have them both in full view.

With just two moorings left to free, Grace was ahead of Shelby and reached the outer hull of the *Southern Cross* first. There she halted.

"What's wrong?" Knute was three or four meters behind. "Keep going, Grace. Don't get ideas."

She pointed, but she did not move. "Look. Can't you see it?"

Shelby followed the line of her arm. For a moment he saw nothing. Then he noticed the tiny sparks of light, twinkling against the blue backdrop of the Messina Cloud. As he watched, the flecks of light strengthened and became more numerous. When they finally dwindled and faded, the space they left behind seemed oddly clear and empty.

"It's nothing." Knute had moved to where he could see it too, and he sounded unimpressed. "It's just a sounder. We're in the channel right between the Portland and Lizard Reefs. It's well known as a sounder alley. I expected we might see one."

Expected, just as Shelby had *hoped* that he might see one—but not in such circumstances. Knute nudged them forward, urging them to continue working. But Shelby could not resist pausing to watch when the sounder itself appeared, and even Knute did not try to force them. Again there was that strange and high-pitched *shreep-shreep-shreep* on the suit communications channels. Again there was the long, tapering body, a kilometer and more of near-perfect blackness. Again there was a great octagonal maw, with its eight blue-white tendrils that like the body distorted the background star field beyond them.

Grace backed up a couple of meters. "It's coming this way. And it's getting awful close."

"We're safe enough." Knute used the barrel of the rivet gun to push her forward again. "You know it's harmless. Get back to work."

"They never come this close. And look at the mouth. It's dilating. And it's getting huge!" Grace backed up farther, bumping into Shelby. "Knute, you have to tell Captain Mossman to get us out of here."

"Are you crazy? I told you, it won't hurt us. Get those moorings free!"

Shelby, standing next to Grace, could see along the full length of the sounder. With a thrill of recognition he saw on the sounder's side a familiar pattern of white dots, in the shape of a running stick-figure man.

"Grace, look at its left side! The markings."

She gasped. "It's the same one! They're all supposed to look different. Shel, it's the same one. It's come after *us.*"

The sounder was closing in, heading directly toward them. The maw was stretching, wider and wider. Now it was easily big enough to engulf the whole pinnace. Still it was growing. Shelby felt strange forces twisting his insides, pulling and squeezing with sensations that he had not felt since his passage through the node network.

"What the devil!" Knute Crispin was sharing the experience of internal body tides, and he did not like it. He began to back up toward the rear of the hold. The rivet gun would be as useless as a packet of pins on a creature the size of the sounder, and Knute knew it. He pointed the gun instead at Shelby and Grace. "Both of you, back inside the main hull. You're right, it's too damn close. I'll tell Pearl to get us the hell out of here."

Grace turned to follow, but Shelby held her arm. She tried to shake herself free. "Shel, let me go." She was close to hysterics. "It's come for us, it's come to get us. It wants us. *Let me go!*"

"No!" Shelby held on, ignoring her cry and her struggle. "Why would it come for *us*? A sounder doesn't even know what humans are. It hasn't come for you or me. It's come for *that.*" He pointed toward Knute Crispin, who had lost all interest in Grace and Shelby and was blundering toward a passage that led to the harvester's interior. "It came for the starfire—for *its own* starfire, the one that we took. That's what it's hunting for. We wouldn't be safe in the ship—not anywhere in the ship. Come on!"

While Grace screamed and struggled in his grip he launched himself outward, dragging her with him away from the harvester's hull. There was a moment when they seemed to be heading right into the sounder's gaping mouth, but Shelby fired his suit jets laterally at maximum impulse while new and stronger forces tore at his body. He and Grace flew sideways, bare meters from the octagonal mouth. They passed by the glowing fringe of deep red and right through the blue-white waving tendrils that surrounded it.

And then they were clear, sliding past the side of the sounder's great body and turning slowly together in space. They both saw what happened next.

The *Southern Cross* had switched on its drive. The high-temperature fusion products of its exhaust flamed directly into the sounder's maw. The monstrous black body shuddered along all its kilometers of length, but the sounder advanced steadily toward the harvester. The mouth opened wider and wider. And instead of flying away at high acceleration, the harvester remained fixed in position, the thrust of its drive somehow neutralized. It did not move as the maw of the sounder slowly engulfed it.

As the *Southern Cross* disappeared, the space around Grace and Shelby became thick-flecked with luminous sparks, filling again with a glittering blue fog.

Grace's despairing cry came over the suit radio. "Shel, it's going to sound! We're too close!"

The great body beside them was beginning to shimmer, a vibrating wall of jet black. The sound came again on the suit radios, impossibly loud.

SHREEP-SHREEP-SHREEP-SHREEP.

It burned into Shelby's brain. "Use your suit jets!" He screamed at Grace, sure she would not hear him. "Get away from the body!"

But he could not perform himself what he was telling her to do. The tidal forces so close to the sounder were too strong, they destroyed brain as well as body functions. Shelby struggled to operate his suit controls, to give the command to use suit jets at their last-resort emergency settings.

He did not do it. He could not do it. The knowledge of that failure filled his mind. As his world dissolved into its own sea of sparks that faded quickly to blackness, his last thought was a hope that Grace would somehow manage to escape.

CHAPTER FOURTEEN

IT WAS the repetition of a nightmare, and the second time was no less unpleasant than the first.

The return of sound before sight; the nausea, the dry throat, the ache in every cell of the body; the hot spikes of pain through the head.

Shelby opened his swollen eyes. The nightmare continued. Again he lay on the floor of a corry. Again a gentle force was pressing him onto something soft. But here at last was a difference. This time he was face-up, staring at the lattice of support struts that met at the corry's apex.

He turned his head to the left, half-expecting to see Logan's multi-armed form again at work by the corry's retaining wall. The result of one small head movement was an immediate and unbearable agony across his neck and shoulders, enough to make him cry out. He froze, unwilling to shift his position another millimeter. He found himself staring at Grace. She was lying by his side, and according to her suit monitors she was alive but unconscious.

After two minutes he felt that he must try to do something, no matter how little. He made a feeble attempt to sit up. The pain in his back forced him to abandon the idea at once, but he had raised his head just enough to see that he was tied down to the floor of the corry by a dozen loops of cable. His effort had made all his joints throb, as though he had been stretched to the limit in every possible direction.

He groaned again and heard a murmur over his suit radio.

"Do not move if you can avoid it. I tied you down for a reason. Both your shoulders are dislocated, and possibly your knees and elbows."

Shelby moved anyway. Gritting his teeth against the pain, he turned his head the other way and confirmed his impression of the voice. On his right, standing at the corry's central controls, was the suited and improbable figure of Scrimshander Limes.

Shelby had been unable to hold back another moan, and at the sound Scrimshander came across to lean over him. Apologetic grey eyes peered into his.

"I am sorry. I did not sedate you, because I thought you would prefer to know what is happening. Would you like me to do so?"

"What about Grace?"

"Her problems are more severe. I have given her painkillers, but I am afraid that she has internal injuries. I cannot determine their extent while she remains in her suit."

"When can you get her out of it?"

"Only when we are again on board the *Harvest Moon*. And before you ask me when that might be, I will confess that I do not know." Scrimshander gestured to the apex of the corry. "Do not try to look, but our harvester lies far off in that direction, beyond the two reefs. Although I followed you as soon as possible when the cable broke, it was necessary to travel a considerable distance before I could reach you. You were in a communications blind spot and traveling fast. In fact, had it not been for the visual sighting of another harvester, I would have had no idea where to look."

"That was the *Southern Cross*. What happened to it?"

"I was hoping that you would be able to tell me. A sounder appeared, and then disappeared. The harvester seemed to vanish with it."

Shelby lay back and closed his eyes. "The sounder got them. Swallowed them up. I saw it happen. The ship, and Pearl Mossman, and Knute Crispin. All gone."

"I feared as much." Scrimshander straightened up. "Now, if you will excuse me, I must attend to our own problems."

"You're flying us back home?"

"Ah—yes. In a manner of speaking." Scrimshander was oddly hesitant. "There is one other thing that I must mention. If we take a straight-line return course toward the *Harvest Moon*, I estimate that the flight between the Portland and Lizard Reefs will require at least ten hours."

"Don't worry about me. I can stand it." Shelby had a terrible thought. "Unless you mean that in ten hours Grace—"

"Be reassured, I judge that she is in no immediate danger of dying from her injuries. However, that is not the problem. It has been a long time since we left the *Harvest Moon*."

"They won't go away. They'll still be looking for us."

"Of course they will. The problem is not with them. It is with us. We each started out with full air supplies in our suits." Scrimshander gave a little cough. "Unfortunately, that as I said was a long time ago. We each have only six hours left before our air is exhausted."

Shelby jerked his head upward and at once regretted it. He groaned and lay back. "Six hours. But you said the trip home will take at least ten."

"That is correct. If we make the direct flight between the Portland and Lizard Reefs, it will be a minimum of ten hours." Scrimshander leaned over Shelby, and again those mild grey eyes stared into his. "We need a velocity boost. I am sorry, but I am afraid that we have absolutely no choice. If we are to have any hope of surviving, we must attempt to thread the eye of one of the reefs."

When he had leaped from the apparent safety of the *Southern Cross* into open space, Shelby was terribly afraid that he would die within the next few hours. Now, watching Scrimshander Limes preparing to enter the eye of the Portland Reef, he was totally convinced of it.

He had told Scrimshander everything that he knew or conjectured about the encounter with the *Southern Cross*, but now he doubted that any of the three of them would live to pass it on to others. To survive a passage through the eye of a reef called for great skill. Only the best pilots in the Cloud dared to think of trying, and only when they were in fully equipped rakehells. How many times had Shelby seen Scrimshander, flying this same underpowered corry with its primitive instruments, roll and yaw and stagger his way to a messy and chaotic rendezvous with the *Harvest Moon*?

The little vessel was rolling now, when the smallest jolt

or turn was agony. Shelby wished that he had asked to be sedated and followed Grace into peaceful sleep. It was so obvious that Scrimshander was inadequate for the task ahead. Even during the approach to the Portland Reef, where the disturbing forces were small, the corry was tilting and jerking in response to the pilot's commands.

The random element of their motion grew more apparent as they approached the outer edge of the reef. Its center lay straight ahead, an eye with a pupil of cloudy black. Turbulent forces began to shake the corry, racking Shelby's back and shoulders with intolerable agony. He did not realize that he was crying out in pain, but as the reef grew from a featureless eye to a rolling funnel of darkness, Scrimshander came rapidly across to his side.

"I must do this now, or not at all. Once we are into the central channel it will be impossible for me to leave the controls even for a moment." He smiled down at Shelby. "Courage now. In less than three minutes this will ease your pain."

The injection went in through the suit's neck access point. Shelby did not even feel it. He wondered if the shot was going to make him unconscious, or if he would be awake and aware at the moment of his own death.

He fixed his eyes on the apex of the corry. The central channel of the reef lay in that direction, a hole in space lined up like a dark target in the crosshairs formed by the corry's thin support struts. A wall of blackness was gradually growing about them, replacing the normal blue glow of the Messina Cloud. They were moving past the safety point, heading into a region of no return. Soon the reef's own forces would drag them in, even if they turned and applied maximum thrust in the opposite direction.

New forces came to buffet the corry, powerful fields arising from within the reef itself. They were compounded by Scrimshander's inept handling of the ship. The surface on which Shelby was lying began to wobble and jerk, but he felt no pain. The shot had taken effect. He was drifting in a state where consciousness was a sometime thing, fading in and out beyond his control.

A tremendous shudder of the whole corry brought him briefly awake. He looked around, knowing that the movement was doing something awful to his neck, knowing that if he lived he would regret it later. Now he felt neither pain nor fear.

They were within the eye of the reef. Blackness lay on all sides, unrelieved by any sign of stars or dust clouds.

In regions of the spectrum beyond those wavelengths visible to human eyes it was not quiet at all. Shelby heard over his suit radio strange bursts of sound and hair-raising banshee screams. Twice there came the *shreep-shreep-shreep* of a sounder, rising and falling in pitch like a siren rushing past them.

How could a sounder be here, within the dark heart of a reef? Trying to understand that, he drifted off into an uneasy doze.

A change in the motion of the corry and a new sound on his suit radio brought him once more awake. The forces he felt were more intense now, but also somehow smoother, as though the ship was sailing on the fields within the reef rather than fighting them.

He looked across toward the corry's central boss. Scrimshander was there, hunched over the controls. In the shrouding darkness of the reef his face showed as a pale patch of white in the control panel's dim light.

Scrim was talking to himself. That was the sound that Shelby had heard on his suit radio.

"Come on, now, you can do it," Scrimshander was saying. "You know you can. We must be close to the halfway point, and we're still in one piece. You just have to hold it together for another hour or two." He gave a gurgling little laugh, almost a giggle, as a new surge of force hit the corry. The lattice of support struts twanged like giant harp strings, and the corry floor shuddered in response. "Oops! Little surprise there. Your own fault. Stay awake. Now's not the time to nod off. You can sleep later."

Shelby, staring at Scrimshander's dim-lit face, wondered how long it had been since the other had slept. They had left the *Harvest Moon* in the middle of the afternoon, with more than twenty-four hours' supply of air. Now—Shelby squinted at his suit monitor—they were down to less than three. He and Grace had been unconscious for much of the time, but Scrim had been awake and obliged to be alert for over thirty hours.

He closed his eyes again. The soft and oddly changed voice went on in his ear. "We're going to make it, you know. Stands to reason. Look at the facts. You were outside at the right time and sitting in the perfect place to see what happened when the kids went shooting off. Two bits of luck right there. Saw the sounder and the *Southern Cross*, otherwise you'd never have spotted those two little suits in the middle of nowhere. Another nice bit of luck. Uh-oh."

There was a swooping lurch of the corry floor beneath Shelby's back, forcing sharp pain even into his drugged mind. The voice in his ear snorted its disgust.

"I didn't like that one bit. Hey, Lady Luck, are you listening? You're not supposed to do that to me. Remember, I'm your best buddy? It's your job to help me. Come on, Lady Luck, make me lucky. Come on, Lady Luck, make me lucky. Come on, Lady Luck . . ."

It was a ritual chant, repeated over and over. After the first half-dozen times Shelby lost count. The corry veered and rolled and shivered and groaned, slithering its way through the gnarled and tortuous sea of force fields that made up the dark heart of the Portland Reef. The voice, the chanting voice of the stranger who was also Scrimshander Limes, went on and on and on: "Come on, Lady Luck, make me lucky. Come on, Lady Luck, make me lucky. . . ."

And Shelby, not knowing how much he heard and saw and how much he imagined, went drifting far off on his own voyage across seas of time and space.

Shelby returned to full consciousness screaming in pain.

"Easy, now," said a gruff voice. "One more go, and you'll feel loads better."

The awful, impossible agony came again, this time on Shelby's other side. He screamed again and opened his eyes.

"There we are." Uncle Thurgood Trask was bending over him, manipulating Shelby's left shoulder in his big hands. "They're both back in place. A couple of weeks and you'll be as good as new."

Shelby realized several things at once. The pain was not as bad as it had been. He was alive. He was on the *Harvest Moon*.

"Grace—" He looked around. There was no sign of her. On a bed next to him lay the silent form of Scrimshander Limes.

"Lana is looking after Grace." Thurgood released Shelby's shoulder. "I'm afraid she's in pretty bad shape."

"Scrimshander?"

"Fine. Just totally exhausted." Uncle Thurgood shook his head. "That man is a living, breathing miracle. He takes two hands to find his own nose, but somehow he threads the eye of the Portland Reef after he's been thirty-three hours without food or sleep. He passed out the minute we pulled him aboard, and he's been out ever since. But if I ever say one bad word to him or about him again, you can paint me purple and dump me out of the lock. If you'd have asked me—"

"He didn't."

"Eh?" Thurgood frowned at Shelby. "Didn't what?"

"Didn't fly through the eye of the Portland Reef."

"Now that's where you're wrong, young man." Thurgood sniffed. "You were probably unconscious, but that's exactly what he did—and I know it's hard to believe, because I found it hard to believe myself."

"It wasn't Scrimshander who did it." Shelby struggled to sit up, winced, and stared hollow-eyed at Uncle Thurgood. "I was awake. I heard what he was saying. The man who flew us through the eye wasn't Scrim. It was Jack Linden. Lucky Jack Linden, the only person to survive the Trachten blowout."

Thurgood Trask jerked back as though he had been slapped. "You mean he said—you mean that he knew—"

"I don't know what he knew. But I can tell you what he said."

Shelby repeated what he had heard on the corry as accurately as he could remember it. As he spoke, Thurgood Trask's ruddy face paled.

"It is, it is." He was squeezing his hands together until the knuckles went white. "Oh, Lord, don't let it happen. Tell me it's not so."

He took a step toward where Scrimshander lay, then hesitated. "He must have his rest, he's totally exhausted. We can't disturb him now. He must sleep until he wakes naturally."

He came back and perched on the end of Shelby's bed. "What did he say in the corry? Tell me again, every word, exactly what he said."

Shelby did his best. At the end of it Thurgood nodded and muttered "Thank you," but it was clear that he hardly knew that Shelby was in the room. His eyes were fixed on Scrimshander's sleeping face. Again and again he half stood up and then subsided, muttering, "He must have rest. He must. He's exhausted."

But Thurgood's face twitched constantly with tension. Finally, after only half an hour, he rose from the bed and turned to Shelby.

"You see, I have to know." He was apologizing, but it was not clear to whom. "I can't help it. I *have* to."

He stepped quickly across, took Scrimshander by the shoulders, and shook him gently. "Scrimshander. *Scrimshander Limes!* Do you hear me?"

The pale grey eyes opened. There was no hint of recognition in them. Thurgood Trask groaned aloud, and his shoulders slumped in despair. "Oh, no! He's gone, he's gone back. It's finally happened."

"He's gone," Scrimshander repeated slowly. "Who has gone, Thurgood? What happened?"

"You know me!" Uncle Thurgood gasped. "You remember my name. Do you know who I am?"

"Of course I do. You are Thurgood Trask." Scrimshander's face clouded and he frowned in perplexity. "But Thurgood, I have had another dream."

"Don't say that." Thurgood stood over the bed wringing his hands. "For God's sake don't say that. I've told you, Scrimshander, that dream you have—it means nothing. It's all imagination. It just means you're overtired, and overexcited, and overworked. You mustn't let yourself think of it. Forget it."

"No, Thurgood." Scrimshander shook his head. "You are wrong. I must *not* forget it. This was *another* dream, not the one that I have had before. And this time it was different. This time I did not stand by helpless while . . . they died. This time—this time I was able to *do something*."

A look of weary peace came to his face. He sighed and placed his cheek flat against his folded hands like a tired child. "Go away now, Thurgood," he said firmly. "I want to dream." The gray eyes closed.

"Scrim*shander* Limes," began Thurgood. "You don't go telling me to—" Then he turned to Shelby and placed a finger to his lips. "Shh! He must sleep. Come on, we have to leave him to rest."

"I can't move." The pain in his shoulders was less, but that allowed Shelby to become more aware of his swollen and throbbing knees and elbows.

"No more you can." Thurgood Trask came again to the bedside. He bent, grunted, and hoisted everything, bedframe and mattress and Shelby, into the air. "You need rest, too. Do you want to go to your own cabin?"

"No. I want to see Grace."

"Mm." Thurgood paused. "I'm not sure that's a good idea."

"I don't care. I must know how she is, even if it's bad—you had to know about Scrimshander."

"Aye. That I did. I had to. All right, then." Thurgood, his shoulders braced against the weight that he was supporting, headed for the exit and sidled his way carefully through into the corridor. "I don't want one word from you to Grace or about Grace," he added, as he carried Shelby through the silent and darkened interior of the harvester. "Not unless Lana says it's all right. You're in good shape, even if you don't feel it. Grace isn't."

The warning was unnecessary. Shelby, craning his head back and to one side as far as the pain in his neck and shoulders would allow, saw Grace at once as he was carried head-first into the ship's little medical center.

His first impression was that she was dead. Her cheeks were white and shrunken, as if all the blood had been drained out of her body. Her eyes were closed and deep set within their bruised sockets.

Lana Trask was sitting by the bedside. She was examining the output from the telemetry sensors festooned about Grace's head and trunk and tenderly adjusting the IVs connected to her daughter's thin arms. She glanced up as Thurgood entered, tiptoeing silently in spite of the weight that he was carrying.

He nodded to her.

"Shel's doing fine." He spoke in a whisper, as though Shelby could neither hear him nor speak for himself. "Scrimshander, too." He gently lowered the bed so that Shelby lay on the other side of Lana from Grace. Thurgood said nothing more, but his face asked the question.

"Internal hemorrhaging has stopped." Lana's own cheeks were almost as pale as Grace's. "But she's lost an awful lot of blood. I'm giving her stored plasma, but she needs another transfusion. We're running out of her type."

"Why didn't you tell me earlier? I'll be glad to—"

"Wrong blood type, Thurgood. We all are. She's type O. Everyone else on board is A, B, or AB. A transfusion from any of us would kill Grace."

"I'm blood type O!" Even if Shelby had remembered Thurgood's order to remain silent, he would have ignored it. "You can take my blood, as much of it as you need."

This time it was Lana Trask's face that asked Thurgood Trask the silent question.

"Dislocations and sprains. No hemorrhaging." Thurgood stood and pondered. At last he nodded. "We could do it." He turned to Shelby. "But you have to understand what you're offering. There's some danger to you if you give blood in your condition, and it will definitely slow your own recovery."

"I don't care." Shelby forced himself to turn his aching

head toward Lana and Grace. "Who cares how long it takes me to get better? I'm not going anywhere. Do it. I'm ready right now."

Thurgood was already moving toward the medical supply cabinets. He paused there with the transfusion equipment in his hands. "Are you absolutely sure of your own blood group?"

"I'm sure. Get a move on!"

"But if you're not type O—"

"Shelby is right, Thurgood." Lana was over by Grace's side, examining the monitors again. "We can't afford to wait for another second. I'll take all responsibility for this, whatever happens."

Lana's tone more than her words told Shelby just how close Grace was to death. He hardly felt the needle go into his own arm, but he saw the thin stream of red, curiously dark, as it moved along the tube of transparent plastic. He watched as Lana attached it carefully to the IV in Grace's arm.

And then came the anticlimax. For minute after minute, absolutely nothing seemed to happen. The blood flowed on, milliliter by milliliter, with only the faint click of a flowmeter to tell him that anything was moving from his body to hers. Grace remained as pale and lifeless as ever.

Even Thurgood was reduced to silence, his eyes fixed on the monitors, until at last he shook his head and muttered, "All so totally pointless. What the devil did they think they were doing? Cutting our cable like that, when if they had full holds they could just have ignored us and headed straight for the node and been first Sol-side."

For the first time, Shelby realized that no one on the *Harvest Moon* had any real idea what had happened. He, Grace, and Scrimshander were the only ones who knew, and two of the three were unconscious. Scrimshander might have sent any number of messages from the corry while Shelby himself was doped with painkillers, but since they were in a communications blind spot for that whole period no one would have received them.

"It had nothing to do with transuranics and full holds," he said. "It was a kidnap attempt. And it almost worked."

Speaking in no more than a whisper, Shelby told everything that had happened from the moment that the collection cable was cut and he and Grace went flying off toward the reefs. He told of the mysterious appearance of the sounder, and the final fate of Pearl Mossman and Knute Crispin. And he explained how, when he and Grace seemed doomed to die, Scrimshander against all the odds had followed them, found them, and rescued them.

"We would have died, too," he concluded, "if Knute Crispin hadn't taken the Cauthen starfire from Grace. It was his own greed that killed him."

"Or *may* have killed him," Lana said. And, when both Thurgood and Shelby frowned at her in perplexity, "What you've just told me might explain something very strange. When you were lost I sent out calls to the other harvesters in the area, telling them that our cable had been cut and we had lost a corry. I asked them to keep a watch and to listen for any possible messages from you. Of course, they didn't hear or see anything. But a few hours ago I had a call back from the *Dancing Lady*, confirmed later by the *Balaclava*. They'd heard nothing from a corry, but making an all-frequency sweep they had both picked up a distress call from a harvester. It was Pearl Mossman—alive. She had some odd and garbled story that the *Southern Cross* had been swallowed up by a sounder. The strangest part, though, wasn't the message itself, it was the frequency that the other ships received it on. It was far lower than the standard frequency for distress calls. If that frequency change was caused by a Doppler shift, then when the message was sent the *Southern Cross* was traveling away at eighty percent of light speed."

"Impossible," Thurgood Trask grunted. "If Pearl Moss-man had accelerated to that speed in such a short time, she wouldn't be talking. She'd be flattened to a thin smear. It takes a full year at one-gee acceleration to reach eighty percent of the speed of light."

"It does." Lana Trask had been studying Shelby's face, and now she stood up and cut off the flow of blood from Shelby to Grace. "I don't think we ought to take any more for the moment. But I wonder, Thurgood, if the sounders know something that we don't."

"An inertialess method for acceleration?" Thurgood shook his head. "Hmph. Fat chance. I've heard talk of that since I was Doobie's age, and I'll believe it when I see it."

"Maybe you saw it today. We'll have to go into this in detail with the other ships when we're all back Sol-side." But Lana did not continue, because she had heard a sound from behind her. She swung around. "Grace? Grace, love, can you hear me?"

The pale lips moved. Grace uttered something between a faint sigh and a moan. Shelby, turning his head with effort in that direction, imagined he could see a touch more color in the waxen cheeks. As he watched, the long eyelashes fluttered.

Thurgood Trask gave a snort of excitement. "Come on, girl," he muttered. "That's the stuff. A little bit more."

Grace's eyes were still closed, but she was turning her head. As she did so she winced with pain. Shelby realized that in addition to her internal injuries she must have suffered the same agonizing stretches and sprains that he had.

Her eyes were opening, to thin slits that showed a gleam of blue iris. She was looking right at him. He was convinced of it.

"Grace? Grace, can you hear me?" He tried to lean toward her. "We made it, Grace. We're home. We're on board the *Harvest Moon.*"

Now he was sure that she was awake. Her eyes had opened farther. But as he watched he saw a tear form, run down to the corner of her eye, and trickle onto her cheek.

"Grace, don't cry." He tried to reach over to her, but the pain in his arms and shoulders was too much. "You're home now. Muv's here, and so's Uncle Thurgood. Everyone's here. Everything is going to be all right." He had a new unpleasant thought. "Is it the pain? I know, it's awful. Just wait a minute and you'll have something for it. Grace, please don't cry."

She was trying to shake her head, but all she could manage was a millimeter of movement from side to side. "It's not that." Her voice was the faintest whisper. "It's not the pain."

"What is it, then? Scrim? He's all right, and so am I."

"Good. But Shel"—a tear welled up in the other eye, and slid across the bridge of Grace's nose—"it isn't that. Shel, I'm so sad. I lost my beautiful starfire."

CHAPTER FIFTEEN

FOR almost a week the *Harvest Moon* had flown steadily toward the node. On the sixth day, when Grace felt well enough to talk, Shelby learned for the first time what she had known for days without being told.

"Half our usual acceleration, at the most," she said. Shelby's bed remained where Thurgood Trask had put it down, alongside hers. "You ought to go flat out at this stage of the game if you have the fuel. And we have plenty of cumes."

"So why?" Shelby was feeling good enough to try to get

up, but Grace was nowhere near that point and a sense of guilt had kept him in bed. "Why are we dawdling along instead of flying?"

"Because of us two. So we won't hurt. Or I won't. I don't think you're hurting much now, judging from the way you keep wiggling about."

"But that's terrible. Suppose the *Harvest Moon* loses because of us?"

"Then we lose." Grace was oddly matter-of-fact. "It's not a big deal, financially. We'll be in at the top of the market, even if we're a day or two behind the first ship through the node. You won't lose even half a percent of your share."

"I thought it *was* a big deal about being first through. Everybody talks about it all the time."

"Psychological. It shows who's the Cloud's top sniffer."

Shelby felt a new and different guilt. "It's my fault, you know. Your mother's the best. She should have won."

"There's no question of it being your fault, or my fault, or anybody's fault except Pearl Mossman and Knute Crispin. Everyone in the fleet knows what the *Southern Cross* did, and they'll understand if we're not first through."

"If I hadn't insisted on going out so we could take another look at the reefs, none of this would have happened. And you'd still have your starfire."

"You don't know that. If Pearl was out to get you, my bet is she'd have found a way."

"She might not. And if I hadn't dragged you outside the ship when the sounder was closing in, you wouldn't have nearly been killed."

"Rubbish." Grace was well enough to argue, and that was a good sign. "If you hadn't dragged me outside, the sounder would have swallowed us along with Pearl and Knute."

"It didn't harm them. Uncle Thurgood listened to their

message. He said they sounded scared, but they were all right."

"Sure. Define all right. For a start, tell me where they are. Nobody's heard a word from them since that distress call, and it's been six days. If we'd stayed with the *Southern Cross* we might be dead. Or alive but a hundred light-years away, with no chance of ever getting back. Jilter is convinced that the sounders exploit some sort of space-time singularities before and after they sound. That's why they seem to come from nowhere, and why they just disappear afterward and you can't find them. I wish we had their trick of inertialess acceleration, though. We could do with it right now."

Shelby sat up suddenly in bed, wincing at the stabbing pains along his back and in his hips. "How do you feel?"

"Compared to what?"

"Don't get smart. I mean, suppose I went along to your mother and said we were feeling well enough to take a higher acceleration for a run to the node. Would you be able to stand the extra weight?"

"Maybe. First, you prove to me that you can walk to see Muv. Then I'll give you an answer."

He had gone too far to back out. Shelby eased himself out of bed and balanced himself on legs that felt like someone else's. He took two careful, painful steps, holding the side of the bed.

Grace giggled, and he glared at her. "I don't see anything funny."

"You're not lying where I am. You're all bent and wobbly, like your own grandfather."

"Wait 'til *you* get out of bed, before you laugh too hard." Shelby released his support hold on the bed and gradually forced himself to an upright position. "Well? I'm up, and I'm walking. Can you stand a higher acceleration?"

"Of course I can. I'm healing fast."

"You'd better be." Shelby took another tottering step. "You're not getting any more of my blood, you know, not even if the acceleration tears your stitches and splits you wide open."

Grace giggled again, which spoiled the effect of his words. Shelby left the medical center with all the dignity that he could manage and headed for the control room. Once he was in the corridor he didn't have to show off for Grace's benefit, and he shuffled along stiff-legged and with tiny steps.

Lana Trask was not in the ship's control room, but Jilter was. He listened to Shelby for about five seconds and shook his head.

"Forget it. Lana will say no."

"But we could lose the race to be first Sol-side."

"No we couldn't. We already did. *The Pride of Dundee* and the *Coruscation* will hit the node tomorrow. We'll be third when we go Sol-side two days after that. No one else is even close. Speeding up now won't change anything."

Sol-side. The realm of J. P. Cheever and Cheever Consolidated Enterprises. Shelby felt a moment's temptation to tell Jilter that it would be all right, that he and his father would make up for any financial loss suffered by the crew of the *Harvest Moon* since they were not first through.

Then he decided not to—and not because he wouldn't be believed. He had had another thought. He made his way back to Grace as fast as his stranger's legs would carry him.

"I failed," he said. "We won't be increasing acceleration."

She visibly relaxed.

"But I need your help," he went on. "Jilter says that *The Pride of Dundee* will pass through the node tomorrow and go Sol-side. You told me that on the voyages when the *Harvest Moon* was first through, other harvesters would ask you to carry messages for them back to the solar system."

"That's right. There's a rule, though: good news only. Nothing about death, nothing about trouble—and nothing that might have commercial value."

"That's all right. This is good news. But I don't know how to send it to *The Pride of Dundee*."

"Jilter would have helped you. Or Muv. Anyone would."

"I know. But I want this to be a surprise for them."

Grace stared at him. "I shouldn't," she said at last. "But I can't resist it. Make me one promise, and I'll tell you how to send a message so *The Pride of Dundee* gets it and no one here but you and I knows it's been sent."

"What's the promise?"

Grace grinned, the first full-fledged and genuine grin since she had lost the Cauthen starfire. "Just make sure that I'm there when it happens, even if you have to carry me. I want to see Muv's face."

CHAPTER SIXTEEN

SHELBY wouldn't believe it until he experienced it for himself. His memory of the last time was too vivid. He tensed as the moment of the transition approached.

"Relax." Grace was still in bed, but she was sitting up and very cheerful. "I'm telling you, it will be all right."

"But I remember going through the node from Sol-side when I first came to the Cloud. My whole body was twisted and pulled. I thought I was coming apart. If that happens now, it will kill you."

"You think Muv would take the ship through if she thought there was any chance that it might hurt us? I'm telling you, Shel, it's all in the mind."

Sheiby stared at the screen that Uncle Thurgood had set up at the foot of Grace's bed. He was unpersuaded. The pearly glow of the node entrance was only a few kilometers away, and he was not keen to go closer. The *Harvest Moon* had paused in its approach, performing some delicate and precise matching of position and velocity.

And then the hesitation was over. The harvester was moving again, heading right into the shimmering hiatus of the node. Shelby tensed and held his breath, waiting for a twisting and tearing that would send agony through his still-bruised joints.

The forces came. He was being pulled in every direction. And it didn't hurt a bit.

Grace was right. The discomfort of passage through the node network was all in the mind. He allowed himself to breathe, and in that same instant the disk of Sol, shrunken and far-off, popped into existence on the viewing screen.

"Yeh!" Grace waved her arm, free of its last IVs. "Hi there, Sun. We're home again."

Shelby sought, and failed to find, any sign of Earth next to the Sun. He knew that it was much too small and dim to see, but he had to look anyway. "How long 'til we reach Terminal?"

"About four hours. It was built close to the node on purpose." Grace pushed back the covers.

"What are you doing?"

"I'm getting up." She was easing her legs over toward the side of the bed. "And you're going to help me."

"You're not supposed to do that. You're too weak." But he obeyed her gesture, and went to stand next to her and support her.

"We'll see how weak I am. Be reasonable, Shel. Look at it from my point of view. You'll be heading over to Terminal, and so will Muv and Doobie and Jilter. That's where all the action is. You think I'm going to sit here and fester, while you're off having fun? I intend to be there, no matter what."

He allowed her to rest her weight on his arm as she slowly took a first hesitant step. Off having fun? He was not so sure of that. It had seemed such a brilliant idea to send a message back to Earth via *The Pride of Dundee*, announcing that Shelby Cheever was alive and well and would be arriving at the Terminal in the Kuiper Belt in two days' time, aboard the *Harvest Moon*. He could imagine Cheever Enterprises taking over the whole Terminal, and the harvester crews' amazement when they learned that all Shelby's stories were nothing more than the exact truth.

But that wasn't all he could imagine.

He supported Grace as she took another couple of steps. "Are you all right?"

She was grunting and cursing under her breath. "I don't hurt, if that's what you mean. But I'm so *weak*. You'd think I'd been lying around here for months." She released her hold on his arm and carefully stood without help. "When do you propose to go inside Terminal?"

"As soon as I can. As soon as we're docked."

"I was afraid you'd say that. So I've got maybe five hours. Not much, but it will have to do. Leave me alone now." She waved him away impatiently. "I have to get dressed, and then I want to sneak over to get a suit. Whatever you do, don't tell Muv. And no, I *don't* need more of your help. I'll see you later."

Dismissed, Shelby had no distraction from his own worries. He went wandering off to the forward observation port and stared out. Terminal, the great docking facility where all the harvesters and rakehells came to sell cargo on their return from the Cloud, was no more than a tiny spark of light among the background stars. He sat, watching and thinking, as the spark grew slowly to a blob, to a lopsided disk, and at last to a solid body with its own ports, locks, antennas, and long-armed gantries. He could see two harvesters already docked at Terminal. They must be the *Coruscation* and *The Pride of Dundee*, which had carried Shelby's message back from the Messina Cloud.

Their crews would be inside Terminal.

And who else?

Shelby realized, for the first time in months, that he hardly knew his father at all. Which did nothing to explain why he was so afraid of him.

J. P. Cheever could not have explained Shelby's fear, either, even if he had known of it, any more than he could explain the secret of his own business success. So far as he was concerned he was just the same with Shelby as with anyone else: friendly, curious, interested, and direct. He knew that Shelby had never responded, but that was a different matter.

Given the news that his son had returned from the dead, surely anyone would behave just as he behaved. Drop everything; put trusted subordinates in charge of business with orders to make no major decisions; and commandeer the fastest method of travel from Earth to the Kuiper Belt.

Within thirty-six hours of receiving that astonishing message from *The Pride of Dundee*, Cheever had learned a surprising amount about harvesters and the Messina Cloud and was making the transition to the Kuiper Belt. Soon after that he had located and was meeting with a co-owner of the *Harvest Moon*. Mungo Trask was a huge, slow-moving and slow-speaking man who unself-consciously bounced three-year-old Danielle, the youngest of the Trasks, on his knee during the whole conversation and obviously had no thought of handing her over to anyone else to look after while they talked.

The discussion had little to do with Shelby Cheever, beyond the fact that he was J. P. Cheever's son and was now aboard the *Harvest Moon*. Shelby was not even a name to Mungo. The two men talked technology, harvesters, transuranics, and markets. Cheever had never before been beyond the Moon, but economics was economics. After three hours he understood the harvester business, as he told Mungo, "about enough to make a fool of myself." Then Danielle demanded food. The talk switched to children, and parenting, and the importance of the education that neither of the two men had ever had.

He left Mungo at last and went to watch *The Pride of Dundee* and the *Coruscation* unload their cargoes at Terminal. Later he talked his way into tours of the two vessels. He listened to the bargaining in Terminal's huge open market and felt rather than heard the subtle shift in negotiating positions that took place when the *Harvest Moon* finally came popping through the node.

And then it became harder to concentrate on business. The time he had spent with Mungo Trask had reassured him in one way. Shelby would have been treated decently aboard the *Harvest Moon*. But how had Shelby behaved? Cheever was under no illusions about his son. A pampered and sheltered childhood on Earth was poor preparation for life in the Messina Cloud—or anywhere else.

He watched the steady approach of the *Harvest Moon*, not knowing that Shelby in the forward observation port of the harvester was staring right back at Terminal, and he did not move until a safe docking had been achieved. Then he retreated from the staging area where the new arrivals would shed their suits and come aboard. He took up an inconspicuous position on a raised platform far at the back, sitting in the shadows with his short legs swinging free.

There were only three crew members when they finally appeared, one man and two women. J. P. Cheever's first inspection was disappointing. Then he took a second look at the man, who was supporting the younger woman on his arm. He saw past the thin body with its pained and careful invalid's walk to the youthful face.

It was Shelby. Fifty pounds lighter, pale, and apparently ten years older, but undeniably Shelby Cheever. Now his son was staring around him with an uneasy expression on his face.

Time to move. J. P. Cheever slipped off the platform and came up behind the three newcomers as they headed toward the open market.

"Captain Trask?" And, as she turned, "I'm Jerry Cheever. I want to thank you for saving my son's life, and for looking after him." He reached out and squeezed Shelby's arm, but he kept his gaze on Lana Trask's face.

Her reaction provided more reassurance. She did not gasp, or look baffled, or ask questions. She gave him one quick comprehending look, glanced at Shelby, and turned at once to the young girl holding on to his arm. "Gracie! You must have been in on this. Who carried the message?"

"*The Pride of Dundee.*"

"I thought as much. You and I will talk about that later."

And then she was turning back to J. P. Cheever, smiling, and saying, "Shel was an asset, not a liability. Any time he wants a crew position on the *Harvest Moon*, he has one."

"Glad to hear that. I must say I did wonder."

"But I thought you lived on Earth."

"I do."

"So how were you able to get here so quickly? *The Pride of Dundee* hasn't been Sol-side more than two days."

"I greased Emigration a little. And I took over the transportation system and the node network for a while."

Grace's hand tightened on Shelby's arm. His father's words were casual, but they implied the possession of enormous wealth. Shelby had told the truth about his background; and Lana Trask must realize now how wrong she had been.

But Grace was disappointed at her mother's reaction. You would never know from Lana Trask's face or voice what she was thinking. She merely nodded at J. P. Cheever and said, "You must want to spend time with your son. And I ought to go and see how my husband and other daughter are doing."

"They're both fine. Danielle is a beautiful little girl."

That produced at least a raised eyebrow from Lana. Shelby knew the feeling. He had been studying his father closely, and he noticed that J. P. Cheever was shorter than he remembered him. His father was quite a little man. He realized that it had never been the height or size or manner that was intimidating. It was J. P. Cheever's habit of always knowing a little more about everything than he could possibly know.

Lana did not ask questions. She merely moved Grace's hand from Shelby's arm to her own and said, "Maybe you two will join us for dinner? It's a tradition for the crew to get together and celebrate on the first night Sol-side. Shelby is a full-fledged crew member, of course, as much as me or Grace, and you will be very welcome, too."

"I'd be honored." Cheever stared at Grace with considerable curiosity, but he did not move or speak until he and Shelby were alone. Then he took his son by the shoulders and gave him a long and silent head-to-toe scrutiny. "What the devil did you and Grace Trask do to yourselves? She looks like she can hardly walk."

"Nothing much. We threaded the eye of the Portland

Reef." Shelby spoke with some pride, then saw that his father had no idea what he meant. "How's—how's Mother?"

"She's fine. Really looking forward to seeing you." J. P. Cheever shook his head. "But no matter what I said, I couldn't talk her into coming out through the node network with me. For the past three months she's regarded it as the monstrous scientific construct that killed her son. She's blamed everybody from me to the ship's crew to the people who built the node. I don't suppose you'd like to tell me what prompted you to make a node transition from the *Bellatrix* alone, and without adequate preparation?"

For the first time in his life, Shelby met his father eye to eye. "I was falling-down drunk. Everything that happened that day was my own stupid fault, and no one else's. Don't tell Mother, though."

"I wasn't planning to," J. P. Cheever said dryly. He grimaced, less the captain of Earth industry than the perplexed husband of Constance Cheever. "I'll keep quiet about the drinking, provided you don't go telling your mother that you got hurt in the Messina Cloud."

"Deal."

"You can tell me, though, anything you feel like." Cheever led the way through the Terminal, to the simple suite of rooms that he had reserved for him and Shelby. "For instance, what's the Portland Reef, and what's it mean to thread the eye? Mungo Trask never got to that."

Shelby settled down opposite his father and started to talk. He didn't intend to say much, but J. P. Cheever had the strange knack of drawing someone on and drawing him out, while barely saying a word himself. Before Shelby was finished he had rambled on about everything. He talked of waking hungover in the Messina Cloud with Logan, and how there were similar smart machines used everywhere but on Earth. He explained harvesting, and how he and Grace had met a sounder between the Portland and Lizard Reefs, and gained a Cauthen starfire and a mass of shwartzgeld. How they had later met the same sounder, lost the starfire, but escaped with their own lives. And how, when those lives again seemed lost, Lucky Jack Linden had steered them through the deadly eye of the reef.

"Except, like I said, he's Scrimshander Limes again now," Shelby explained. "You'll meet him tonight, him and Uncle Thurgood. They're a turn together you shouldn't miss."

"I'm looking forward to it." J.P. had absorbed every word, and he understood more than his son imagined. "Sounds like you really enjoyed yourself on the *Harvest Moon*."

"Not at first."

"But you'd go back?"

"Any time." Shelby's voice filled with enthusiasm. "It's where the future is. Lana Trask says we don't know one-tenth of what there is to learn in the Cloud. The sounders apparently have some form of inertialess drive. It permits unlimited acceleration, without any of the physical effects of a high-gee—"

"Whoa. You've lost me. Remember, you're talking to someone whose science education stopped when he left school and ran away at thirteen."

"You ran away?" Shelby stared at his father.

"Tell you about it some other time. Don't let it give you ideas. Anyway, the drive?"

"It's something that apparently people have talked about for centuries. But it won't be developed on Earth, because there's no particular use for it there. It's a tool for deep space. And the people in the Belt and the Cloud simply don't have enough development capital. You know, if you were just to take part of Cheever Consolidated Enterprises and move it to the Kuiper Belt and out to the Messina Cloud, there's no limit to what might be done."

"Could be. Who's been getting to you? Lana Trask or Gracie? Both of them, I guess. Son, how old do you think I am?"

"Huh?" Shelby, lost in his own enthusiasm, stared at his father. "How *old* you are? I don't know. Fifty-five?"

"I'm seventy-three. I'm in good shape—for my age—but it's too late for a dog like me to learn new tricks. It's all I can do to keep on top of things on Earth. Space belongs to the Trasks, and to all the other miners and harvesters. They are earning the rights to it with every voyage and every kilo of metal and transuranics that's shipped down to Earth." He glanced casually away from Shelby. "But we owe Lana and the rest of your crew a great deal. I was just wondering how I can repay them. I can give them cash, of course. But how much?"

He saw from the corner of his eye the change in Shelby's face and heard the anguished "Not money! For God's sake don't offer them money. Especially not Captain Lana."

It was, to J. P. Cheever, a highly satisfying answer. "You think not?" he said. "All right, then, no money. What would you suggest?"

"We-e-ll. I have an idea for one of them." Shelby could finally ask a question that had plagued him since his first meeting with Doobie and Grace. "J.P.—"

"I'd prefer Dad."

"Uh—yeah. All right. Dad"—the change came out awkwardly—"I know I'm rich. But just how much money do I have?"

"Total? I have no idea. It would take the accountants a while to value your assets. And most of them aren't liquid, so you couldn't easily spend them. Why do you ask?"

"I wondered, could I buy a harvester if I wanted to?"

"I'm sure you could. You have enough ready money for that." J. P. Cheever was on solid ground with this one. He had been over the economics of Cloud harvesting with Mungo. "Half a dozen of them, if you felt that way inclined. Are you considering it?"

"No. But I was thinking of buying a Cauthen starfire. For Grace. She lost hers, like I said, when we left the *Southern Cross*. It was the most precious thing in the world to her, and if I got her a replacement . . . What's wrong?"

J.P. Cheever could not see his own face, but he suspected that it had taken on the same look of distress with which Shelby had greeted the proposal of a cash reward to Lana Trask.

"Your money is your own, son. It's not my job to tell you how to spend it. But if you'll listen to a word of advice, I don't think you ought to buy Grace Trask a starfire."

"Why not?"

"Think about it. The two of you have a great adventure together, and you win a starfire. It's the most exciting thing that's ever happened to her. Even if she does lose it, she'll always remember the thrill of how she got it. Then you come along, and you say, Hey, Gracie, you lost your starfire? No big deal, not for rich-boy Shelby. Here's another one I just bought for you—and I'll get you two or three more like that if you want 'em."

Looking at Shelby, J.P. Cheever realized that while he might not have known the son that he had lost very well, he certainly didn't yet know the one who had come back to him. He had gone on for far too long. Shelby had seen the point and looked stricken even before his father started to answer.

"What, then?" Shelby asked. "I'd like to give Grace and Lana and the rest of them something, and so would you. But what?"

"We'll have to stew on that. Mungo Trask gave me an

idea or two, but I have to fit it in with some other plans." J. P. Cheever put his hand on Shelby's shoulder. "Let's sit awhile and talk about what *you* want to do next."

But Shelby was glancing at a clock on the wall. "It'll have to be later. I didn't realize we'd been sitting here talking so long. My fault—I've been babbling. But the final cargo tally for the *Harvest Moon* will be starting any minute, and I have to be there."

"The others can't do it without you?"

"Not so well." Shelby stood a little straighter, put one hand in his pocket, and stuck out his belly. It didn't work as well as it had once, because there was really no belly to push out. "I'm the best tallier on the ship. Even Uncle Thurgood says so, says I have a natural talent."

"Better get to it, then," J. P. Cheever said gravely. He had caught that faint reflection of the earlier Shelby. "Work is work. But I'd like to watch for a while. Come on, and we can talk as we go. Then I want another word or two with Lana and Mungo Trask."

The first dinner Sol-side, according to Grace Trask, was always a fun occasion. Everyone let his or her hair down and there were no rules.

So was it Shelby who was ruining everything, or his father, or something else? All he could be sure of was that the atmosphere while they ate wasn't relaxed at all. It was positively grim. Uncle Thurgood didn't bully Scrimshander once. He didn't rise to the bait when Doobie started to talk about "tar-farming" in the Messina Cloud. All he did was gloom over his food and scowl at J. P. Cheever. At the earliest possible moment he excused himself and dragged Scrimshander away with him.

After he was gone, Lana Trask stared accusingly around

the table. "All right. Who did it, and what was it?"

Jilter merely shook his head. Doobie said, "I haven't spoken one word to Uncle Thurgood, or to Scrimshander, since we finished tallying," and Shelby nodded agreement.

"Gracie?" Lana turned to her daughter.

"I *talked* to him, sure I did. Just before dinner." Grace's face displayed bewilderment, but no trace of guilt. "He ought to have been pleased with what I told him."

"Which was?"

"Only that Shelby's father has lots of clout back on Earth, and that's where they have the best facilities for treating people with mental problems. I told Uncle Thurgood that maybe we could arrange for a cure for Scrimshander."

"Which explains everything." Mungo Trask, who had sat through dinner with his returned family in contented silence, scowled and sighed. Suddenly he looked like his brother Thurgood. "Grace, I have one question for you. Can you tell me what a *cure* would be for Scrimshander Limes?" And, when Grace sat in awkward silence, "Would it be going back to become Lucky Jack Linden again, remembering exactly how his wife and family died? Is that a cure? I don't think so. I didn't speak to Thurgood today, but he spoke to me. He was as happy as I've ever seen him. He told me that Scrimshander has never been as much at peace as he is now, because when he dreams it's not about the Trachten blowout. It's about piloting a corry with a couple of young idiots aboard and bringing them safe home against all the odds."

"Sorry." Grace's face was white. Shelby had the feeling that Mungo Trask never spoke like that to his children.

"That's all right." Mungo looked around the table. "I'll talk to Thurgood, and I'll reassure him. And we're all like family here, so it won't go any farther."

Before anyone could react to that curious statement, J. P. Cheever had jumped in. "I guess that was my cue. For the past two days, ever since I learned that Shelby was alive, I've been puzzling over two things: What should he be doing with himself now? And how can I ever thank the crew of the *Harvest Moon*, and all the harvesters, for what they did for him?" He gave Shelby a reassuring glance that said *Don't worry. I'm not going to suggest money.* "I didn't have any idea, though, until Mungo and I had a talk and found we agreed on two things: Being a parent is hell; and the thing that the two of us lack and always regret missing is any sort of real education. It's particularly hard to get out here, in the Kuiper Belt, and damn nigh impossible in the Cloud.

"So Mungo and Lana and I are proposing a deal, and here it is. You, Shelby, will go back to Earth and be educated. After that, if you want to, you return to the Cloud and help with its development. Now, wait a minute." J. P. Cheever held up his hand to cut off Shelby's protest. "This isn't just for you. The same offer goes for all the teenage children in the Cloud, Grace and Doobie and Nick Rasmussen and all the rest of them. There will be a free education for each of you, courtesy of Cheever Enterprises, the best that you can get on Earth—which also means the toughest. Five years or more of hard grind, with emphasis on science and technology. And *then*—but only then—Cheever Enterprises will begin a major development program in the Messina Cloud."

Grace and Doobie had been giving Shelby questioning looks. He realized that he was being appointed as the spokesman.

"What do you mean," he asked, "a major development program? Do you mean that you'll come out to the Cloud in five years and manage things?"

"No." J. P. Cheever shook his head. "Definitely not."

"Then if you won't, who will? Me?"

"Maybe, but not necessarily." J. P. Cheever waved his arm vaguely around the table. "It could be Grace, or Doobie, or maybe someone I've never met. You and the others will be evaluated on a fair and equal basis. No favoritism. The best-qualified of you, whoever that turns out to be, will be in charge. I can be sure of inherited money, you see, though I don't have a high regard for it. What I can't guarantee is inherited *ability*, to manage a development program or to do anything else that's worth doing. You may or may not have it. You get an equal chance, with everyone else. Fair enough?"

He was staring at Shelby. They all were. Shelby could tell, if he said yes, that Grace and Doobie would go along. He thought of them, and of Nicky and Mooks and Skip and the rest of the harvester teenagers. That would be his competition. Tough competition, too, but he believed that he could handle it. And the prize for the winner was the Messina Cloud development program, with a freer hand in its direction than he had ever dreamed of.

And suppose he *didn't* beat the competition? Then it meant that there was someone in the group smarter and better qualified than he was. And he would learn from that person.

The others had been watching him closely, observing the changing expressions on his face. When finally he nodded and said, "Fair enough," Lana Trask, Mungo Trask, and his father shared a three-way smile.

And when Lana spoke she was facing Shelby, but her words didn't seem to be addressed to him at all. "Now I see where he gets it from," she said.

Her words seemed clear enough. It was five more years before Shelby understood what they meant.